BLIZZARD

This Book Belongs

To: Ruth Van-Nes

OTHER BOOKS BY AL LACY

Journeys of the Stranger series:
  Legacy (Book One)
  Silent Abduction (Book Two)

Battles of Destiny (Civil War series):
  Beloved Enemy (Battle of First Bull Run)
  A Heart Divided (Battle of Mobile Bay)
  A Promise Unbroken (Battle of Rich Mountain)
  Shadowed Memories (Battle of Shiloh)
  Joy From Ashes (Battle of Fredericksburg)

JOURNEYS OF THE STRANGER • BOOK THREE

BLIZZARD

AL LACY

MULTNOMAH BOOKS

BLIZZARD
© 1995 by Lew A. Lacy

published by Multnomah Books
a part of the Questar publishing family

Edited by Rodney L. Morris
Cover design by Multnomah Graphics
Cover illustration by Bill Farnsworth

International Standard Book Number: 0-88070-702-X

Printed in the United States of America.

For information:
Questar Publishers, Inc.
Post Office Box 1720
Sisters, Oregon 97759

95 96 97 98 99 00 01 02 03 — 10 9 8 7 6 5 4 3 2 1

For Marshall Stevens, who is not only my pastor,
but also my adopted son.
Thank you for the way you have promoted my
Questar books to the people of Calvary Baptist Church.
Thank you for loving me...and thank you for staying
true to the Lord Jesus and to His Word.

I love you more than you will ever know.
III John 4

ONE

Dawn was a slight hint of gray on the horizon as the three men ran northward across open fields, hopping ditches, bounding over high spots, darting through low spots, and zigzagging their way amongst patches of brush.

Their lungs burned and their legs felt the strain of pushing hard without letup. They would waste no breath on words at the moment. The only thing on their minds was to get as far as they could from the Colorado Territorial Prison and Canon City before the guards discovered they were missing.

The Rocky Mountains lifted their jagged heads against the star-lit western sky off to their left, bold, black, and high. Ord Grabow, Treg Taggart, and Jack Slattery were headed for the nearest farm to steal horses. Once they had horses under them, they would head due west into the hidden glens of the mountains and veer north again.

They had run better than a mile at a hard pace when they topped a grassy rise and dropped into a brush-lined ravine. Grabow—who had worked out the escape plan—stopped, gasping for breath, and said, "Let's hold up...for a minute."

The trio bent over and sucked hard for air. After a bit, Jack Slattery looked at Grabow and snapped, "You lied to me, Ord! You said you'd have Frank's cell door fixed so it wouldn't lock, just like you did ours. But Frank's wouldn't budge!"

Grabow swallowed hard, licked his lips, and growled, "That no-good brother of yours is the one who got us caught in the first place! I wasn't about to take him with us."

"Ord's right, Jack," Treg Taggart said. "Frank ain't got your smarts. If he'd kept his head about him, our pals wouldn't be dead, and we'd never seen the inside of that rotten prison."

Slattery's mind flashed back to some three weeks earlier when their gang, led by Casey Baldwin, robbed the El Paso County Bank in Colorado Springs. There was a shootout, and four of the gang members, including Baldwin, were killed. Grabow, Taggart, and the two Slattery brothers, cornered by too many guns, had surrendered.

The gang had already murdered more people than they could remember, and a quick trial brought convictions for murder and robbery. They were taken to the prison at Canon City where they were to be hanged on October 27. It was now October 19.

"Your stupid brother was supposed to be on watch outside the bank while we cleaned out the safe and the tellers' cages," Grabow said. "He got himself occupied with somethin' else—who knows what?—and let those federal deputies surround us. We don't need no ignoramus like him with us."

"Frank had no idea those government tin stars were closin' in on us, Ord! Any more than the rest of us did. We knew that town marshal was outta Colorado Springs that mornin', and Frank wasn't thinkin' about no federal marshals! He—"

"Aw, come off it, Jack!" countered Grabow. "We left him out there to keep a sharp eye out, and he let us down! It's as simple as that. And that's the reason I didn't include him in this break. Now, I don't wanna hear no more about it!"

"He's my brother, Ord, and you left him there to hang! That cuts me pretty deep. You—"

"I could've left *both* of you there! You ever think of that? It was me who engineered the escape, wasn't it?"

Jack looked at him silently, mouth drawn in a thin line.

"Well, wasn't it?" pressed Grabow.

Jack licked his lips and nodded in short, jerky movements. "Yeah."

"Then I could've just taken Treg with me and let you stay and hang, too, couldn't I?"

Jack knew it was true. He hated to think of his brother going to the gallows, but he was glad Ord had taken him along.

"Well *couldn't* I?" snapped Grabow.

"Yeah. You could've."

"Then be thankful for that, and shut up about Frank."

Suddenly the sound of the prison's huge bell echoed over the hills. Their escape had been discovered, and soon the guards would be coming on horseback to track them down.

"Let's go," said Grabow. "I can see the farm from here."

The trio covered another half mile in a matter of minutes, and made their way into the yard of the old farm. They vaulted the split rail fence of the corral, eyeing four saddle horses that regarded them warily.

They found bridles and saddles inside the barn, picked the three animals they wanted, and hastily made ready to ride. They had them just about saddled when the farmer, a man in his late fifties, came around the corner of the barn inside the corral and leveled a rifle on them from behind, blaring, "Hold it right there, you jail birds!"

All three were drawing up the cinches when the surprise came. They halted and looked around at the farmer, his jaw jutted with determination.

"Back away from them horses!" commanded the farmer. "This is as far as you go. Won't be long till the guards'll be here, so we'll just wait."

Grabow moved slowly away from the horse and toward the man, keeping a close watch on the rifle. "Look, mister," he said, "we were sent up on a false charge. We want to clear ourselves, but we can't do it locked up in the prison. I'm askin' you to have some mercy, here. We need these horses to make good our escape."

As he spoke, Grabow inched his way closer to the farmer. "I promise you—as soon as we clear this thing up with the law, we'll bring the horses back, and we'll pay you for the time we used 'em. How about it?"

Ord was now within reach of the rifle. Its muzzle was pointed directly at his chest. The farmer's eyes showed that he was thinking on Grabow's words.

Ord smiled, keeping his voice low and soft. "How about it? You'll be doin' a mighty good deed if you'll give three innocent men a chance. You wouldn't want to see us rot behind bars for something someone else did, would you?"

The farmer began shaking his head. "How do I know you're tellin' me the truth? I think it'd be best if we just wait till them guards show up. Then we can—"

Grabow grabbed the barrel of the rifle with both hands and wrenched it from the farmer's grasp. It discharged, sending the slug into the ground. He swung the rifle and connected with the farmer's head, knocking him down and out.

The rifle was only a single-shot, and there wasn't time to locate more cartridges. Grabow threw it down and headed for the horse while Taggart opened the corral gate and Slattery mounted up. As they were about to ride away, the farmer's wife emerged from the back door of the barn and dashed to her husband. She knelt beside him and screamed at the outlaws as they galloped away.

The trio rode hard, heading due west for twenty miles, then hauled up in a rock enclosure just outside the small town of Spike Buck to give the horses a breather. While the animals blew and snorted, Taggart climbed atop a tall rock and checked their back trail.

"See anything?" Grabow asked.

"Nope. No sign of 'em yet."

"They'll find our trail sooner or later," put in Slattery. "They want us real bad."

The Casey Baldwin gang had murdered a large number of people while robbing banks, stagecoaches, and trains in the brief two years they had been together. Their faces were on wanted posters all over Colorado, Wyoming, and New Mexico Territories. Lawmen had felt great relief when they learned that Baldwin and three of his men had been killed and the other four were in prison and due to hang October 27.

"Yeah, they want us real bad," nodded Grabow, "but they ain't gonna get us. We're gonna make it to the hideout, and there ain't no lawman anywhere who has any idea where it is." The gang had a cabin hideout high in the Elk Mountains just south of Crested Butte.

Grabow glanced at the eastern sky. "Won't be anybody on the streets of Spike Buck for another couple of hours," he said. "Let's break into the gun shop and arm ourselves, then we'll bust into a clothin' shop and find somethin' to wear besides these prison duds."

Little more than a half hour later, Grabow, Taggart, and Slattery had accomplished both tasks. They took their prison garb with them and rode northwestward toward the town of Buena Vista, riding through streams and rocky areas so as to leave no tracks.

The October wind whipped down from the towering peaks above them, bringing cold air off the snow that had already fallen in the high country. The unsightly trio was glad they had taken heavy coats and hats while they were outfitting themselves.

Though the sun began to warm the flatlands east of the Rockies, the shadows hung on in the canyons where the outlaws rode. The air was thin and bracing, and the raw wind that gusted through the canyons was rich with the pleasant odors of the mountains.

It was nearly noon before the sun reached them with its warmth. They stopped to remove their coats, and began to talk about what they should do for food.

"Well," said Grabow, "since there ain't no towns between here and Buena Vista, looks to me like we'll have to drop by a cabin along the way somewhere and see if we can't fill our bellies."

An hour later, Grabow, Taggart, and Slattery found themselves in a weather-rutted defile passing up through a ridge strewn with boulders and rocks. When they reached the summit, they spotted a small cabin nestled among the pines some fifty yards away. A stream bent abruptly behind the cabin and dropped toward them on its way down the mountainside.

"Maybe whoever lives up there will share some food with three weary travelers," Taggart said.

"They will whether they want to or not," chortled Grabow.

Moments later, they hauled up to the front porch and dismounted. Tiny wisps of smoke trailed upward from a metal chimney at the back of the cabin.

"Has to be somebody home," Slattery said, eyeing the smoke.

Grabow stepped onto the porch and was about to knock when the door came open, revealing a wrinkled old man with a long gray beard and hair that dangled to his shoulders. He wore a battered, greasy hat. He ran his squinted gaze over the faces of his visitors and asked in a cracked voice, "What kin I do fer ya, boys?"

"Well, sir," Grabow said politely, "we've been travelin' for quite a while, and somehow we got a little mixed up. Could you tell us if we're on the right trail to reach Buena Vista?"

"Shore can, and you are," came the ready reply. "Jist aim your noses due north. You cain't miss it."

"Much obliged, sir," nodded Grabow with a slight grin. "We...uh...we haven't had a morsel to eat since yesterday. Been travelin' from the south, and since we got somewhat mixed up, we also haven't been where we could get somethin' to eat. I was wonderin' if—"

"So you're hungry, eh? Well, I jist et 'bout a hour ago, but I think ol' Barney, here, kin fix ya up." Extending his gnarled old hand, he said, "Name's Barney Fletcher, mister. Whut's yours?"

Grabow introduced himself and his partners, telling the old man they were traveling through to Denver from Canon City way.

"Well, c'mon in, fellers," cackled Fletcher. "We'll rustle ya up some grub."

The trio took seats on rustic chairs and watched as the old man added wood to the stove. As he worked, Fletcher spoke over his shoulder, "So you boys're from Canon City, eh?"

"That's right," Taggart said.

"Anythin' excitin' goin' on over at the prison?"

The outlaws exchanged furtive glances.

"Nothin' much," said Taggart.

"They hang anybody lately?"

"Not lately," replied Grabow.

"Too bad," grumbled Fletcher, dropping the cast iron lid in place on the stove. "I think they're gittin' too soft on criminals these days. When they break the law an' the jedge sentences 'em to hang, I think they oughtta hang the same day, not git to sit around in a cell fer awhile before they stretch a rope. That's my sentiments, anyways. Whut do you fellers think?"

"I think we're hungry, Pops," Grabow said. "How soon do we eat?"

"Won't take long," replied Fletcher. "I'll have you some victuals right soon. You like biscuits n' gravy?"

"I think we can tolerate 'em," Slattery said. "How about whiskey? You got any of that while we're waitin' for the biscuits and gravy?"

The old man screwed up his face. "Nope. Ain't got none o' that stuff. It'll rot your gut and burn up your brain, don't you know thet?"

Slattery looked at his friends and sighed. "How about coffee, Barney? You got any coffee?"

"Yep. Shore do," nodded Fletcher, turning to the rickety old cupboard that stood close to the stove. "I'll have it fer ya in a jiffy." He pulled a coffee can from the cupboard and picked up a blackened coffeepot, shook it, and said, "Oops! I gotta go git some water at the stream. Be back in two shakes of a lamb's tail."

When the old man stepped off the porch, bucket in hand, Taggart ran his gaze to his partners and said, "I think maybe he suspects somethin'."

"Whaddya mean?" Grabow asked.

"Well, his askin' about the prison and all. If he suspects we might be escapees, he's liable to head south and let that stupid warden know he saw us, and tell him which way we're headin'."

"He's not suspicious of us," Slattery said. "If he thought we were escaped criminals, he wouldn't go on about hangin' 'em quicker."

"Yeah, but what if that was just a cover-up to mask his real feelin's?" Taggart said. "I think we'd better do him in before we leave."

"Naw," said Grabow. "I'm with Jack. The old duffer don't suspect us. 'Sides, I ain't in a killin' mood today. I ain't for killin' nobody unless they're a threat, and that old geezer ain't no threat."

Taggart hunched his shoulders. "Okay. I hope you boys are right. I'd sure hate to find out later that he blabbed to the law about our whereabouts."

They heard Fletcher's shuffling feet, and seconds later, he came through the door, carrying the bucket. "Now, we'll git that coffee goin'," he said, pouring water into the coffeepot.

An hour later, Barney Fletcher sat at the table and watched his visitors eat. He figured all three were in their thirties, though Grabow appeared the oldest. They were all hard-eyed and had a mean look to them. He wanted to ask what business they were in, but his good sense told him to leave it alone. Instead, he talked about the mountains and how much he enjoyed living in them.

"How long you lived up here, Barney?" Taggart asked around a mouthful of biscuits and gravy.

"I forgot. I s'pose a hunnerd years or so."

Treg laughed. "You always been alone?"

"Not zactly. Had a missus fer forty years, but she died. That was when we lived down by Pueblo. I was in the shippin' business. Now I'm in the hermit business. But I ain't really alone, neither."

"No?"

"Got an ol' mule in that shed out there. Ol' Willie. Me an' ol' Willie git along jist fine. We don't need nobody else."

"The shippin' business, eh?" said Grabow, sipping at his coffee. "What kind of shippin'?"

"Well, I run a wagon 'tween Pueblo an' Denver, haulin' all kinds o' supplies. You know...whatever the folks in Pueblo needed that was comin' in at the rail head at Denver from back East."

"So you moved up here after your wife died?"

"Yeah. It's just me an' ol' Willie now...but we're happy."

The men finished their meal, thanked Barney for his hospitality, and mounted their horses. Barney stood grinning on the porch and said, "So you boys are goin' through Buena Vista an' on to Denver, eh?"

"That's right," Grabow nodded. "Thanks again for the victuals."

"Yore welcome. So long."

When the trio had ridden out of sight into a dark canyon, Barney Fletcher closed up the cabin and went to the shed. "Well, ol' Willie, we got a leedle trip to make."

"Ord, I've got a feelin' the old buzzard suspects us," Taggart said as they rode away from the cabin. "I vote we go back and snuff 'im out. We could weigh his carcass down with rocks and throw him in that stream."

"Treg, you ain't got no grace about you. That little old man ain't gonna do us no harm. Forget him."

"Okay, okay. Just a hunch in my gut, that's all," Taggart grinned. "Let's make tracks."

"That's exactly what we *don't* want to do," Slattery said.

Taggart snorted. "You know what I mean."

The trio arrived on the outskirts of Buena Vista an hour after dark. They found trash burning in an ash pit behind a large house and threw their prison garb into the fire. Since they had no money, they decided to break into the general store and steal food after the town had gone to bed.

At dawn the next morning, Grabow, Taggart, and Slattery awakened in their heavy coats. They got up from the pine needle beds they had made beneath the towering pine outside of Buena Vista and ate stolen hardtack and beef jerky for breakfast. Before the sun was up, they were in their saddles.

They faced better than seventy miles of tough riding through the deep canyons and over the lofty passes of the Continental Divide before they would reach the town of Crested Butte. The lowest pass over the Divide was almost twelve thousand feet. They rode a shallow stream with the soft sound of the wind in the tall pines overhead and birds singing from the branches.

"How long you think we'll need to hole up, Ord?" Taggart asked.

"I figure a coupla months, at least."

"That'll take us into December," Slattery said. "If we're gonna plan to stay that long, we probably oughtta lay up enough food and supplies to stay till spring."

"Naw," Grabow replied. "I'd go nuts bein' cooped up that long. Even if we get some heavy snows, there'll be days we can ride for low country. After a coupla months, I'll be ready to start robbin' banks and stages and trains."

"Me, too," Taggart said. "But I ain't seen my pa nor my four brothers and my sister for quite a spell. I want to go down to pa's cattle ranch once it's safe to venture outta the hideout."

"Well, if you can sneak real good, you can prob'ly go down even before a couple months," said Grabow. "We'll talk about it in a month or so."

Slattery set his mouth in a long, hard line and his eyes grew cold. "Nice you can see your brothers again, Treg. My only brother is gonna hang in a few more days."

"I told you to be glad I let *you* go with us," Grabow shouted. "I don't want to hear no more about your stupid brother, you got that?"

Slattery wanted to lash back, but he knew it was best he say no more. Deep inside, he nursed a grudge against Ord Grabow for leaving Frank at the prison to hang.

CHAPTER

TWO

Three days before Ord Grabow, Treg Taggart, and Jack Slattery rode away from Barney Fletcher's cabin toward their mountain hideout near Crested Butte, Deputy U. S. Marshal Ridge Holloway dismounted in front of the Old Buffalo Saloon in Laramie City, Wyoming.

Holloway turned twenty-eight in August. He had been a deputy sheriff in El Paso County, Colorado, since he was twenty, and became so well known for tracking outlaws and bringing them in—some dead, some alive—that Chief U. S. Marshal Solomon Duvall in Denver offered him a job as one of his deputies. Holloway had been a federal officer, working out of the Denver office, for just over two years. On assignment by Chief Duvall, he had been trailing Sal Durant and Fenton Millard for three days. Though they had worked hard at covering their trail, Holloway was now standing beside their horses in front of the Old Buffalo Saloon.

Holloway cast a glance toward the saloon door, which stood open in spite of the cool October air. The brilliant morning sunlight made the interior of the saloon a dark maw. He slipped up close to the first horse and loosened the cinch, then did the same to the second.

Holloway removed his badge and dropped it in his shirt pocket. He tested his Colt .45 for freedom of movement in its holster, then made his way across the boardwalk toward the saloon door. He thought of how it never used to bother him to enter a saloon until that wonderful day some six weeks ago—September 10, to be exact. *Sunday,* September 10.

Ridge had first met Marlene Daniels when buying grain for his horse at her father's feed and grain company nearly two years ago. Marlene was kind and friendly to him, but when he asked her for a date, all she would say was that if he would come to church, she would sit by him in the pew.

This went on for over a year before Ridge finally broke down and went to a service. True to her word, Marlene sat by him. Ridge had never given much thought to Jesus Christ or His death on the cross, but ever since that first Sunday, he had attended services except when he was out of town on assignments. Then on September 10 of this year, Deputy U. S. Marshal Ridge Holloway found himself walking the aisle at the end of the sermon to lay claim to what Jesus had done for him in His death, burial, and resurrection.

Now that Jesus Christ lived in his heart, Ridge felt a repugnance every time he entered a saloon. He had to enter them quite often in his work, but he was amazed at the difference in how he felt about such places since he had become a Christian.

Ridge tried not to look like a lawman as he pushed his way through the doors. It took a few seconds for his eyes to adjust to the dark. As the adjustment came, Ridge saw two men at a table off to his left and three men at a table on the other side of the room to his right. There was no one else in the saloon except the bartender, who was behind the bar, wiping glasses with a dirty towel.

The two to his left were Sal Durant and Fenton Millard. The outlaws glanced at him, then went on with their quiet conversation. Ridge sized up the situation as he moved through the room and saw the three men on his right look up at him as he stepped up to the bar. The bartender, a stout, bald man, grinned and said, "What'll it be, pal?"

"Just some information," replied Holloway. "Lookin' for a friend. I thought he might be in here. But I—"

Suddenly one of the men to his right stood up and said loudly, "Well, if it ain't the Deputy U. S. Marshal Ridge Holloway himself! How ya doin', Marshal?"

Ridge recognized the man's face, but couldn't place him.

"Guess you found him," chuckled the bartender.

Holloway's attention went immediately to Durant and Millard. They were looking at him warily, their hands dropping slowly to their sidearms.

Ridge had to move fast. He whipped out his gun and shouted, "Get back!" Durant's gun was out and coming up on him. Ridge fired, hitting him square in the heart. By the time he could swing his weapon on Millard, the outlaw had dropped his hammer.

Millard's gun boomed, and Ridge felt the slug claw at the sleeve of his left arm. A burning sensation followed. He fired, hitting Millard in the upper chest on the left side, and the outlaw went down, his gun slipping from his fingers.

Ridge had his gun cocked and ready to fire again as he stood within twenty feet of Millard, who was breathing hard and looking at his revolver only inches from his right hand.

"Don't even think about it, Fenton," Ridge warned. "You'll end up as dead as your partner. You're under arrest."

"You ain't takin' me in, lawman," breathed Millard. "I ain't gonna rot in no federal prison."

"Be better than dyin'," retorted Holloway, moving slowly toward him. "If you go for that gun, I'll have to shoot you again."

The words were still coming out of Holloway's mouth when Millard grabbed his revolver and started to bring it to bear. A second shot boomed from Holloway's gun, sending a slug through the outlaw's wrist. The gun fell from his hand, but Millard was determined. Swearing, he grabbed the weapon with his left hand and swung it on Holloway.

Ridge was left with no choice. His gun roared again, and Fenton Millard slumped into a lifeless heap.

Warden Burl Hedge was at the main gate of the Colorado Territorial Prison to meet the six mounted guards when they returned at sundown. His head guard, Murray Deppert, slid from the saddle while the others rode through the gate.

"I see you didn't get them," said Hedge glumly.

"No sir. They conked a farmer and stole three of his horses. We followed their trail to Spike Buck. They broke into the gun shop and a clothing shop there, and we followed their trail a few miles north of town, then it led into a stream. We rode the stream banks for hours, but couldn't find where they came out. They flat gave us the slip."

Hedge rubbed the back of his neck and said, "I'm sure you did all you could. Take your horse to the stable, then bring Frank Slattery to my office. He probably knows where they've headed."

"But will he tell you?"

"I don't know. Maybe, since they didn't take him with them."

Frank Slattery moved through the door of the warden's office with Murray Deppert behind him. A single chair sat in front of the desk. Hedge pointed to it and said, "Sit down, Frank."

Frank Slattery was two years younger than Jack, but looked a great deal like him, both in face and body. His features were grim as he obeyed, easing himself onto the hardback chair.

Deppert closed the door, then leaned his back against it, choosing to stay on his feet though there were other chairs in the room.

Hedge leaned forward, placing his elbows on the desk, and looked the condemned man square in the eye. "Where'd they go, Frank?"

"How should I know?"

"Don't give me that," blurted the warden. "Your brother and those other two cold-blooded killers know they've got to hole up and lie low for a while. I want you to tell me where they'll hole up."

Frank Slattery's face was like granite. "I have no idea."

"You're lying, Frank!" The warden's neck went red at his collar, and the color worked its way up into his jowls.

"What makes you think I'm lyin'? There ain't no special place. They could've gone most anywhere."

"My patience is running low, mister," he warned. "Now tell me where they went."

"I don't know."

"You liar! You do too know!"

The words echoed off the walls of the warden's office. Murray Deppert was a big man and was known to be strong as an ox. He moved up behind Slattery, laid both hands on his shoulders, and squeezed down hard. "Now, why don't you just come clean and tell Warden Hedge what he wants to know?"

"How can I tell him somethin' I don't know?" Slattery whined through clenched teeth.

Deppert squeezed even harder and growled, "I'll bet a couple dislocated shoulders would help loosen your lyin' tongue!"

Slattery slid down in the chair, ejecting a pained wail.

"Enough, Murray," Hedge said with a wave of his hand.

Deppert let go and took one step back. "I can get it out of him, sir."

"We can't use those methods, Murray, as much as I'd like to." Then to Slattery, Hedge said, "You're a fool, Frank."

"Whattya mean?"

"Jack and those other two don't care a fig about you, or they'd have taken you with them."

Frank's mouth pulled tight, but he said nothing.

"They're just as guilty as you are, Frank," Hedge said, his eyes narrowed. "But you're gonna hang, and they're gonna go scot-free."

Slattery met the warden's hard gaze with one of his own, but said nothing.

"Pretty dirty of them, don't you think, Frank? Left you to die alone. You could pay them back real easy."

Frank adjusted himself on the chair. "I don't care about Grabow or Taggart, but I ain't gonna sic no law on my brother!"

Hedge eased back in his chair. "So if you chose to, you *could* sic the law on Jack, right?"

"What?"

"You just said you aren't gonna sic the law on Jack. Well, sounds to me like if you wanted to sic the law on him you could, because you know where he's gonna hole up."

Frank stared at the warden, adjusted his position on the chair again, and cleared his throat. "Okay, so I know where Jack is gonna hole up. You ain't gonna find out where from me."

"Like I thought—mush for brains. You'll protect Jack, but he couldn't care less about you. Some kind of brother you've got. While you take the plunge, Jack'll be sitting in the hideout all safe and snug. He won't shed a tear on October 27. He proved that he cares nothing about his little brother. You're a fool."

"Jack would've taken me if he could've!" Frank screamed.

"Open your eyes, Frank! Jack could've taken you along if he'd wanted to! Look me in the eye and tell me I'm wrong."

Frank stared at the floor. Silence prevailed.

"If Jack is such a good and loyal brother, Frank, why didn't he take you with him?"

The words came out cold and shaky. "I ain't tellin' you nothin'."

Hedge released a big sigh of disgust and said, "Get him outta here, Murray, before I lose my temper and let you dislocate his shoulders."

It was just after seven o'clock the next morning and Burl Hedge was having a cup of coffee at his desk, rubbing his eyes. He had slept very little during the night. There came a knock at the door.

"Yes?" he called.

"It's Murray, Warden."

"Come in."

The door came open, and Deppert took one step inside. "Sir, we've got a little old man down in the reception room. Says he wants to talk to you."

"About what?"

"Well, sir, he rode up to the gate on a droop-eared mule and asked the guards if there'd been a prison break within the last couple of days. They told him of Grabow, Taggart, and Slattery breakin' out, and he asked what they looked like. When he heard their description, he told the guards he had information for the warden about them."

"Bring him to me," Hedge said, rising to his feet.

Moments later, Murray Deppert ushered the grizzled hermit into Hedge's office. Hedge extended his right hand and said, "I'm Warden Burl Hedge."

"Barney Fletcher," grinned the oldster, meeting his grip.

"I understand you have some information for me."

"Yep. Yore guards described the very no-goods that showed up at my cabin yeste'day. I had a funny feelin' 'bout 'em all along. Shore was right, wasn't I?"

"Yes," nodded Hedge. "Now, exactly what is it you wanted to tell me?"

"Thought you might be interested in which way they're headin'."

"Well, we know they were heading northwest until the guards I had tracking them lost their trail in a stream."

"Mm-hmm. Well, when they came to my cabin, they ast if they was on the right trail to Buena Vista."

Hedge and Deppert exchanged glances.

"They said they was goin' through Buena Vista to Denver."

"Denver?" queried Hedge.

"Thet's whut they said. 'Course, they coulda been lyin'."

"I very much appreciate this information, Mr. Fletcher," said Hedge. "Now, exactly where is your cabin?" The old man gave them a detailed description of his cabin's location.

"They no doubt were headed for Buena Vista, Warden," Deppert said, "but I think they were lyin' about goin' on to Denver. I've got a feelin' they're gonna hole up somewhere in the mountains."

"I think you're right," replied Hedge. Then turning to the old man, he patted him on the back and said, "I can't thank you enough, Mr. Fletcher. You've been very helpful. What you've told me may just help us apprehend them."

Barney shrugged his shoulders and grinned. "Just doin' my duty, Warden."

When Fletcher was gone, Hedge said, "Only thing we can do now, Murray, is put it in the hands of the United States marshal at Denver."

It was five minutes before eight o'clock when Chief U. S. Marshal Solomon Duvall dismounted in front of the federal building that housed his office on Tremont Street in Denver. He looked up to see two of his deputies talking to the Western Union delivery boy, Billy Thompson.

Billy was holding a yellow envelope, and turned to smile at the chief as he rounded the hitch rail. "Got a message for you, sir," said the fifteen-year-old. "It's from Warden Hedge at the prison in Canon City."

"Thanks, Billy," grinned Duvall, who bore the look of a seasoned and aging lawman. He had a set of rough, raking eyes deep-set in a face the color of an old boulder. Silver hair showed under the broad brim of his hat, matching his bushy brows and droopy mustache.

"You're welcome, sir," said Billy, placing the envelope in Duvall's hand and hurrying off.

Duvall looked at Deputies Todd Traeger and Jess Vine. "Well, boys, we'd better open shop. No doubt the bad guys in these parts will give us something to do before the sun gets much higher."

The U. S. marshal's office, strategically located in the Rocky Mountain region at Denver, was bolstered with fourteen deputies. All but three were on assignment, tracking down outlaws in every direction. Duvall kept three deputies around the office at all times in order to handle local problems. His third deputy on this day was Lou Watson, who rode up just as Duvall was unlocking the office door. Watson had just joined Duvall's staff two days earlier.

Duvall entered his private office, sat down, and read Warden Hedge's lengthy telegram. He sighed deeply, then strode into the outer office where Traeger and Vine were helping Watson with some paper work.

"Bad news, boys," he said.

All three turned to hear it, eyes fixed on their boss.

"Ord Grabow, Treg Taggart, and Jack Slattery broke out of Canon City Prison yesterday morning."

"Oh, no!" Vine said.

"Nothing about *Frank* Slattery, sir?" Traeger asked.

"Not much more than that they didn't even try to take him with them," responded Duvall.

"That's strange," Watson said. "I mean, Frank is Jack's kid brother."

"Hedge give you any idea which way they headed, Chief?" asked Vine.

"North. Hedge sent guards after them, but they lost their trail. Seems they stopped at an old hermit's shack in the high country, and told him they were heading for Denver through Buena Vista."

"Coming here?" Watson said, raising his eyebrows. "Going to make it easy for us, eh?"

"Don't think so. Hedge says he thinks they were lying to the hermit. He squeezed pretty hard on Frank and learned that they're going to hole up somewhere. I seriously doubt they'd come here. Frank let it slip that he knows where the hideout is, but refuses to tell."

"So we've got to start combing those mountains, Chief?" Jess Vine asked. "Why, they could be anywhere. There's no way we can find them with no more than that to go on. Seems to me Hedge needs to lean hard on Frank and make him talk."

Duvall scrubbed a hand over his mouth, absently toying with his mustache. "I'm afraid torture is out, Jess. But I...ah...I know a man who's smart enough to get the location of the hideout from Frank Slattery without hurting him. He's a genius at this sort of thing."

"And who is this genius, Chief?" Lou Watson asked.

Duvall smiled and glanced at his other two deputies. "You men know who I'm talking about."

Both nodded as Traeger said, "Your friend John Stranger."

Watson said, "Wait a minute. You're telling me you have a friend whose name is actually *Stranger? John Stranger?*"

"That's the only name anyone in these parts knows him by," replied Duvall. "He's a mysterious sort, but one fine gentleman. Has insight on human behavior like you've never seen. He can squeeze the information we need out of Frank Slattery, all right.

Only problem is, I don't know where John is. It'll take some time to run him down. Maybe several weeks."

"So what's this John Stranger do for a living, Chief?" Watson asked. "He a lawman of some kind?"

Duvall looked at the other two deputies and smiled. "Sometimes. But he doesn't do it for a living. He does it to help me out when I have a need for his services. He does the same thing for other lawmen."

"Other times," Traeger volunteered, "Stranger does some doctoring when there isn't a doctor around. Does some ranch work now and then. Helps people who are in trouble. Gives money to people who are in need."

"He's some kind of preacher, too," Vine said. "Puts the heebie-jeebies down your spine."

Watson looked at Duvall. "He really that good, Chief?"

"He wouldn't know," chuckled Vine. "He's never heard him."

Duvall's face tinted. "Church just isn't my cup of tea. John's talked to me about the Bible, and heaven and hell, and that kind of thing, but I've got other things to think about. Other than his preaching at me now and then, I love to have him around. Anyway...my point is, I've got to find him and get him to Canon City before it's time for Frank Slattery to hang—and that could take weeks."

"If it does, Chief," Traeger said, "there's no way we'll ever catch Grabow, Taggart, and Slattery. Once Frank is dead, there'll be no way to find the hideout. They'll hole up till they think it's safe, then they'll go on a robbing and killing spree again."

"We've got to make time work for us," Duvall said.

"How?" asked Traeger.

"Two things. First, I'll go see Judge Waymore and ask him to put a stay on Frank's execution until I can locate John Stranger. Once we find out where their hideout is, we'll be there in a hurry. Hopefully they'll still be holed up, and we can haul them back to Canon City...and the gallows."

✷ ✷ ✷ ✷ ✷

Late that afternoon, Murray Deppert knocked on Burl Hedge's door. He entered at the warden's call and closed the door behind him. "You get a reply from Chief Duvall, sir?"

"Yes," Hedge nodded, gesturing for Deppert to sit in the chair in front of the desk. "Duvall talked to the judge and got an open-ended stay of execution on Frank. Duvall has some genius friend he thinks can come here and get the hideout location out of Frank by using some kind of mental trickery or something. It may take a few weeks to find this friend."

"Well, I guess anything's worth a try."

"Can't argue with that. We'll sit tight and wait till this friend of the chief's can get here. Duvall said once his friend gets the information out of Frank, he and his deputies will move on the hideout. If Frank's information is proven to be true, he'll be hanged immediately, and hopefully the marshals will capture the others so we can put a rope on their necks."

The next morning, Duvall began wiring sheriffs and town marshals within a five-hundred-mile radius, giving John Stranger's name and description. He asked them if they saw Stranger to have him wire the Denver office immediately.

If Duvall did not locate Stranger in time, he would instruct Warden Hedge to simply tell Frank Slattery that the execution had been temporarily postponed for reasons undisclosed. Duvall hoped against hope that wherever the three killers were holed up, they would stay there long enough to be caught like rats in a trap.

THREE

———◆———

I t was mid-morning the day after Chief U. S. Marshal Solomon Duvall sent out his wires to lawmen in the area. Two of Duvall's deputies had just returned from tracking, unsuccessfully, a pair of train robbers into Kansas, and they sat in front of Duvall's desk, explaining the problems they encountered. Deputies Todd Traeger, Jess Vine, and Lou Watson leaned against a side wall, listening.

"Chief, we'd've had those skunks if Nick's horse hadn't broken its leg," Deputy Fred Upshaw said. "We were closing in on them, sure as anything. We rode double all the way into Goodland, but the extra load slowed my animal down, and...well, we just couldn't keep up with them."

"Time I could buy a horse in Goodland, and Fred and I could get back on their trail, there wasn't any trail," Nick Pond said. "They just seemed to disappear into thin air."

Solomon Duvall leaned back in his chair and pulled at an ear. His countenance showed that he was displeased, but his voice held no ire as he said, "Guess all I can say, fellas, is that I wish you'd caught up to them before they crossed the Kansas line."

"We gave it our best, sir," Upshaw said, "but when the wind kicked up that dust storm, we had no choice but to take refuge and wait till it was over. We knew those two outlaws were having to hole up just like we were, but there was no way we could—"

Upshaw's explanation was interrupted by a knock at the door.

"See who that is, will you, Watson?" the chief said to the newest man on his force.

Lou Watson opened the door and found Billy Thompson standing there, smiling. "Howdy. I have a wire here for Chief Duvall."

"Bring it here, Billy," Duvall said.

The boy hurried to the desk and handed Duvall the yellow envelope. "Would you like me to wait so's if you wanted to send a reply, I could take it to my pa?"

"Not necessary, son," smiled Duvall. "If it demands an answer, I'll send one of my men over with it."

"Yes, sir," nodded the boy, and was gone.

Before opening the envelope, Duvall stood and said to the two deputies who sat before him, "We can't catch them all, fellas. Thanks for giving it your best. I know you're tired, so go on home and get yourselves some much-needed rest. Report back to me in the morning."

When Upshaw and Pond had gone, Duvall said, "Well, you fellas have some paper work to do, so I'll turn you loose on it."

The other three deputies moved to the outer office and picked up where they had left off when Upshaw and Pond had arrived. Traeger and Vine said they would be glad when they could be sent out on an assignment and some other poor deputies could take over the tedious part of the federal lawman business.

Watson, who was just learning the paper work part of the job, grinned and said, "Well, my pa always said you gotta take the bad with the good."

"Sounds like your pa and mine went to the same school," chuckled Traeger.

"And mine," Vine said.

Just then Duvall came out of his office and said, "Wire's from Marshal Rayburn Blair in Heber City, Utah, fellas. Says John Stranger was in his town about a month ago, but he has no idea which direction he went. Doesn't help me any, but at least it's good to get such a quick response."

"Guess your friend Mr. Stranger can move a long ways in a month," Vine said. "Who knows where he might be by now?"

"All depends," replied the chief. "If John sees people with a need or a wrong that needs to be righted, he sticks with it till its taken care of. Sometimes he'll be in one locale for quite a while... then there are times when he moves a long ways in a hurry. I've known him to load that black gelding of his on a train and move several hundred miles in a jiffy. Oh, well. Since Judge Waymore signed that stay of execution, there's no need to get nervous about where John Stranger might be. Sooner or later, one of those lawmen I wired will know where he is. Until then..."

Duvall's attention was drawn to the window where he saw Deputy Ridge Holloway ride up, leading two horses. A dead man was draped over the saddle of each animal.

"What is it, Chief?" Traeger asked, turning to look out the window.

"It's Ridge," replied Duvall, moving toward the door. "Looks like he got his men."

Solomon Duvall and the three deputies stepped out onto the boardwalk as Ridge Holloway swung down and wrapped his horse's reins around the hitch rail. People on the street gawked at the bodies draped over the horses' backs.

"Looks like you shed some of your own blood on this one, Ridge," Duvall said, nodding at Holloway's left arm. The sleeve of his heavy shirt was ripped just above the bicep and showed a large stain of dried blood.

"It's not bad. Just a scratch," Holloway said.

"Looks like more than a scratch to me," said Duvall. "You lost quite a bit of blood. You got a bandage on it?"

"Yeah. It'll be okay."

Duvall moved closer to the hitch rail and eyed the lifeless forms, their heads and arms dangling. "Where'd you catch up to them?"

"Laramie City. One of the saloons. Tried to take them alive, but they thought they could shoot their way out."

Duvall grinned, shook his head, and chuckled, "The fools. They didn't realize who they were up against."

Duvall turned to Vine and said, "Jess, you take the bodies over to the funeral parlor, then put the horses at Sideler's stable. Tell Yates the U. S. government will pay him for burying the outlaws, and tell Ben to sell the horses, take out his fee for boarding and selling them, and to pay our office the difference…if there is any by the time they're sold."

"Right," nodded Vine, and moved to lead the horses away under the gawking eyes of the townspeople.

"Todd, you watch the office while Lou and I walk over to Doc Goodwin's office," Duvall said.

"While you do what?" asked Holloway.

"Oh, by the way," Duvall said, ignoring the question. "Ridge, I want you to meet our newest deputy, Lou Watson. He's replacing Harry Sloane."

Deputy Harry Sloane had been killed in the line of duty a few weeks previously. The sound of his name lanced a cold shaft through Holloway's heart. He and Sloane had been good friends. But Ridge managed a smiled and shook hands with Watson, welcoming him to the force.

"I want Lou to meet Doc Goodwin," Duvall said to Holloway, "since Doc is our official physician."

"We have an official physician?" Watson said.

"Mm-hmm. Denver has three good doctors, but we chose Doc Goodwin to patch up our men because his office is closest to ours. I think you should meet him *before* he has to see you in his official capacity. I mean, since I'm walking Deputy Holloway over there anyway."

"Fine with me," said Watson.

"Now, look, Chief," argued Ridge, "I wrapped the wound up. Believe me, it'll be all right."

"Nope," retorted Duvall, shaking his head. "By what I see on that sleeve, you've lost too much blood for it to be minor. I want Doc to look at it, and the only way I can be sure you'll go over to his office is to walk you there myself. C'mon. Let's go."

Holloway wagged his head back and forth, grinning. "You know what, Chief?"

"What?"

"You'd make somebody a good mother."

The three lawmen made their way down Tremont Street toward Dr. Lyle Goodwin's office, which was a block and a half from the federal building. About halfway, they were passing Denver's largest clothing store when two young women came out, carrying packages. They took one look at Holloway and cried, "Ridge, what happened?"

"Just got a scratch while trying to capture a couple of outlaws. Nothing serious."

"It sure looks serious," one of them said.

"It's really not. Danielle, Maisie, I'd like you to meet my chief, U. S. Marshal Solomon Duvall and the newest member of our force, Lou Watson. Men, this is Danielle Fontré and Maisie Sanborn."

The two young women did a slight curtsy and the lawmen lifted their hats, smiling and saying how happy they were to meet them. Ridge explained that Maisie and Danielle were members of the same church he belonged to, and that they taught children's classes in the Sunday school.

Danielle eyed the bloody sleeve again, and asked, "Does Marlene know you've been wounded, Ridge?"

"No. No, she doesn't even know I'm back yet. I'll be seeing her this evening, I'm sure."

"Ladies, you'll have to pardon us," Duvall said, "but we really need to get Deputy Holloway to Dr. Goodwin."

Ridge told the young ladies he would see them on Sunday, and the three lawmen moved on down the street. When they stepped into Dr. Goodwin's waiting room, a young nurse sat at the desk, making notes in a patient's file. Looking up, she smiled and said, "Well, what have we here? Three federal lawmen at once! Am I being arrested?"

When she saw Ridge Holloway's bloody sleeve, she stood to her feet and asked, "Is that a bullet wound, Ridge?"

"Yes, ma'am. I bandaged it up, and I think it'll be all right, but Mother Duvall here thinks Doc should take a look at it." He paused, then said, "Oh! Miss Breanna, I should introduce you to our newest deputy, Lou Watson."

The nurse offered her hand and welcomed Watson to Denver.

"Nurse Baylor is one of the rare C.M.N.s we have in the West, Lou," said Duvall. "You know what that is, don't you?"

"Yes," said Watson, having a hard time keeping his eyes off the nurse's face. "Certified Medical Nurse."

Breanna Baylor smiled at him again and said, "I'm actually what we call a 'visiting nurse.' I usually am traveling about, but Dr. Goodwin is out of town for a couple of days, and I'm filling in for him. Anything I'm not qualified to handle, I refer to one of Denver's other doctors."

Breanna turned to Holloway and said, "Let's go on into the clinic and let me take a look at that wound, Ridge." She led Holloway inside the examining room and gestured toward the table. "Sit right there, and we'll see how bad you're hurt."

Ridge and Breanna knew each other well. They both attended the same church and had shared many conversations, especially after he became a Christian. Breanna knew her Bible well and had answered many questions for him.

Breanna cut away the sleeve, removed the crude bandage Ridge had made for himself, and began carefully examining the wound.

"What do you think, Miss Breanna?" Duvall asked.

"Didn't go real deep, but he's going to need stitches. I'd say it will take about ten." Then to Ridge, "Lie down here on the table, and I'll get started."

Breanna moved to the cupboard and began gathering the materials she would need. Over her shoulder, she said, "Chief Duvall, you and Deputy Watson can sit out in the waiting room while I take care of this."

"We really need to get on back to the office, ma'am," said Duvall, "but I need to ask you if this wound is going to be a problem for Ridge. You know…as far as him doing his work. I have an immediate assignment for him, which I haven't even talked to him about yet, but it'll take him out of town as usual."

Breanna carried her supplies to a small stand beside the table where Ridge lay. "I assume it could involve gunplay," she said.

"Yes'm."

"If it was his right arm, Chief, I would say not to send him. But these stitches shouldn't cause much problem. He should be able to do his job just fine."

"Good," grinned Duvall. "Ridge, we'll talk about this when you get back to the office, okay?"

"Sure, Chief. I'll be there in a bit."

Watson moved close to the table and looked down at Holloway. "Pretty as she is, you'll probably not even feel the needle when she puts in those stitches."

Ridge grinned and Breanna gave Watson a mock frown, saying, "Vamoose, Deputy!"

Duvall and Watson laughed and headed for the door.

"Thanks for fixing up my man, Miss Breanna," the chief said.

"Oh, you're welcome. I'm to bill your office as usual, right?"

"Yes'm."

When they reached the street and headed back toward the federal building, Watson said, "Perky little gal, isn't she? Not to mention her good looks."

"That she is," Duvall said.

"You think a lot of Ridge Holloway, don't you, sir?"

"That's an understatement. He's the best man I've got. Has a lot of good common horse sense, knows how to use his brain, and when he's pushed, he knows how to handle his gun. Pretty good with his fists, too, I might add."

"How long's he been with you?"

"Just a couple of years. He was deputy sheriff in El Paso County, down in Colorado Springs, when I learned about him. Has a knack for tracking down outlaws and bringing them in—some dead, some alive. I contacted him, offered him a job on my force, and he's been with me ever since."

A wagon rolled down the street toward them. The driver, an elderly man, waved and called, "Howdy, Sol!"

Duvall waved back, then said, "I was afraid for a while that Ridge might ruin himself as a lawman, but it didn't work out that way."

"How's that?"

The chief cleared his throat. "Well, I…ah…I don't know anything about your religious preferences, Lou, but I'm leery of these Bible-thumpin' Christian types."

"Don't worry, sir, I'm not one of them," Watson said. "But I rubbed elbows with a lot of those types in the Civil War. Some of them may be a little off in the head—of course, I know some non-religious types like us who are, too—but some of the finest and bravest men I fought with carried Bibles and weren't ashamed to be known as followers of Jesus Christ. There was a chaplain—Baptist, I think—who was working on me. A lot that he said made good sense, but he got killed at Petersburg, and I haven't heard any preaching since."

"Well, I don't mean to offend anyone," Duvall said, "but that kind of thing just doesn't appeal to me. Anyway, what I started to say was that a little over a year ago, Ridge began going to church every time he was in town. Same church Nurse Baylor goes to, by the way."

"Oh? She doesn't act like a fanatic."

"Well, she's got her feet on the ground, I'll say that," chuckled Duvall, "but the little scamp has preached to me a few times."

"I wouldn't mind *her* preaching to me at all," Watson said. "I'm sure I could sit and listen to her for hours!"

"I don't mean pulpit preaching. I mean she preaches to me one-on-one every once in a while."

"I wouldn't mind that, either."

"Anyway, as I was saying...several months back I noticed that Ridge was showing a lot of interest in Marlene Daniels. When I saw him going to church with her every time he was in town, I got worried. I was afraid if he got converted, it would ruin him as a law officer."

"So he got converted, I assume."

"Yes. About six weeks ago."

"Hurt him any?"

"Not in the least. He's still just as persistent in his pursuit of outlaws as he was before. Those two he just brought in—Sal Durant and Fenton Millard. Mean. Killers through and through. I haven't gotten the details yet, but Ridge obviously did his job. And those two are numbers six and seven Ridge has tracked down and brought in since he got converted. Three of the other five he brought in alive. They've already been hanged. The other two, he had to take out in gunfights."

"Well, I guess becoming a Christian didn't ruin your best man, Chief. Like I said, that chaplain made some good sense. If I ever get converted, I hope I'll still be the lawman I ought to be. I'd like to be your number *two* man, anyway."

"Well, you just work at it," chuckled Duvall.

✻ ✻ ✻ ✻ ✻

Breanna Baylor had completed taking the stitches in Ridge Holloway's arm, and he was sitting up on the examining table while she bandaged it. They heard the door of the waiting room open and close, then there was a knock at the clinic door.

"I'll be with you in a moment," called Breanna. "Right now I'm with a patient."

"Miss Breanna!" came Marlene Daniels's harried voice. "Is Ridge in there?"

"Yes. Come in."

Marlene entered the room and hurried to the examining table. "Oh, Ridge! Maisie and Danielle told me you'd been shot! Is it bad?"

"Just a scratch," he replied.

"Just a scratch?" she said. "You don't use that much bandage on a scratch! How bad is it, Breanna?"

"Well, I'll have to say it was a little more than a scratch. It took ten stitches."

"Ten stitches! Oh, Ridge. Did you lose much blood?"

"Not a whole lot," Ridge replied, grinning. "I still have enough."

Tears filmed Marlene's dark eyes. "This is awful! Just awful! I can't stand it, Ridge! I can't stand it!" Suddenly, she began to weep, throwing her hands to her face.

Ridge gave Breanna a what-do-I-do-now look.

Breanna took Marlene firmly by the shoulders and said, "Get ahold of yourself, Marlene! Ridge is fine. I've already approved his going on another assignment very soon. The wound is not serious. The bullet didn't touch the bone. All it did was tear a little flesh."

Marlene turned to Ridge and said, "So this one isn't serious. I'm thankful to the Lord for that. But it could have been serious. The bullet could have plowed into your heart instead!"

Breanna touched Marlene's arm and said, "Honey, this kind

of thing is to be expected in the life of a lawman. Especially one as active as Ridge."

"That's just exactly what I've been trying to tell him, Breanna!" Marlene said. Then to Ridge, "See there? Even Breanna knows what happens to lawmen!"

Ridge picked up his shirt and slipped into it, trying to keep the bloody sleeve out of Marlene's sight. He met Breanna's steady gaze and said, "We've been discussing marriage, ma'am. But Marlene wants me to give up my badge and do something else for a living."

"Daddy has offered him a good job with his company," Marlene said, "but he won't even consider it. He would be a full partner in a few years, and we would be quite well off. But no...Mr. Stubbornness here thinks he has to wear a badge. I told him I won't marry him unless he finds another line of work, even if it's not with Daddy. But he thinks if he holds out long enough, I'll give in and marry him anyhow. Well, I won't!"

"Marlene, listen to me," said Ridge. "I—"

"No, you listen to me! I am not going to be a lawman's wife! For one thing, I don't want to live every day wondering if you'll come home all shot up or even dead. And for another, I don't believe a Christian man ought to wear a badge."

Breanna and Ridge exchanged glances.

Marlene set tear-filled eyes on the nurse and said, "Breanna, don't you agree that a Christian shouldn't be a lawman—that he shouldn't wear a gun and be in a position where he has to kill people? Daddy doesn't wear a gun, and neither does Dr. Goodwin. It just doesn't seem right to me now that Ridge is a Christian for him to wear a badge and a gun."

Ridge was tucking his shirt under his belt, looking at Breanna with expectant eyes. He wondered which of them she would agree with.

Breanna responded quickly and readily. "I think you're wrong, Marlene. Christians have no right to live in a society where they are protected by lawmen who lay their lives on the line every day...and refuse to be lawmen themselves."

"But what about—?"

"Just a minute, honey," cut in Breanna, raising palms forward. "Let me finish. You will agree with me that there's a war on between the men who wear badges and those who threaten the lives and property of law-abiding citizens, won't you?"

Marlene bit down on her lower lip. "Yes," she said weakly.

"Well, when a country is threatened by an aggressor in a time of war, what are Christian men supposed to do? If a Christian man refuses to take up arms and fight to protect his family and his country, what right has he to expect non-Christian men to do it?"

Marlene folded her arms across her chest and stared blankly at the floor. "It's not the same thing as being a lawman."

Ridge wanted to get into it, but Breanna was doing a good job. He would let her proceed.

"What's the difference?" she pressed. "War is war, whether it's a national war or a local one. The outlaws here in the West have declared war on good, decent citizens, and men like Ridge have taken up arms to fight them so people like you and me can lead safe and peaceful lives. They lay their lives on the line, yes. They also have to take lives to preserve ours. It's all part of it, Marlene."

Ridge set soft eyes on Marlene and asked, "Do you see the picture, now?"

Marlene jutted her jaw and said, "How about the sixth commandment? You *have* learned the ten commandments by now, haven't you? And I'm sure Breanna knows them. What about *Thou shalt not kill?* It is never right for one human being to take the life of another!"

"Scripture always sheds light on itself, Marlene," said Breanna. "I have a Bible in the desk out in the waiting room. Let's take a look and see what *Thou shalt not kill* means according to the Lord Himself."

FOUR

B reanna Baylor returned from the waiting room and moved up close to Marlene, opening her Bible. "Here, let's take a look at Genesis 9, verses 5 and 6. These are the instructions of Almighty God to Noah and his family when He sent them out of the ark after the flood. Look at the latter part of verse 5: *At the hand of every man's brother will I require the life of man.* You can see the subject here is the life of man. Right?"

Marlene nodded.

"All right. And what did God say? He said He would require the life of man at the hand of every man's brother. See that?"

Marlene nodded again.

"Okay, now look at verse 6: *Whoso sheddeth man's blood, by man shall his blood be shed: for in the image of God made he man.* According to this verse, Marlene, when one man has murdered another, who is to execute him?"

Marlene Daniels blinked. Her lips quivered slightly as she replied, "It says by man shall his blood be shed."

"That's right. Romans chapter 13 talks about this same thing and makes it very clear that those in authority must protect society by bearing the sword against evildoers. The Lord recognizes civil law and says we should obey it. Ridge just tracked down two evildoers who were a threat to society. Even if he had brought them in alive, they would have been hanged. Capital punishment originated with God Himself for the protection of law-abiding citizens. Thank God, though all our civil leaders are not Bible-believing Christians, they believe in the principles laid down in the Bible. That's why they hang killers. Woe be to this country if our leaders ever cast aside God's principles and go soft on outlaws. Nobody will be safe."

"But the Bible still says *Thou shalt not kill*," argued Marlene.

"You're right, it does," smiled Breanna. "Do you think God contradicts Himself?"

"Of course not!"

"Then what do we do with these two seemingly contradictory statements?"

Marlene thought for a few seconds. "I guess we have to let Scripture shed light on Scripture."

"Yes, you're exactly right," nodded Breanna, turning to the New Testament. "Let's let Jesus settle the problem for us."

She found Matthew chapter 19 and placed the page in front of Marlene. "In this passage, Jesus is listing for the rich young ruler some of the commandments in the moral law. Look at verse 18: *Thou shalt do no murder, Thou shalt not commit adultery, Thou shalt not steal, Thou shalt not bear false witness.* The adultery, the stealing, the lying all have their counterparts when we read the commandments in the Old Testament, don't they?"

"Yes."

"Okay, *Thou shalt do no murder.* Which commandment does that correspond to?"

Marlene thought a moment. "It would have to be *Thou shalt not kill.*"

"That's right. So Scripture casts light on Scripture. Jesus tells us that *Thou shalt not kill* is talking about murder. It is not murder when you kill someone in self-defense. Nor is it murder when civil leaders execute evildoers. They are obeying the command of God.

It was not murder when Ridge killed those two outlaws he just brought in, nor has it been murder when he has had to take the lives of other lawbreakers. In His wisdom, God laid out this order for the protection of society."

Marlene stiffened. Her eyes were unrelenting. "I still won't marry a man who wears a badge and carries a gun. Either turn in your badge and find other employment, Ridge, or we're through."

Ridge looked stricken and said nothing for a long moment. Then he looked at Breanna and said "Thanks for patching me up. I'm much obliged." With that, he headed for the door.

"You're welcome," Breanna called after him.

Ridge was through the door and gone, and Marlene stood with her mouth agape, staring at the spot she had last seen him. "Well! How do you like that?" she breathed, looking at Breanna. "How rude! He just walked out without saying a word to me!"

Breanna looked her straight in the eye. "Are you really in love with Ridge?"

"Of course."

"Would you take some advice from an older woman?"

"Older woman? You're not much older than I am. What…six or seven years?"

"Something like that. But I've been farther down life's road than you have, and I think you're wrong to do Ridge this way. If a woman truly loves a man, she will marry him for what he is, not what she wants him to be. If you really love him, accept him for what he is and marry him. Believe me, Marlene, you'll lose him otherwise."

Marlene stiffened. "You're not married, Breanna. What makes you the expert on how to keep a man?"

Tears surfaced in Breanna's eyes and her voice quivered as she said, "I know what it is to love a man, Marlene. And…I know what it is to lose him because of a foolish mistake."

"Well, I'm sorry about that," Marlene said, heading for the door, "but I'll prove you wrong in this situation. I'll get Ridge to turn in his badge and marry me, too."

When the door closed, Breanna broke down and cried. She wept for several minutes, then heard the outer door open, followed by anxious voices. Within minutes, she was busy stitching up a bad gash on a farm boy's arm.

That night, lying in her bed in the darkness, Breanna found sleep elusive. She kept going over her conversation with Marlene Daniels. Again she wept and said, "Oh, John, I miss you so terribly! I love you so much! How could I have made such a horrible mistake?"

She wiped her tears on the sheet, and sat up and fumbled for a match on the small bedstand. She found one, struck it, and lit the lantern. She crossed the room, sniffling and wiping more tears from her cheeks, and opened her purse and pulled out a silver medallion the size of a silver dollar. She returned to the bed and angled the medallion toward the lantern's light. It bore a raised five-point star in its center and was emblazoned with these words around its edge: *THE STRANGER THAT SHALL COME FROM A FAR LAND—Deuteronomy 29:22.*

Breanna eyed the medallion for a long moment, then doused the light and slipped back between the covers. The room was pitch-black around her as she clutched the medallion to her breast and let her mind trail back to that fateful day in Wichita, Kansas, when she sent John Stranger out of her life. "Oh, John, where are you tonight? Dear Lord, take care of him. Please Lord…please bring us together so I can tell him how much I love him, and how very foolish I was to send him away."

Breanna rolled over in the bed and adjusted the position of her pillow. She was wide awake. She closed her eyes and thought of all the times she and John had spent together and of how his presence had been both comforting and disconcerting. There was a gentleness in him like she had never seen in a man, yet the mysterious aura about him kept her off balance. The latter began to fade as she got to know him better, and she recalled the indescribable expression in his iron-gray eyes that drew her like a magnet.

The more time they had spent together, the weaker she found her resistance to him. John had made his feelings known to her, and they were definitely of the romantic kind. He had fallen in love with her.

John Stranger was a wonderful man, but she must never let herself be hurt again.

Breanna found herself sitting up in bed, wiping tears. She squeezed the medallion tight in her fist and breathed, "Oh, John…I will always love you." Then lifting her eyes upward, she looked into the pitch-black void and prayed, "Dear Lord, please…please bring him back to me."

Breanna pulled her legs up and wrapped her arms around them. Resting her face against her knees, she thought of the times John had been near her since that cold day in Wichita when she sent him away. He had even saved her life since then, but without letting her see him.

She stayed in that position for several minutes, then sighed and said, "Breanna Baylor, you'd better get some sleep. You have to be Dr. Lyle Goodwin again tomorrow."

Deputy U. S. Marshal Ridge Holloway arrived at the U. S. marshal's office after having his wound stitched up by Breanna Baylor. He found that Chief Solomon Duvall was in a private meeting with a deputy who had just returned from an assignment. Deputy Lou Watson told Holloway he was to get a good night's rest and be at the office at eight o'clock in the morning.

The time was five minutes before eight the next morning when Duvall met Holloway in the outer office and ushered him into the inner office for a conference.

When both men were seated, Duvall smiled and asked, "How's the arm this morning?"

"A little sore, but not bad. Miss Baylor is good at what she does."

"You sound like all her other patients…including me," chuckled Duvall.

"So what's up, Chief?"

Duvall eased back in his chair behind the desk and informed Holloway of the prison break at Canon City. Ord Grabow, Treg Taggart, and Jack Slattery were last known to be headed north toward Buena Vista. The guards had lost their trail just north of

Spike Buck, but an old hermit had seen them and reported to Warden Burl Hedge that they were heading for Buena Vista. Duvall went on to explain Frank Slattery's unwillingness to reveal the location of the hideout where the escapees would be holing up.

"So I assume I'm to find this hideout," said Holloway.

"Well, yes, but I want you to have more to go on than the word of an old mountain hermit."

"What do you have in mind?"

"You've heard me talk about John Stranger."

"At least a million times. Somehow I've always been out of town when he's been here."

"I've told you about his uncanny way of worming information out of outlaws."

"I think you've told me everything about the man...except one thing."

"What's that?"

"Why you want him around when he preaches to you so much."

Duvall sighed. "Well, as has been so well said so often, you have to take the bad with the good."

Holloway snorted and laughed. "Chief, you ought to give the Lord a chance. You might just find out this Bible stuff is better than what you've got."

Duvall shook a finger playfully at his favorite deputy. "Now, look, pal...I take the pressure from Stranger, but I'm not takin' it from you."

"Well, just so you get a dose now and then. Maybe one of these days you'll see your need for the Lord. Anyway...you brought up your friend John Stranger. I take it you're plannin' on sendin' him to Canon City to worm the location of the hideout out of Frank Slattery."

"Right."

"You know where Stranger is?"

"No. I've put out wires to every lawman in a five-hundred-mile radius. Somebody will see him sooner or later and tell him to contact me."

"Well and good, Chief, but isn't there a date set for Slattery's execution?"

"Yeah. The twenty-seventh."

" *This* twenty-seventh? October twenty-seventh?"

"Yep."

"Well, seems to me you're about out of time."

"Not quite. I got Judge Waymore to grant an open-ended stay of execution until I can locate Stranger and get him to Canon City."

"Well, good. So you're confident Stranger can get Slattery to tell him where the hideout is?"

"Stranger'll get it out of him, all right."

"I hope you're right. Grabow, Taggart, and Slattery are vicious killers. They've got to be tracked down and executed *muy pronto.*"

"I agree," said Duvall. "So...here's where you fit in. I want you to go over to the western slope. Delta Valley. Taggart's father has a cattle ranch there. Old man's name is Otis. It wouldn't surprise me any if the hideout is on the Taggart ranch. Maybe we can get a jump on those three before I find John Stranger."

"Worth a try, Chief," Ridge said.

"That's what I figure, and you're the best man I've got for the job. I want you to secretly observe the Taggart place."

"Have any idea how big the spread is?"

"Not really. I know Otis has five sons that work the ranch with him...total of six sons, with Treg. Has a daughter that lives on the ranch, too, I understand. Wife's dead."

"So, how soon do I go?"

"Tomorrow. You'll take the train over to Grand Junction, rent a horse, and ride south to Delta Valley. It's about fifty, sixty miles from Junction. If you should see any sign of the escapees or anything that would cause you to suspect they're being harbored on the place, wire me for instructions on your next move."

"All right."

"You can keep contact with me through the office of Delta County Sheriff Luke Prisk. Check in there every day to see if I've left any messages."

"Okay."

"If you feel confident Treg and his two cronies aren't being hidden there, wire me, and I'll send you further orders. Possibly by that time, I'll have found John Stranger and he'll have the location of the hideout squeezed out of Frank. If the hideout is within reasonable distance of Delta, I'll want you to put together a posse with Sheriff Prisk's help and head for it immediately."

Holloway rubbed his wounded arm and said, "I would imagine that Sheriff Prisk would've checked out the Taggart ranch by now on his own. Certainly he's been notified of the prison break, hasn't he?"

"Of course. And Prisk no doubt has thought of the possibility that Treg may be hiding there, but if he'd seen anything suspicious, he'd have notified Warden Hedge. Since I haven't heard from the warden, I must assume it's because Prisk has nothing to report. He's got a whole county to look after and can't watch the Taggart place every day. You can."

"I'll get my gear together and take the next train to Grand Junction," Holloway said, rising from the chair.

Situated in the heart of Delta Valley, Colorado, the town of Delta was the county seat. It was built on the banks of the Gunnison River, nearly three hundred miles southwestward across the Rockies from Denver.

Local rancher Roy Lynne and his family had ridden into Delta in one of the ranch wagons to do some shopping. The wagon was parked in front of the Delta Gun Shop while Roy was inside buying ammunition. His wife Nelda—who just had her forty-first birthday—waited with her two offspring, twenty-year-old Autumn and seventeen-year-old Adam. While the son and daughter sat quietly in the wagon, Nelda talked with Mable Dyer, the wife of another local rancher. The Dyers had recently moved into the area and were slowly getting to know their fellow ranchers and the people of Delta. Mable was smiling broadly because she had just learned from Nelda that the Lynnes were Christians.

"Oh, how wonderful!" she exclaimed. "Jim and I were hoping we'd find some other Christians in the valley. The one thing we are unhappy about is that there's no church here. Isn't it hard for you, too?"

"Yes, it is," nodded Nelda. "There are several other Christian families in the area who feel the same way. We meet on Sundays and have services in different homes. Our husbands take turns bringing Bible messages. We're praying that the Lord will send us a God-called preacher who will found a church and be our pastor."

"Oh, wonderful!" said Mable, clapping her hands together. "Just wait till Jim hears this! Where are you meeting next Sunday?"

"Well, it happens to be at our house. We start at ten o'clock, and the Sunday evening service is at seven. We'd sure love to have you come."

"You can bank on it, honey," replied Mable.

A wagon rolled down the street and hauled up in front of Mauldin's General Store directly across the street.

"Look, Autumn," Adam said. "It's Lulu."

"Who's Lulu?" Mable asked, casting a glance toward the driver of the wagon.

"Lulu Taggart, Otis Taggart's only daughter," Nelda said. "He's got six sons, but Lulu's the only girl."

"I heard about his oldest son," Mable said. "An outlaw and killer. Going to hang at the prison in Canon City in a few days."

"Yes."

"Looks like a man to me," Mable said, her eyes fixed on Lulu as she climbed down from the wagon seat.

"I know," said Nelda. "I suppose it's because she's been raised with those six brothers."

"She also cusses like a man," Adam said.

"Autumn has befriended her and tried to talk to her about the Lord," said Nelda, "but so far she hasn't been interested."

"And I'm going to keep trying," Autumn said. The sun shone brilliantly on Autumn's long auburn hair and her dark-brown eyes flashed.

"Her father makes fun of the Lord and those of us who believe in Him," Nelda said. "Rails at the Bible and says it's no better than Aesop's Fables. He has reared his sons and daughter to be just like him."

"Too bad," Mable said. "I hope the girl can be reached."

Lulu Taggart nearly bumped into Sheriff Luke Prisk as she passed through the door of Mauldin's General Store.

"Oops!" said the sheriff, sidestepping to avoid a collision. At twenty-six, Prisk was the youngest man to wear a sheriff's badge in all of Colorado Territory.

Lulu gave him a grim look and said, "Excuse me."

"My fault, Lulu," grinned Prisk. "Wasn't watching where I was going."

"Don't worry about it," she said, moving past him.

"So what does your pa think about the prison break?" Prisk asked.

"Prison break?"

"Yeah. Your brother."

"Treg?"

"Yes."

"Escaped from Canon City?"

"That's right. Three days ago. Sounds like you didn't know about it."

"I didn't. Pa doesn't either."

"You wouldn't lie to me, would you, Lulu? I mean, Treg and his pals aren't hiding on your place, are they?"

"No, they're not! And what do you mean 'pals'? Who else escaped?"

"Ord Grabow and Jack Slattery."

"Jack? What about Frank?"

"Frank's still there. He's still slated to hang on the twenty-seventh."

"Oh. Well, Sheriff, you can believe what you want to, but we don't know anything about the break."

"Lulu, you do understand, don't you, that harboring wanted criminals is a felony? If you're lying to me and Treg is hiding on your place, you, your father, and your brothers could go to prison for a long, long time."

Lulu's face flushed with anger. "I ain't lyin', Sheriff! I told you we don't know anything about Treg breakin' out of prison! My pa knows the law about harborin' wanted men, and he ain't hankerin' to go to prison. If Treg shows up at the ranch, pa'll send him on down the road!"

"I'd like to believe your pa would do that, Lulu, but I have a feeling he'd hide him. And anybody else Treg had with him."

"I don't give a tinker's toot about your feelin's, Sheriff! Are we through with this conversation?"

"Looks like we must be," he said calmly.

"Good!" she rasped, wheeling about. "I've got things to do."

Suddenly Lulu was aware that George Mauldin and several of his customers had been listening to the conversation. She gave them all a hard look and pushed her way up to the counter. "Is Taggart money still good in your store, Mr. Mauldin?" she asked curtly.

"Why, yes, of course," came a flustered reply.

"Fine. Then I need to buy some things."

"I'll be with you in a moment," nodded Mauldin. "Soon's I finish with Mr. Talley, here."

Lulu glanced around at the other customers, male and female, who were looking on, and growled, "What're you starin' at?"

They turned away and began looking at the merchandise on the shelves. When Bob Talley walked away from the counter, carrying his packages, Lulu told George Mauldin that her father had sent her to buy some tools. She listed what she needed, then waited impatiently at the counter, exchanging hard looks with the other customers.

Ten minutes later, Lulu passed through the door, carrying a box heavily loaded with tools. A man in his forties was just coming in as she moved onto the boardwalk. "Hello, Lulu," he said, smiling. "Can I carry the box to the wagon for you? Looks plenty heavy."

She glared at him and snapped, "I can handle it!"

"Well, excuse me," he said, and moved on inside.

Lulu carried the heavy box to the rear of the wagon, hoisted it over the tail gate, and dropped it hard and loud. The horses jumped with a start, snorted, and swished their tails.

She was heading for the front of the wagon when she saw Autumn Lynne coming across the dusty street, smiling at her. Beyond Autumn, Lulu could see Nelda and Adam standing together, talking to a local rancher and his wife.

Lulu swore under her breath. She liked Autumn but detested what she stood for. Otis Taggart had taught his daughter—as well as his sons—to stay away from "Bible-totin' religious fanatics."

Autumn drew up, smiling, and said, "Hello, Lulu."

Lulu laid her hand on the front wheel of the wagon, nodded without a smile in return, and said, "Autumn."

"Sheriff Prisk crossed the street to speak to us when he came out of Mauldin's. He told us about the prison break. We hadn't heard, yet."

"Mmm," Lulu nodded again.

"He said you didn't know about Treg breaking out until he told you a few minutes ago."

"Well, that's right."

"What'll your pa do if Treg and his friends show up at the ranch, Lulu?"

"What would your pa do if the situation was his, Autumn? Hmm? Treg's still part of our family, and I can tell you right now...Pa and the rest of us will do everything we can to keep the law from catchin' Treg again if he shows up. That's what. He's family, kid, that's enough. Us Taggarts stick together."

"You're very unhappy, aren't you?" Autumn said softly, giving Lulu a compassionate look.

"Whaddya mean?"

"Well, you never smile, and you're always carrying a chip on your shoulder. I don't know when I've ever heard you laugh. Life doesn't have to be like that, Lulu."

The Taggart girl sighed. "Yeah, I know. If I'd let Jesus come into my heart, I'd be happy all the time...just go around gigglin' and cuttin' up."

"I never told you that a Christian is happy *all* the time, Lulu," Autumn said softly. "As long as we're in this troubled world, we'll have our unhappy days. But when Jesus lives in your heart, and you know all your sins are forgiven, and you know you're going to heaven when you die, even unhappy days are easier to get through. When you know the Lord, everything in life takes on a new meaning, and you can face the hard times with joy and peace of mind. Not only that, but Jesus gives you something to live for."

"Look, Autumn," Lulu said in a level tone, "I like you. You've always been nice to me. But my pa has always taught me to stay away from that church stuff. He says hymn-singin' and hell-fire-and-brimstone preachin' is a foolish waste of time. Pa says the Bible is no different than Aesop's Fables...and that there ain't no heaven and there ain't no hell. He says when we die, it's the same as an animal dyin'. That's the end of us. So why bother with all that Jesus stuff?"

Heavy of heart for Lulu, Autumn said, "You told me before that you know there's a God."

"Yeah. This universe is here. I can't believe it just came from nowhere and nobody. Has to be a God."

"Doesn't it make sense, then, that since we were created by God, He would make contact with His creatures?"

"I guess," Lulu replied, shrugging her shoulders.

"That's what He has done in giving us the Bible, Lulu. It's His Word."

"Well, if He wants to contact us, instead of givin' us a Book, why doesn't He just come down here and talk to us?"

"He's done both," Autumn said, laying a hand on Lulu's arm. "He gave us the Bible, and He sent His Son into the world to die on Calvary's cross for our sins. Lulu, death is *not* the end for human beings. We either go to heaven to be with Jesus, or we go to hell to spend eternity away from Him. It all depends on whether we are willing to put our faith in Him."

Lulu's face went bone-white. She turned away from Autumn and climbed hurriedly into the wagon. "I've got to get home. Pa wants these tools right away."

"Down deep in your heart, you know what your father has taught you is not true, don't you?" Autumn said.

"I've got to get home."

"The church services are at our house this Sunday, Lulu. Ten o'clock in the morning and seven at night. Won't you please come to at least one of them?"

Lulu gave Autumn a blank look, snapped the reins, and drove away without answering.

Lulu Taggart had a miserable ride home. Why did it upset her so whenever Autumn talked to her about Jesus? Was there really something to this salvation stuff? Was her father wrong? *If Jesus is all the Bible says He is, why don't more people believe in Him? Why doesn't Pa believe in Him?*

Lulu's thoughts were interrupted by the sight of Sheriff Prisk riding toward her at an angle. He was coming from town cross-country, rather than following the road.

Prisk reached the ranch gate seconds ahead of Lulu and stopped his horse directly in front of her. Lulu pulled rein, rolled the rattling vehicle to a halt, and eyed him with disdain. "What're you doin' here, Sheriff?"

"I decided to come and check the place out. I want to make sure Treg and his pals aren't hiding here."

"I told you they ain't here. Until you informed me of the prison break, I didn't know nothin' about it. Neither does Pa. I told you that. Are you callin' me a liar?"

"Take it however you wish, but I'm not going to rest till I look the place over."

Lulu refused to look at Prisk as he rode alongside the wagon to the ranch house. When they hauled up at the front porch, Prisk saw Otis and his sons, Wick, Nate, Cliff, Jeb, and Van walking toward the house from the corral. The look on Otis's face showed that he was displeased to see the lawman on his property.

Lulu hopped out of the wagon and moved toward her father and brothers, telling them quickly about the prison break and of the sheriff's insistence he search the place for Treg. Prisk saw the look of surprise on all six faces. Were they putting on a good act, or were they really surprised? With the Taggart clan, there was no way to know. Prisk would have to follow his mission through. He slid from the saddle and met the clan stone-faced as they drew up.

Otis grinned and said, "So Treg's done got hisself outta that rotten prison, eh, Sheriff?"

"Yeah," nodded Prisk.

"Lulu says you think Treg's here."

"Just came to check and see."

"I don't rightly appreciate you callin' my daughter a liar, Sheriff. She said she told you Treg ain't here."

"I'll start with the house, Otis," Prisk said.

"You ain't got no right to come here and snoop, Sheriff!" Otis said.

"Oh, but I do. You live in Delta County, and if you'll look close at my badge, you'll see it says I'm sheriff of Delta County. I'm going to start with the house, and if I don't find Treg in there, I'll check out the barn and all the outbuildings. If I still haven't found any trace of him, I'll take a ride over every square inch of this place."

"Now, look here, Sheriff!" Otis bellowed. "You ain't—"

"And if I find that you're harboring Treg, you and your sons and daughter will all go to prison!"

"You ain't goin' one inch farther than you've already come, Prisk!" Wick Taggart said. Wick was next to Treg in age at twenty-eight and had a special dislike for lawmen, whom he considered to be crooks with tin stars on their chests. "Best thing for you to do is turn your horse around and ride off Taggart property while you're still healthy! Unless you can come back here with an army big enough to conduct a search, you'd best forget it!"

Prisk turned to Otis and said, "You'd better teach this smart aleck to keep his mouth shut. It could get him in real trouble. Now I'm telling all of you—if I have to come back here with enough men to force a search, you'll be jailed for obstructing justice! You got that?"

Van, the youngest son at twenty-one, blurted, "You deaf, Prisk? Didn't you hear what Wick said? Be best if you ride on out while you're still healthy. You're kinda pushin' your luck, aintcha?"

"Otis, either you call off your hounds and give me leave to make my search, or the bunch of you are going to be plenty sorry!"

Wick, face bloated with anger, moved toward the sheriff. Prisk was bracing himself when Otis leaped in front of Wick and took hold of his shoulders. "Let it go, son," Otis said. "We ain't got nothin' to hide." Turning to Prisk, he mumbled, "Go on and make your search, Sheriff."

Otis and his sons followed the sheriff everywhere he went in the house, barn, and outbuildings. Lulu planted herself in the kitchen and stayed there.

When the buildings were cleared, Prisk mounted his horse and told the Taggarts he would ride the place over. If he found no trace of Treg, they would be cleared for the moment. Before he rode out of the yard, he looked at Otis and said, "If you're telling me the truth and Treg isn't here, you are bound by the law to turn him in if he shows up. You harbor him for five minutes, and you're guilty of a felony. Understand?"

Otis gave him a hard, stony look. "I understand."

The sheriff could feel the hot eyes of the Taggart clan burning his back as he guided his horse out of the yard. He knew they would never turn Treg in.

CHAPTER

SIX

———◆———

The Taggart brothers sat at the supper table with their father and began gobbling their food. Lulu waited on them and ate in between pouring coffee and hurrying back and forth between the men and the stove to add more food to the table.

Wick laughed and said, "Good ol' Treg! Got himself outta that prison before they could hang 'im! Wonder how he did it?"

"I got a hunch it was Ord who came up with the escape plan," Jeb said. "He's a pretty smart cookie."

"Wouldn't doubt it," Cliff said. "Ol' Ord has a brain and a half in his head."

"What's got me puzzled," Nate said, "is why'n blue blazes they didn't take Frank along. I'd think Jack would've made sure Frank went with 'em."

"Maybe there jist wasn't no way," said Otis. "Set-up at the prison might not've been so's they could take Frank along."

"So ol' Frank'll hang by himself," said Wick. "Well…main thing is that Treg don't hang."

"For sure," grinned Otis. "Ain't no doubt in my mind Treg'll show up here as soon as it's safe. We need to plan on how to hide him when he does. He might have Ord and Jack with him, too."

While the men discussed what to do when the escapees arrived, Lulu Taggart was having a battle inside. Autumn Lynne's words kept biting at her like vicious dogs: *Down deep in your heart, you know what your father has taught you is not true, don't you?*

Lulu paid no attention to what her father and brothers were saying. She kept thinking of what Autumn had said about God sending His Son to die so sinners wouldn't have to perish if they believed in Him.

After a while, Wick noticed that his sister was preoccupied and absently picking at her food. "What's the matter, Lu? You're actin' funny."

Lulu raised her head, met his gaze, and said, "What do you mean, I'm actin' funny?"

"Well, you were starin' at your plate like a sick hound dog and just pushin' your food in circles. You in love or somep'n?"

"That's a dumb question. Course I ain't in love."

"Then what's ailin' ya?"

By this time, all eyes were fixed on Lulu.

"Nothin's ailin' me. I'm…just worried about Treg. Maybe the law'll catch up to him and he'll hang anyhow."

Otis studied her for a moment, then said, "Lulu, I think you're storyin' to Wick. You ain't showed this much worry over Treg before. I ain't seen you lookin' like a sick calf 'bout his bein' in prison and about to be hanged like you're actin' now. Out with it, girl. I wanna know what you're upset about, and I wanna hear right now. Don't try to pull no wool over your pa's eyes…that'll just git my dander up."

Otis Taggart had a way about him. None of his offspring could fool him. Lulu knew she was in trouble if she didn't tell him the truth. Her hands were trembling. She drew a shaky breath and said, "Okay, Pa. I…I saw Autumn in town today. She was talkin' to me about God and Jesus, and heaven and hell again."

Otis exploded into a long string of profanity, stood up, and shoved his chair backward, knocking it over. "I've told you to quit talkin' to those religious hypocrites, Lulu! Haven't I? Well, haven't I?"

"Yes, Pa, but—"

"But nothin'!" he stormed, his face getting red. "All that ever happens when you talk to that Lynne girl is you get upset! Why don't you listen to me and stay away from her?"

Tears were spilling from Lulu's eyes. "Autumn's the only person my age in this whole valley who'll even speak to me, Pa. She's always nice to me. I put up with her religious talk just to have someone to talk with."

Wick scowled at Lulu and said, "I think maybe you're startin' to believe that religious stuff, Lu!"

Every eye was on Lulu. "I ain't startin' to believe it," she said. "But it don't make a person bad just because they believe in God. Maybe believin' in God ain't so bad, anyway."

A deep frown ridged Otis's brow as he swung his head sharply toward his daughter and stared at her. "I knew it! You *are* startin' to believe that stuff!"

Lulu's eyes bulged with fear. "N-no!" she stammered. "All I said was—"

"You shut up, girl!" blared Otis, stabbing a finger at her. "Come on, boys. We're goin' to the Lynne place right now! I'm tellin' Roy Lynne face to face to make his daughter stay away from Lulu!"

"No, Pa!" Lulu sobbed. "Autumn is the only friend I've got! Please! I won't let her persuade me! I promise!"

Otis pointed his finger at her again. "I told you to shut up! You stay here and clean up the kitchen. Your brothers and me are gonna take care of this problem once and for all!"

Lulu knew better than to say any more. She stood in the middle of the kitchen with tears streaming down her cheeks and watched her father and brothers storm out of the kitchen and head for the barn.

✳ ✳ ✳ ✳ ✳

The moon was lifting off the eastern horizon as the five Taggarts rode west toward the Lynne ranch, putting their mounts to a steady trot. While they rode, Otis said, "I'm tellin' you boys right now, if one of you ever departs from what I've taught you about this God stuff, I'll bash your head in! There ain't no God! That Bible is fairy tales, just fairy tales. If there ever was a Jesus Christ, He's dead and gone like any man. Don't you ever believe that stuff about Him comin' back from the dead. Ain't no man never come back from the dead. When a man dies, that's the end of 'im. Ain't no heaven. Ain't no hell. Ain't no God anywhere in the picture. Ain't no God to have to answer to for our deeds. Men created God. We live our lives like we want to, and we die. That's it."

Otis cast quick glances at his sons and said, "I wanna hear it from you boys right now. That's what you believe, ain't it?"

"Exactly, Pa," said Wick.

"Jeb?" Otis turned to his next eldest.

"Sure, Pa. I believe what you've taught me."

"Nate?"

"Same here, Pa."

"Cliff?"

"I believe just like you, Pa."

"Van?"

"There ain't no God, Pa."

"Good! You boys just hold to that, and you'll be all right. Now let's take care of this business with Autumn Lynne."

At the Lynne ranch, Autumn's boyfriend Doug Price was their guest at the evening meal. The Lynnes approved of Doug as a potential husband for their daughter, though the couple had not yet become officially engaged. Autumn was expecting any time that

Doug, who was partner with his father at the Delta Hardware and Gun Shop, would have a man-to-man talk with her father, asking for her hand in marriage. Autumn was ready. Doug would get an emphatic "yes" when he asked her to marry him.

"Doug, did I hear you say when you came in the door that you'd talked to Sheriff Prisk this afternoon?" Roy asked.

"Yes, sir," Doug nodded and set his coffee cup in its saucer. "It was just before I left town to ride out here. Sheriff Prisk said he did a thorough search of the Taggart ranch and found no trace of Treg. He said he still expects Treg to show up there sooner or later."

"Sure he will," Aaron said. "Those Taggarts are a tight-knit clan. Treg will come home when he thinks it's safe to travel out in the open."

"Did the sheriff say he was going to keep a close watch on the Taggart place?" Roy asked.

"He said he wishes he could, but there's no way he can. With his duties to the whole county, he can't very well be out there in the bushes on the Taggart ranch watching for Treg."

"Won't the U. S. marshals be on Treg's trail, Daddy?" asked Autumn.

"I'm sure they will, honey. From what I know, those other two who escaped with Treg are as cold-blooded as he is. I'd think they'd be on their heels immediately."

"Sheriff Prisk told me they sent out guards from the prison to track them down," Doug said, "but they lost their trail after only a few hours. He's expecting to hear soon from the U. S. marshal's office in Denver as to what's being done to find them."

"Well, I hope they catch them before they show up around here," said young Adam. "It's bad enough just havin' the Taggarts in the valley…but to have Treg with 'em, and two more just like him, nobody'll be safe."

"That's for sure," agreed Nelda, looking around the table. "Anything else I can get for anybody?"

Everyone was sufficiently full.

"Autumn, I'll do the dishes and clean up the kitchen," Nelda said. "You and Doug can take yourselves a little moonlight walk, okay?"

Autumn shook her head and said, "I'm not going to leave you with all of this work, Mother. We'll do the dishes and clean up together. Then you can have your evening and there'll still be time for Doug and me to take our walk."

Doug pulled out his pocket watch, looked at it, and said, "Maybe we'd better postpone the walk till another time, Autumn. I have to be home to help Dad in about an hour."

Nelda stood up and said, "So it's settled. You two go on and take your walk. I can handle this project."

"I'll help you, sweetheart," Roy said. "These lovebirds need a little time together."

Doug and Autumn glanced at each other shyly.

"Mom, I'd help with the dishes and all, but I have a bone in my hand," Aaron said.

Nelda laughed. "How dreadful. I certainly couldn't expect you to do a thing in the kitchen when you've got a bone in your hand."

"I'd help, too, Mom," said Adam, "but I've got nails in the ends of my fingers."

"Oh, poor baby," said Nelda, frowning in mock concern. "We certainly can't ask you to help when you've got nails in your fingers. I don't suppose your handicaps will keep you boys from playing checkers for the rest of the evening, though."

Aaron and Adam grinned at each other.

"Get out of here, you two miserable bums!" Nelda laughed.

The night air was crisp as Autumn and Doug, wearing light coats, walked hand-in-hand down the lane that led to the road about a half-mile from the ranch house. The lane was lined with towering cottonwoods, which had lost nearly all their leaves, their naked limbs like skeletal claws against the moonlit sky. The night breeze whisked fallen leaves across the road in front of them with a dry, rustling sound.

Autumn hoped Doug would talk about the two of them and their plans for the future, but he talked instead about the prison break and what might happen if Treg Taggart showed up in the valley.

After they had walked about fifteen minutes, Doug said, "Well, Autumn, we'd better turn around. I don't want to keep my dad waiting."

"What kind of work are you and your father doing tonight?"

"Book work. We've got a stack of invoices to go through, and we need to work on new orders. A never-ending job."

"Guess you wouldn't want it to end, or you'd be out of business."

"Can't have that, now, can we? Delta Hardware and Gun Shop has to stay in business."

Autumn was hoping Doug would add that the company must stay in business so one day they could become husband and wife and have a good living, but the words did not come.

They were near the ranch house when they heard the rumble of hooves behind them. They turned and saw six riders galloping up the lane.

"Who do you suppose that is?" asked Autumn.

"I can't tell for sure yet, but I think it may be Taggarts!"

"What could they possibly want? We don't have anything to do with them!"

"I guess we're about to find out," said Doug, as they moved closer to the porch steps.

Otis Taggart hauled up to the sound of snorting horses and snapped, "Roy home?"

"He is," nodded Autumn. "What do you want to see him about?"

"I'll tell him when I see him. Tell him I want him out here."

Autumn felt the beginning of a surge of anger. "I'll take the message to my father if you'll tell me what your business is."

"My business is to tell your old man I'm not puttin' up with any more of your shovin' your religion down my daughter's throat! He's gonna put a plug in your mouth, or else!"

Autumn looked to Doug for backing, but he stood numb and silent. "I haven't shoved anything down Lulu's throat, Mr. Taggart, least of all religion! How could I shove something down Lulu's throat that I don't have?"

"Why, you lyin' little snip! Don't tell me you ain't got religion! You're whole family's just a bunch of religious fanatics!"

"You've got that wrong, sir," Autumn said. "We do not have religion. We have salvation in Jesus Christ. Salvation and religion are not the same thing. You are the one who is religious!"

"*Me?*"

"Yes, you! The Bible says, *The fool hath said in his heart, There is no God!* You worship your foolishness. You're the religious one, sir, not me. There's a big difference between salvation and religion."

Otis swore and spit on the ground. "I wanna talk to your old man!"

"I'm right here, Otis," Roy Lynne said as he crossed the porch with Aaron and Adam on his heels. Nelda paused at the door, looking on.

Otis and his sons fixed their eyes on the tall rancher as he demanded, "What are you screaming at my daughter about?"

"I came here to tell you *and* her that I want her stayin' away from Lulu! She's always upsettin' Lulu with all that religious talk!"

"I think you didn't hear Autumn, Otis," said Roy. "We are not religious people. We are saved people. There's a big difference. And you...you're supposed to be an atheist, right?"

"You bet I am!"

"And you say there's no God?"

"That's right!"

"Well, I just heard you ask God to damn something. Who were you talking to, Otis, if not to God?"

The older Taggart looked around at his sons, then back at Lynne and blared, "Don't you get smart with me, mister!"

"Who's getting smart? I heard you and so did your sons. You asked God to do something. If He doesn't exist, why do you talk to Him?"

"I've had enough of this, Lynne! And I've had enough of your daughter tryin' to convert Lulu! You make Autumn stay away from her, y'hear?"

"The girls have become friends, Otis. You can't lock Lulu away from everyone who doesn't share your hypocritical atheism."

"Whaddya mean, hypocritical?"

"Well, you say there's no God, yet you call on His name. That's hypocrisy if I ever saw it."

Otis Taggart was nonplused.

"You lay offa that talk to my pa, Lynne!" Van bellowed.

Aaron Lynne stepped to the edge of the porch and hissed, "You're on Lynne property, Van! Or have you forgot? You watch your mouth!"

"Yeah? Well, you watch your own mouth, buddy, or I'll shut it for you."

Aaron hopped from the porch, shouting, "You aren't man enough!"

Before anyone could stop him, Van vaulted from his horse and made a mad dash for his challenger. Aaron made a quick move to the side, seized Van by the collar, and slammed his face into the edge of the porch. The impact split his forehead open and he fell to the ground, dazed.

The Lynne men were not armed. When Aaron saw the Taggarts clawing for their sidearms, he bent down and whipped Van's revolver from its holster. He had the gun cocked and ready to fire before Otis and his sons could get their weapons out of their holsters.

"Hold it!" roared Aaron. "First guy that pulls a gun gets it!"

The Taggarts froze, eyes blazing with fury.

"Some Christian you are," Wick said, "puttin' a gun on your fellow man! I thought you Christians were supposed to believe in bein' peaceful."

"We do when it's possible," countered Aaron. "With Taggarts, it isn't possible. I'm warning you...don't put your hands near your guns."

"Look what you did to my son!" boomed Otis. "He's bleedin' somethin' terrible!"

"Pick him up and take him into town to the doctor," Roy said.

"Wick, pick your brother up and put him on your horse," Otis said. "We gotta git him to the doc. Cliff, you bring Van's horse along."

Wick slid from his saddle, giving Aaron a venomous look. Van's head was clearing, and he moaned pitifully as Wick hoisted him into his arms and carried him toward his horse. Cliff guided his mount to Van's horse, leaned from the saddle, and lifted the reins over its head so he could lead it.

"Better tie a bandanna around his head, Wick," Otis said. "Gotta slow that bleedin'."

Jeb glowered at Aaron and hissed, "You ain't heard the last of this, mister!"

"That's right!" Nate said. "We're gonna finish the trouble you Lynnes started!"

"You have a short memory, Nate!" Roy said. "It was you Taggarts who rode onto Lynne property spoiling for trouble! No Lynne started this."

"It's you with the short memory!" Nate retorted. "We rode over here because your daughter's been tryin' to make a Christian outta Lulu! Wasn't no bloodshed till that oldest son of yours slammed Van into the porch!"

Van was sitting on the ground beside his horse while Wick wrapped a bandanna around his head. Wick glared at Aaron and said, "This ain't over till you pay the piper, mister!"

"I don't cotton to threats, Wick! Best thing for you Taggarts to do is to stay off other people's property. If you'd stayed home, none of this would've happened."

"You got that wrong!" Otis half-screamed. "If that sister of yours hadn't upset Lulu with her Jesus talk today, none of this would've happened!"

Autumn left her mother's side and walked resolutely to the edge of the porch. Arms held stiffly at her sides, she said, "My purpose in talking to Lulu was not to upset her, Mr. Taggart. She's a very lonely and unhappy young woman. Is it so wrong to want to make someone's life better…and their eternity? I'm going to heaven when I leave this world, Mr. Taggart, and—"

"Enough of that claptrap!" Otis roared. "You just stay away from Lulu, girl! You understand?"

Otis turned to see Van on Wick's horse and Wick settling in the saddle behind him. Otis looked back at Autumn and jutted his chin. "You stay away from Lulu! I mean it!"

"You're gonna pay for what you did, Aaron!" Wick growled. "You're gonna pay!"

Roy moved up the steps and put an arm around his daughter's shoulders as the Taggarts rode down the lane. Nelda and their two sons joined them.

When the Taggarts passed from view, Aaron eased the hammer on the revolver. "Whew! Thought for a minute there I might have to back up my words!"

Doug was still planted where he had been when the trouble started. He was visibly shaken as he turned and looked up at Autumn. "I'd better get home. Dad's probably wondering what's happened to me." The Lynnes bid Doug goodnight and watched him ride away.

Autumn turned to her father and said, "Daddy, what should I do?"

"Don't let this keep you from witnessing to Lulu, honey. She's not a child. If she's willing to talk, you go right ahead and talk to her. She needs the Lord."

Autumn pressed against her father's side. "I'm glad you feel that way, Daddy. I can't imagine not talking to her about Jesus."

CHAPTER
SEVEN

———◆———

The long grass was becoming tawny on the rugged hills of eastern Utah Territory, and the vagrant winds that swept down from the peaks and distant purple mountains carried a skin-biting nip to them, a bleak reminder that winter was on its way.

The lone rider tightened the black, flat-crowned hat on his head and guided the black gelding beneath him up the rocky trail that seemed to run all the way to the azure sky. When horse and rider reached the trail's crest, they were on a lofty promontory that overlooked the long sweep of the valley below. At the south edge of the valley lay Green River, Utah.

The rider drew rein and let his smoke-gray eyes roam over the breathtaking scene. "Well, Ebony, there's Green River. We'll buy us some more cartridges and keep moving toward Grand Junction."

As if he understood, Ebony bobbed his head, swished his tail, and nickered softly.

The rider was a tall man with a powerful upper body. His features were craggy and rugged with a square jawline that gave evidence of his forceful personality and doggedness. His skin was dark complected, and his high cheekbones often caused observers to wonder if there was Indian blood among his forebears. His right cheekbone bore a pair of jagged, white-ridged scars. His black hair was neatly groomed, and on his upper lip he wore a well-trimmed mustache. His medium-length sideburns and the hair at his temples were slightly flecked with gray.

The tall man was dressed in black, with frock coat, white shirt, black string tie, and shiny black boots. On his narrow hips was a black gunbelt with a bone-handled Colt .45 Peacemaker in a tied-down holster.

The rider gave Ebony a slight nudge and urged him down the winding trail toward Green River as the wind plucked at his hat and ruffled the horse's mane. An hour's time brought horse and rider to the outskirts of the town, and soon they were moving onto Main Street at a slow walk.

Green River's main thoroughfare was wide and dusty, running some four blocks between weather-worn, false-fronted buildings. Residential sections spread out a quarter mile on either side.

It was a tough town, like all towns west of the wide Missouri in those early years that followed the Civil War. And like the rest of them, Green River had its share of drifters who rode with their hands on their guns and their eyes on their back trails...men who lived by the speed of their draw.

Green River's residents frowned on the steady parade of drifters who often brought trouble with them and left shed blood behind. There was a special graveyard on the east side of town where the slow-handed drifters were buried. Outlaws, troublemakers, and gunslingers could not be buried in the town's regular cemetery among the respectable citizens.

As the tall, dark man rode down the middle of Main Street, he gave off an air of alertness, of perpetual watchfulness. His eyes roamed the wide street and his right hand idly touched the bone-handled .45 snugged close to his hip, freeing it from saddle crimp. Then he lowered his right hand, letting it hang idly by his side as he passed a blacksmith shop and glanced into its dark interior. The smithy's hammer rang against red-hot metal, and the forge fire released its acrid tang into the cool mid-morning air.

The rider moved past a saloon where four tough-looking men stood eyeing him with a cold, intent scrutiny. He had experienced the same wariness in countless towns before.

He rode two blocks at a leisurely pace, feeling the watching eyes of men and women. He couldn't blame them for being cautious about strangers. Though he was dressed far better than most drifters, he was still an outsider, an invader of their territory, and so many outsiders rode into towns bringing with them trouble, heartache, and death.

Two men on the porch of the Green River Hotel rose from their chairs and strode to the railing. The bat-wing doors of another saloon swung open, and two men moved onto the boardwalk.

A stagecoach rumbled into town behind him, and he gave it room to pass. He noticed a faded wooden sign a few doors beyond the Wells Fargo office: *Woodley's Gun Shop*. He swung around the stagecoach as driver and shotgunner slid to the ground and passengers emerged. The lone rider caught the eye of the driver and nodded with a smile. The driver nodded and grinned in return.

The tall man swung down, patted his horse's neck, and wrapped the reins around the hitch rail. He could still feel the eyes of some of Green River's citizens on him as he moved into the gun shop and closed the door.

Next door to the gun shop was a millinery store. Inside, Norma Walters was seated in front of a mirror trying on hats. A small baby girl lay in her lap. Her three-year-old son was running about the store, being watched carefully by the store's owner, Florence Benson.

Norma tilted her head from side to side before the mirror with a large plumed hat on her head. "Bobby, I can't see you! Where are you?"

"Over here, Mommy." The boy was in a far corner looking for something, *anything* that would interest a lad his age.

"I told you to stay where I can see you," the mother said. "Now, do as I say."

Bobby moved toward his mother with a hop, skip, and jump, then did three complete turns with arms outstretched like wings.

Florence shook her head and smiled. "I wish I had the energy he has in the little finger of his left hand."

"Me, too," sighed Norma, adjusting the hat to a different angle on her head. "He's full of it."

Across the street from the Wells Fargo office, two teenage boys looked on as a third boy showed them the new Winchester .44 rifle he had received for his birthday. Cal Freeman cocked the hammer and swung the weapon upward as if to shoot a bird, making firing sounds with his mouth.

"Cal, is the gun loaded?" asked Derrold Smith.

"Yeah, it's ready to fire."

"You shouldn't be swinging it around so carelessly," Benny Page said. "It could go off and hit somebody."

Cal chuckled, ignoring his friends, and fired more imaginary bullets at imaginary birds. "I ain't gonna hit nobody. I just want to get the feel of my gun for when I really go huntin'."

Norma Walters made her purchase and emerged from the store into the sunlight, her baby girl in one arm and the hatbox in the other. Bobby was ahead of her on the boardwalk. Norma looked up to see a close friend coming toward her, twirling a parasol on her shoulder. "Hello, Nancy," she smiled.

Nancy Allison smiled back. "Hi, Norma. Got a new hat, eh? Can I see it?"

Nancy took the baby in her arms while Norma untied the string and removed the lid. While the women were discussing the hat, Bobby looked across the street and saw a big shaggy dog he had petted oftentimes before. It belonged to the owner of the land office directly across the street.

Bobby pointed at the dog, which was coming toward him, threading its way through the light traffic of horses, wagons, and buggies. "Look, Mommy! It's Shep!"

Norma was engrossed in conversation with Nancy and didn't hear Bobby's words.

Bobby stepped off the boardwalk and shouted, "Here, Shep! Here, boy!"

Shep was not yet halfway across the street when he spotted Bobby. He barked and wagged his tail and waited to let some vehicles go by. Bobby moved toward him, calling his name.

The stagecoach stood in front of the Wells Fargo office up the street, the six-up team still in the harness. The driver and shotgunner were inside. Across the street from the stage, Cal Freeman was carelessly swinging his Winchester around when suddenly the hammer came down and the weapon discharged. The bullet ripped across the rump of one of the lead horses in the stagecoach team, the sound of the shot clattering amongst the false-fronted buildings.

The man-in-black had just left the gun shop, and his attention was drawn to the teenage boys at the sound of the rifle, as was that of Norma Walters and her friend. Then they heard the rattle of harness, the whir of wheels, and the thunder of hooves as the frightened team galloped full-speed down the street. The unoccupied coach fishtailed behind them.

A woman in front of the land office screamed, and the man-in-black saw the horses and stagecoach bearing down on little Bobby and Shep.

Norma's eyes bulged when she saw the man-in-black drop his paper bag of cartridges and dash toward her son and the dog. Frozen in horror, she screamed Bobby's name.

The man made a dive for Bobby and sent the two of them rolling. Huge clouds of dust followed the bounding stage as it sped down the street toward the end of town and out into the open fields.

The man rose to his feet, holding the boy, as Norma ran toward them, crying, "Bobby! Oh, Bobby!"

When she reached them, the man handed Bobby into his mother's outstretched arms and said, "He appears to be all right, ma'am."

Norma burst into tears and hugged her son. "Thanks to you, he's all right! Thank you! Oh, thank you!"

The tall man noted that some angry men were gathered around the teenage boys and railing at the owner of the rifle. He looked down at the weeping mother and dusted himself off. "You're welcome, ma'am. I'm just glad I happened to be here when I was needed."

Norma was about to say something else when the man excused himself and moved to the center of the street where several men were gathered around the dog. Bobby had been spared the pounding hooves and spinning wheels, but Shep had not. He lay dead in the dust.

Shep's owner had come out of the land office and stood looking down at him, tears filming his eyes. The man-in-black dusted himself off some more and said, "I assume the dog was yours, sir."

"Yes, he was."

"I'm sorry I couldn't save him, too. It was all I could do to save the boy."

"I understand. I'm so glad you got to Bobby in time."

"We all are, mister," said one of the men who stood beside the dog's owner. "That was a mighty fine thing you did. You could've been killed."

"Didn't consider that," the man-in-black said quietly. With that, he turned and walked back to the grateful mother, who was explaining to Bobby what had happened.

Norma held the baby, bouncing her in her arms, and said to the stranger, "I hope the dog didn't suffer."

"Don't think so. I think it was over real quick for him."

"I don't think I've ever seen you before," Norma said.

"Probably not, ma'am. I've been through Green River before, but chances are pretty slim that you've seen me. I'm just passing through again. Needed some ammunition—oh, my cartridges," he said, looking toward the spot where he had dropped the paper sack.

Mort Woodley, the owner of the gun shop, stood with the sack in his hands.

"Excuse me, ma'am," the tall man said, and he stepped toward Woodley. The shop owner grinned and said, "I had to replace the sack, sir. The first one split open when you dropped it. I saw the whole thing. God bless you for what you did."

"Thank you," the man said, taking the sack. He turned back to the young mother and started to say something when his attention was drawn to the stage driver and the shotgunner who went running by, heading after the runaway stage.

A dozen or so citizens stood nearby, talking about the incident and watching Shep being carried away for burial.

Bobby pressed close to his mother as she looked up at the tall man with the twin scars on his cheek and said, "I'm Norma Walters. This is baby Jessica, and I think you already know my son's name."

"Yes, ma'am," the man replied, reaching out to stroke the baby's cheek. "Hello, little Jessica."

Norma looked down at the boy and said, "Bobby, I think you should thank this man for saving your life. He did a very brave thing to keep you from being run over."

Bobby cocked his head, squinted up at the man he thought might be a giant, and said, "Thank you, mister."

A strong hand mussed up Bobby's hair. "You're welcome, little pal."

"You haven't told me your name, stranger," Norma said, smiling at the broad-shouldered man.

He smiled warmly. "That's good enough."

"Pardon me?"

"Stranger, ma'am. That's what folks call me."

"Stranger? That's your name?"

"Yes'm. Folks just call me John Stranger."

Norma was enamored with Stranger's deep, resonant voice, and yet he spoke so softly. "Well, Mr. John Stranger, I would like to invite you to the Walters home for dinner tonight. My husband will want to express his gratitude for what you did. Will you come? We just live about a block and a half from here."

Stranger released another broad smile. "I'd sure like to, ma'am, but I have to keep moving. I'll be a far piece down the road by suppertime. Thank you for your generous invitation though."

"There's no way you can stay over? We have a spare bedroom. You could get a good night's sleep after a nice supper and ride out fresh in the morning."

"Sorry, Mrs. Walters, but I really do have to keep moving."

Disappointment shadowed her eyes. "Maybe some other time? When you're passing through?"

"That'd be something I'd look forward to."

"Fine! Just remember. Greg and Norma Walters."

"And Bobby and little Jessica, too."

"Yes. You can ask anyone in town. They all know where we live."

"I'll do it, ma'am. Next time I pass through." John Stranger reached into the pocket of his frock coat and said, "In the meantime, let me give you something so you won't forget me."

"Forget you?" Norma gasped. "Are you kidding? Forget the man who risked his own life to save that of my son? Never!"

"I appreciate that, Mrs. Walters, but let me give it to you anyhow."

Norma's eyes widened as he laid a shiny silver medallion in her hand. It was the size of a silver dollar and centered with a five-point star. Beautifully engraved around its circular edge were the words: *THE STRANGER THAT SHALL COME FROM A FAR LAND—Deuteronomy 29:22.*

Norma stood staring at the shiny disk, and those townspeople who were near began to close in. When she looked up, the tall man-in-black was stepping into a stirrup. "Thank you," she said.

John Stranger settled in the saddle, touched his hat brim, nodded with a smile, and rode away.

"Let us see it!" said an elderly woman, who pushed close to get a look at the object in Norma's hand.

Others crowded around, and Norma held it so all could get a good look. A middle-aged man repeated the words in a solemn tone, "The Stranger that shall come from a far land. Deuteronomy 29:22. That's Bible, isn't it?"

"Yes," nodded Norma, raising her eyes to look in the direction John Stranger had gone.

He was already out of sight.

"What do you suppose that means?" asked a young woman with two small children at her side.

"I don't know," Norma said, still staring at the spot where she had last seen the man. "I don't know what far land he came from, but I can tell you this much…God sent him here today to save Bobby's life."

"Could he be an angel?" an elderly woman suggested. "The Bible says we can entertain them and not even know they're angels."

Norma shook her head slowly and said, "I don't think angels have scars on their faces."

"Well, whoever he is, and wherever he came from, your little Bobby is still alive because of him," an elderly man said.

Tears began to spill down Norma's cheeks. "Yes," she said with a quiver in her voice. "Thank You, dear Lord. Thank You for John Stranger."

Two days after the incident in Green River, Utah, Mesa County Sheriff Woody Worland was sitting in his office in Grand

Junction, Colorado, some ninety-five miles due east of Green River. Worland had a stack of papers on his desk and was using a fat stub of a pencil to scribble notes as he read through the papers.

Suddenly Worland heard rapid footsteps on the boardwalk outside, and the door burst open. Stanley Myers came in, gasping for breath. "Sheriff! We got trouble!"

Worland looked up and asked, "What kind of trouble?"

"Duke Vedic's in town!"

"Vedic?" Worland said, licking his lips.

The sheriff knew the name too well. Grand Junction, like all other western towns, had its share of gunfighters passing through. But Duke Vedic was not a run-of-the-mill gunslick. Most traveled about looking for gunnies higher on the list than themselves. They would find those men, challenge them, and either walk away knowing they had raised their status...or they would be buried in the nearest graveyard.

Duke Vedic didn't care who he challenged. Worland had seen him on two occasions—once in the small town of Olathe some sixty miles to the south, and once right here in Grand Junction. Vedic had killed three men in Grand Junction, and Worland had ordered him to leave town and not come back. Vedic had started trouble with all three men to get them to go for their guns, and Worland could not arrest him because the other men had drawn first.

Duke Vedic's name was spoken in hushed tones all over the West. Though he was short and light of build, he was lightning-fast, dead-accurate, and cold-eyed. Wherever he roamed, he had a way of getting men to draw against him, then walked away laughing as his victims lay dead on the ground.

Some of the best gunfighters had challenged Vedic and learned the hard way that he was a born killer.

Worland rose from the desk, sighed and said, "Thanks for letting me know, Stan."

Myers scrubbed a shaky hand over his mouth. "What you gonna do, Sheriff?"

"Put the pressure on him," Worland replied. "I warned him the last time he was here that he'd face real trouble if he ever showed up again."

Stanley's eyes bulged. "Y-you gonna put him in jail?"

"Can't do that unless he breaks the law."

"You gonna tell him to leave town?"

"I'm not exactly sure what I'm going to do," Worland replied, heading for the door. "But if I have anything to say about it, Mr. Vedic won't be in town long. With him here, it'll be a miracle if there's no bloodshed. He breeds trouble, and his kind of trouble always ends up with somebody being buried."

"Yeah. Too bad that somebody ain't him."

The sheriff reached the door, paused and looked back. "You haven't told me where he is."

"He's at the Buckboard. You want I should round up some men to help you?"

"No," said Worland, opening the door and stepping out onto the boardwalk. "I'll handle him."

"You ain't gonna draw against him, are you? I...I mean, no offense, Sheriff, but he's faster'n a rattler's tongue."

"I know how fast he is, Stan," Worland said, moving down the boardwalk. "I'm not going to draw against him, but like I said...I'll handle him."

Stanley stayed on the sheriff's heels all the way down the street to the Buckboard Saloon. When they reached the door, Stanley stopped and said, "Be careful, Sheriff."

Worland took a deep breath, let it out slowly through his nose, and said, "Yeah."

Loud, angry voices could be heard coming from inside the saloon, and the sheriff recognized Duke Vedic's as one of them. The feisty little gunfighter had just ridden into town, and there was trouble already.

Since cool weather had come, the batwings were out of use. Worland opened the door and stepped inside, closing it behind him. He saw Vedic at the bar in an argument with a local rancher, a man in his late twenties named Chet Ferris. A half-dozen men stood close by, looking on. The bartender remained behind the bar, a frightened look on his face.

Ferris was a tall, lanky man, and he towered over Vedic. The rancher wore a sidearm, as did nearly every man in the area.

Vedic's hawk-like features were beet-red as he stood looking up at Ferris with fire in his eyes and gusted, "What's the matter, big-mouth? You got a yella belly, do you? If you're not chicken-livered, then prove it! Come outside! Let's square off and settle this thing!"

Vedic's back was toward the door. He had not seen the sheriff come in.

"Duke!" Worland shouted. Vedic jumped at the sudden sound of his voice. He wheeled around and set his beady eyes on Worland. "You wanted to say somethin' to me, Sheriff?"

Worland drew close and fixed him with a steely stare. "Yeah. At it again, aren't you?"

"Huh?"

"Trying to crowd Chet into drawing against you."

"He's got a big mouth. I was just gonna shut it for him. It'd be a fair fight."

"Who started the argument, Chet?" Worland asked.

"He did," came Ferris's quick reply.

Vedic opened his mouth to protest, but Worland beat him to it. "That right, boys?"

To a man they spoke their agreement.

From behind the bar, the bartender said, "They're tellin' it right, Sheriff. Vedic started it. There wasn't any trouble here at all till he came in less than fifteen minutes ago."

Worland turned back to the gunfighter and said, "You're not in town even a quarter-hour, Duke, and already you're goading someone into a gunfight. Let me put it in plain English. You're not welcome here. The last time you were in Grand Junction, I told you not to come back. Now, I want you on your horse and out of town immediately."

Vedic bristled, stood as tall as possible, and gave Worland a wicked leer. "You own this town do you, Sheriff?"

"No, but it's in my county and it's my responsibility."

"Am I breakin' some law?"

"Not at the moment."

"Then by what precept of the law am I being ordered out of town?"

"You aren't. You're being ordered out of town by *me.*"

"Oh? So Sheriff Woody Worland is a law unto himself, now, eh?"

Worland's face reddened. The little gunfighter had him on this one. There was no legal way he could make him leave Grand Junction. The sheriff's voice was cold and hard as he said, "All right, Duke. I have no legal power to make you leave town…but you listen, and you listen good. Your presence spells trouble wherever you go. I'm issuing you a solemn warning. You start any more trouble like I just walked in on, and you'll see the inside of my jail for a long, long time. You savvy?"

Vedic squared his bony jaw and lowered his eyelids. "You might have a hard time takin' me to jail, Sheriff."

"Don't push it, Duke. I learn of one minute's trouble you cause while you're here, and I guarantee it. You'll be locked up."

Worland turned, strode across the floor, and moved outside. Vedic looked around at the unfriendly faces and said, "Guess I'll go do my drinkin' elsewhere."

"Good idea," the bartender said.

Vedic gave him a cold look and headed for the door. When he moved out into the brilliant sunlight, he saw the sheriff standing across the street watching him. He showed the lawman a deadpan face and moved on down the street.

CHAPTER

EIGHT

———◆———

I t was late afternoon and the sun threw long shadows across Grand Junction's main street as the tall man-in-black rode into town.

John Stranger looked toward the depot and saw the train pulling out to the clanging of its bell and screech of its whistle. "Oh, well, Ebony, we can catch the train tomorrow," he said, sighing.

Stranger knew the Denver & Rio Grande train made one round trip a day between Denver and Grand Junction. It usually arrived in Grand Junction about three o'clock in the afternoon and pulled out for the return trip around five-thirty. He had hoped to make it in time to put Ebony aboard a stock car and get himself a seat in one of the coaches, but now he would have to wait until tomorrow.

John Stranger's reason for going to Denver was a beautiful blond nurse. The thought of Breanna Baylor lanced his heart. He pictured her in his mind and thought again how much he loved her.

Stranger boarded his horse at the stable, then draped his saddle-bags over a shoulder and walked a half-block to the Mesa Hotel. He signed in and paid for one night's stay, mounted the stairs, walked down the hall, and entered his room. It had been a long ride, and he was tired. He decided to lie down for a while before going to supper.

Stranger pulled off his boots, lay down on the bed, and stared at the ceiling, thinking of Breanna. He thought of the day they first met when he saved her from a cattle stampede on the plains of Kansas. The young nurse was the most beautiful and wonderful woman he had ever met.

Stranger lay there, thinking about the sweet times they had spent together over the next several weeks. A coldness gripped his heart when he recalled that wintry day in Wichita when Breanna shakily asked him to step out of her life. As he had a thousand times since, Stranger could hear himself say, "Good-bye, lovely lady. I will be out of your life, but you will never be out of my heart. From time to time, I may be looking at you, but you'll not know I'm near. I'll respect your request."

For a few moments Stranger relived the times he had seen Breanna after that—even saving her life more than once—and each time without them coming face to face. It had been several weeks since Stranger had been able to look in on Breanna, and he was eager to do so. He would go to Denver. If she was on assignment elsewhere, he would learn the location from Dr. Lyle Goodwin and go to where she was. He had to know she was all right.

The sun had set and darkness was settling over Colorado's western slope as John Stranger left the hotel and walked to the nearest café. He ate alone at a table in a corner. As he ate, he became aware of a pair of eyes staring at him from a table near the door. He was about to finish his meal when the man approached him.

John saw the badge on his chest and gave him a smile. "Howdy, Sheriff."

"Evening, sir," replied the lawman. "I'm Sheriff Woody Worland. Pardon my boldness, but does your name happen to be John Stranger?"

"Why, yes," he said, rising to his feet and extending his hand. "We've not met, have we?"

"No, sir. You fit the description I was given by wire from a friend of yours who's trying to track you down."

"Oh?"

"Chief U. S. Marshal Solomon Duvall in Denver."

"Yes, we know each other well. You say he's trying to find me?"

"Asked if I saw you to tell you to wire him immediately."

"You have any idea what it's about?"

"No, sir. He didn't say. Sounded urgent, though."

"Thank you. I'll wire him first thing in the morning."

"Western Union office opens at eight," Worland said. "How about I buy your breakfast at seven right here?"

Stranger grinned. "Sounds good to me."

The two men shook hands again, and John Stranger headed back for the hotel. When he entered the lobby and moved to the stairs, another pair of eyes fell on him.

Duke Vedic was sitting in an overstuffed chair, puffing on a cigar and reading a Denver newspaper. The towering stature of John Stranger had caught his eye, and when Vedic got a good look at him, his heart quickened pace. He watched the tall man-in-black mount the stairs and disappear down the hall, then dropped the newspaper and hurried across the lobby to the desk.

"What can I do for you, Mr. Vedic?" the middle-aged clerk asked.

"Question. That tall man who just went up the stairs..."

"Yes, sir?"

"What name did he register under?"

"Probably not his real name," chuckled the clerk.

"I'll bet he signed in as John Stranger."

"Yes, that's it. Sounds phony to me. Who ever heard of anybody named Stranger?"

"How long's he stayin'?"

"Just one night."

"What room's he in?"

"Mr. Vedic, I don't know if I should—"

"*What room's he in?*" boomed the gunfighter, grabbing the clerk by the shirt collar and pulling him hard against the counter. Smoke drifted from the cigar in his mouth into the clerk's eyes. "What's your name, pal?"

"Harry."

"Harry *what?*"

"D-Dorman."

"Well, Harry D-Dorman, I asked you what room John Stranger's in, and I want an answer…now!"

"Room t-twelve."

Vedic released him and looked toward the stairs.

"Please, Mr. Vedic. Not in the hotel," the nervous clerk said.

Duke's head whipped around. "Not *what* in the hotel?"

"A gunfight."

Vedic grinned. "Don't worry, Harry. I ain't gonna go up there and challenge 'im. No, sir! When I brace John Stranger, it'll be right out there in the middle of the street where everybody can watch me kill that hotshot gunslinger. Then watch what happens to Duke Vedic's reputation when word spreads that I took out the dude who killed Tate Landry!"

Harry Dorman licked his lips nervously. "Yes, sir."

Vedic chewed on the cigar at the corner of his mouth and looked hard into the clerk's eyes. "Now, Harry…"

"Yes, sir?"

"You keep all this under your hat. Don't breathe a word about it to anybody…and don't you inform Stranger that I'm in town. You understand?"

"Yes, sir."

"If I hear that you breathed a word of this to anybody, you're a dead man. Y'hear?"

"I won't do that, Mr. Vedic. I promise."

"Good. You just make sure you keep that promise, okay?"

"Yes, sir. I won't forget."

The next morning, John Stranger rose early, bathed, shaved, read his Bible, and spent time in prayer. Placing the Bible in his saddlebags, he draped them over his shoulder and left the room. Duke Vedic was sitting in the overstuffed chair with the same newspaper in his hands, using it to cover his face. He watched Stranger bid the clerk good-bye and pass through the lobby door onto the boardwalk.

Vedic followed Stranger down the street, then drew up when he saw him meet Woody Worland in front of the Blue Mesa Café.

When Stranger and Worland emerged from the Blue Mesa almost an hour later, they were unaware that Vedic was following them at a distance of about half a block. They entered the Western Union office, and Vedic crossed the street and waited between two buildings, keeping a sharp eye on the door.

Inside the telegraph office, Sheriff Worland introduced John Stranger to agent Paul Steffen and explained that Stranger needed to send a wire to Marshal Duvall in Denver. Stranger wrote out the message, informing Duvall of his whereabouts, and Steffen clicked it off on the telegraph key. Then they sat down to wait for Duvall's reply. An hour had passed when the telegraph unit began to click, and the agent hastily put the message on paper. When the clicking stopped, Steffen rose from his desk and said, "Here you go, Mr. Stranger."

Stranger took the paper and began reading the lengthy message. When he finished, Worland said, "From the look on your face, I'd say it's something serious."

"It is. You know about the prison break at Canon City a few days ago?"

"Yes. Ord Grabow, Treg Taggart, and Jack Slattery. I don't suppose they've been caught yet?"

"No. Guess you also are aware they left Slattery's brother behind. Frank's scheduled to hang on the twenty-seventh, but he refuses to tell where the other three are holed up. Duvall wants me to go to the prison and see if I can squeeze the location of the hideout out of Frank."

"Well, I hope you can," sighed Worland. "From what I've read about those three, they're bad medicine. But can you make it there before the twenty-seventh?"

"I doubt it, but the judge who sentenced them has signed a stay of execution to give me more time."

"Well that's good."

"Yeah. Duvall also says he's sending his best deputy on the train that'll arrive here this afternoon. Name's Ridge Holloway. Know him?"

"Sure do. Good man. Great tracker. Fast with his gun and his fists, and knows how to handle outlaws. So what's he sending Holloway here for?"

"Duvall wants Holloway to rent himself a horse and for the two of us to ride down to Delta Valley. He thinks the three killers might be hiding at a ranch there owned by Taggart's father. If we find that the fugitives are at the Taggart ranch, well and good. We'll enlist help from the Delta County sheriff and move in. If not, I'm to proceed as quickly as possible to Canon City and do my best to make Frank talk."

Worland was studying Stranger. "You used to be a lawman?"

"Maybe," nodded Stranger, his eyes on the sheet of paper. A broad grin broke across his craggy face.

"What's so funny?" Worland asked.

"Duvall. I've helped him out like this on numerous occasions. He always offers to pay me handsomely for my services."

"You mean you don't take money for it?"

"No. I do it just to help out when I can."

"Then how do you make your living?"

Stranger turned to the agent and said, "Mr. Steffen, I need to send a wire right back."

"Okay," Steffen said, picking up pencil and paper at his desk.

Stranger leaned on the counter and said, "Tell the chief I'll follow his instructions to the letter, beginning with meeting Deputy Holloway at the depot today. We'll wire him and keep him posted on what's happening."

"That all?" asked Steffen.

"Just close it off by saying he's a crotchety old duffer."

"Really?"

"Mm-hmm," Stranger nodded, pulling out his wallet. "He and I are good friends and I rib him a lot. What's the damage, here?"

While John Stranger finished up in the telegraph office, Duke Vedic was across the street, trying to watch through the window. His attention was diverted when he heard a voice from the boardwalk say, "Well, if it ain't my ol' pal, Duke!"

Vedic looked up to see two drifters he had known for years. Rudy Helms and Max Kisner were inseparable. Both in their early fifties, they had roamed the West together ever since the Civil War came to an end. They existed by doing odd jobs wherever they drifted.

Surprised to see them, Duke figured they were going to put the bite on him as they had done countless times before. He was tight with his money, but Helms had saved his life once down in El Paso, which put the drifter high on his list of friends. An envious gunfighter was about to shoot Vedic in the back when Helms called out a warning, giving Duke time to draw, whirl, and kill the would-be shooter. Since Rudy and Max were close, whatever Duke would do for Rudy, he would do for Max.

"Well if it ain't my ol' buddies!" Vedic exclaimed, moving from between the buildings onto the boardwalk. "Ain't seen you guys since—where was it? Santa Fe?"

"Guess it was," said Helms. "What? Nine, ten months ago?"

"Somep'n like that. How you doin'?"

"Well, to tell ya the truth, gettin' work has been a little tight of late," Helms said. "Don't suppose—"

"Okay, okay. How much you need?"

The drifters exchanged glances.

"I s'pose twenty dollars apiece would hold us fer a while," Helms chuckled, showing a mouthful of dirty, yellow teeth.

Vedic was reaching in his pocket when he saw John Stranger and Sheriff Worland emerge from the telegraph office across the street. Vedic didn't want Stranger to get out of town before he could challenge him to a gunfight. Stranger headed down the boardwalk, and Worland, having spotted Vedic with the drifters, came across the street.

Duke swore under his breath and fished a wad of bills out of his pocket. Before he could count out forty dollars, the sheriff drew up and said, "What's going on here, Duke?"

"Just chattin' with a couple ol' pals I happened to run into, that's all," Vedic replied, letting his eyes roam to Stranger, who was almost out of view.

"Be nice if when your pals leave town, you leave with them."

"Am I breakin' some law by standin' here talkin' to my friends, Sheriff?"

"No, but like I told you yesterday, you're not welcome here. Seems you'd want to be in a place where you feel welcome."

Stranger was now out of sight. Vedic was about to lose the opportunity to brace him and lift his name several notches on the gunfighters' roster. "That tall fella I saw you with...he looks familiar. Like I might know him. Where'd he go?"

"He's leaving town, Duke. Like you ought to do." Walking away, he said, "Remember my warning about starting any trouble. If you left town today, I'd be real happy about it."

The drifters stared after the sheriff until he was out of earshot, then Max said, "That lawman there don't seem to like you much, Duke."

"So what's new, eh?" chuckled Vedic. "I never met a lawman yet who likes me. Scared of me, that's what they are."

Vedic gave the drifters their forty dollars, told them good-bye, and hurried down the street toward the stable. He arrived there and asked the hostler about the tall man-in-black, only to learn he had saddled up and ridden away. No, he had not said where he was going.

Vedic headed back down the street and cursed the drifters for getting in his way. He entered the first saloon he came to, bellied up to the bar, and ordered a stiff drink. He would stick around Grand Junction for another couple of days. Lots of gunfighters drifted through here. Maybe he'd have a chance to brace one of them if he stayed.

After he had belted down a few drinks, Vedic returned to the hotel to reserve his room for another day or two. He passed through the door and approached the desk.

Harry Dorman had just taken payment from a customer who was walking away. As he placed the money in a drawer, he saw the wiry little gunfighter moving toward him and forced a smile. "Hello, Mr. Vedic. Something I can do for you?"

"I want my room for a couple more days, Harry."

"Yes, sir. That'll be four-fifty. Two and a quarter a day, as you know." The clerk was visibly nervous in Vedic's presence; it made him feel good to intimidate people.

"You haven't said anything to anybody about what we discussed last night, have you?" Vedic said as he pulled out his money wad.

"Absolutely not, sir," Dorman said with a quaver in his voice. "Apparently you weren't able to challenge to Mr. Stranger?"

"Naw. I got detained by a coupla old friends, and he got outta town before I could arrange it. I went over to the stable to see if I could catch him, but the hostler said he'd already rode out, and didn't say where he was goin'."

Dorman leaned over the desk and lowered his voice. "I thought something like that might have happened, Mr. Vedic. And I've got good news for you."

"What's that?"

"Mr. Stranger came in here—apparently while you were tied up with your friends—and paid for another night. So he'll be back sometime yet today."

A smirk twitched at Vedic's lips. "Oh, really?"

"Yes, sir. And I thought you might want to know that he also rented a room for a deputy U. S. marshal for tonight. Marshal's name is Ridge Holloway. He'll be coming into town this afternoon."

Vedic's smirk evolved into a wide smile. He reached across the desk and patted Dorman's shoulder. "You're a good man, Harry. A good man."

Dorman grinned, relieved to have accomplished his goal of getting on Vedic's good side. "Thank you, sir. If I learn anything else that I think will be of interest of you, I'll sure tell you."

Vedic thanked Dorman again and went back to the street. He would position himself so he could see John Stranger when he rode back into town. When he returned, Duke Vedic would be there to brace him.

John Stranger decided to use his time wisely. Since he had nearly all day before the train arrived from Denver, he would pay a visit to some dear friends.

Byron and Della Mulvane owned a small ranch a few miles east of Grand Junction. About two and a half years ago, their place had been burned down by Ute Indians. John Stranger had not only financed the price of lumber and materials, but he had also helped them rebuild the house, barn, and outbuildings with his own hands. He would visit them again and be back in town in time to meet Holloway at the depot.

Duke Vedic had been on the street without a break all day. He was seated on a bench in front of a women's dress shop not far from the hotel. His view also took in the stable. Not only were his eyes sharpened for Stranger, but he watched every rider who went by to see if he was wearing a badge. Whatever business John Stranger had with the deputy United States marshal, it wouldn't come to pass. This was John Stranger's day to die.

John Stranger rode into town from the north end. His black gelding cast a bold shadow on the street. He hauled up at the hitch rail in front of the railroad station and moved up the few wooden steps and across the platform. He took a seat near the ticket window, which was close to where the train would grind to a halt. He checked the arrival time on the schedule that hung on the wall, then eyed the big clock over the ticket window. The train was due in twenty minutes.

Stranger watched with interest as the crowd gathered on the platform to meet family and friends. His mind went to Breanna. Chief Solomon Duvall's request for help would delay his checking on her. He breathed a prayer for her safety, while his heart longed for her and his arms yearned to hold her.

NINE

Deputy U. S. Marshal Ridge Holloway sat next to a window on the Denver & Rio Grande train and enjoyed the majestic beauty of Colorado's Rocky Mountains. The huge iron-horse engine had pulled the three passenger cars, plus coal car, baggage and freight coach, and caboose over 10,666-foot Vail Pass, and now was on the downward run toward Grand Junction. The lowering sun cast its golden light through the coach windows in slanted shafts, filling it with a warm glow.

Ever since the train left Denver, Ridge had watched a young couple a few rows ahead of him across the aisle. They were on their honeymoon, and it was evident they were deeply in love.

Ridge's thoughts went to Marlene Daniels. He shook his head as he observed the happy couple and told himself he and Marlene could never be happy together. She was too demanding and self-centered. Since that day in the doctor's office when Marlene issued her ultimatum, Ridge's feelings for her had begun to cool. Ridge decided that when he returned to Denver, he would break it off with her.

Ridge was sure that somewhere God had a young woman picked out for him who would love him and marry him for what he was, not for what she hoped to make him.

Holloway's thoughts were pulled from Marlene when he overheard the conversation of two middle-aged men who sat in the seat in front of him. He had introduced himself to them when they first boarded the train in Denver. Harvey Wilcox was from Grand Junction and rode the train quite often. Rupert Hall was on his way to visit a son, daughter-in-law, and grandchildren who lived in a small settlement just south of Grand Junction.

"Gold, eh?" said Hall.

"Yes, sir. Lots of it. Comes from the mines in the mountains southeast of Grand Junction. Periodically this very train hauls a gold shipment to Denver to be sold in eastern markets. They bring it to the railhead in Junction under heavy guard."

"I can see why that would be necessary," said Hall.

"Plenty of greedy outlaws around these days. So anyway, they load the gold on this train, along with several men to guard it, and ship it to Denver."

"Good thing they don't expect the railroad people to keep it safe. Be a pretty big responsibility."

"Yep, and they don't want to shoulder it. Gold's carried in the baggage and freight car, and the guards ride right in there with it."

"Well, that sure oughtta help deter any robberies."

Suddenly they heard the conductor's voice above the rumble of the coach and the click of the wheels. "Grand Junction, fifteen minutes! Train will arrive in Grand Junction in fifteen minutes!"

Passengers began gathering their belongings, making preparation for arrival. Ten minutes later the train began to slow, and soon the uneven rooftops of the town could be seen. At exactly three o'clock, the big engine chugged into the depot, bell clanging. Ridge Holloway was eager to finally get to meet John Stranger.

Carrying a small bag, Ridge followed slowly as the passengers in the coach filed their way to the door. He watched the happy newlyweds alight, laughing together. *Somewhere, Lord, You have the woman of your choice waiting for me. In Your own time, I know You will cross our paths.*

Ridge's eyes were roaming the crowd when he saw a black, flat-crowned hat towering above the other heads and coming his direction. Within seconds the wearer of the hat was in full view. He was very tall and dressed in black with frock coat, white shirt, and string tie like a preacher...or a gambler.

As the man drew near, their eyes met, and John Stranger released a smile when he saw the badge on Holloway's chest. "You must be Ridge Holloway," he said, extending his hand.

"Yes, sir, Mr. Stranger. Glad to meet you."

"Let's start this off right," Stranger said as they shook hands. "Since we're going to be partners, you call me John."

"Okay, John," smiled the younger man. "Let me say that I'm very glad to finally meet you. I've heard so much about you from Chief Duvall. By the way, he said to tell you if he's a crotchety old duffer, you're a smart-aleck young whippersnapper."

Stranger laughed, then asked, "You have anything in the baggage coach?"

"No. All I brought is this bag in my hand."

"Well, then, let's head on over to the hotel. We'll get you settled in your room, then we'll go to supper. My treat."

"No, sir," said Ridge, shaking his head. "We'll go to supper all right, but Chief Duvall gave me money to pay for our meals. He says you're always paying for everything and won't take anything for your services to the U. S. government."

Stranger laughed again. "Well, you see, I'm filthy rich. Don't need any money, and I'm always looking for somebody who needs a little financial help."

Stranger led Holloway to where he had left Ebony at the hitch rail, then they walked together toward the center of town with Stranger leading his horse. As they walked, they discussed Duvall's orders to spy on the Taggart ranch and what they were to do if there was no sign of the escapees. Stranger then told Holloway he could rent a horse at the stable where he kept Ebony. They would ride south together at sunrise the next morning.

The late afternoon traffic was quite heavy, and there were many people walking the streets. As Stranger and Holloway neared the hotel, they saw a small, wiry man leave the boardwalk and head toward them. He had the cut of a gunfighter.

"You see what's comin' our way?" Ridge said.

"Yeah," nodded John. "Trouble. It's written all over his face."

Duke Vedic fixed himself directly in their path at the edge of the street so they had to either stop or veer into traffic to get around him. "Pardon us, mister. You're in our way," Stranger said.

"Do tell," sneered Vedic. "Well, I'm here to do a little business." He ran his bland gaze over Holloway and said, "My business ain't with you, lawman, so I'd appreciate it if you'd take the horse and move out of the way."

John Stranger had faced many a gunfighter and had laid eyes on a number of others. He had never seen this man before, but he was sure he had already made a name for himself. Stranger had no doubt he would recognize it when he heard it.

"And just what business do you have with me?" Stranger asked. "Far as I know, we've never met."

"You're the one who took out Tate Landry up in Lander, aint'cha? I was there. I saw ya."

"So?"

"I wasn't ready at the time for the dude who outdrew the top dog, but I am now. You're on, Stranger."

John Stranger resisted the temptation to slap Vedic's face. "You're still not ready, son. Go on home and tell your momma she wants you."

"You don't know who you're talkin' to, Stranger. I'm Duke Vedic!"

Stranger recognized the name as belonging to one of the top gunfighters in the West. What better way to make a quick move up the ladder than by challenging and killing the man who had taken out the infamous Tate Landry? But Stranger was not intimidated.

"Like I said, Duke, you're still not ready. Now, go on your way."

Vedic's face went red, and he bellowed so everyone nearby could hear, "I'm Duke Vedic, folks! And I'm callin' John Stranger, here, to a shootout! Y'hear me? I'm darin' this dude to draw against me!"

People began to gather around. Vedic grinned when he saw it and glowered at Stranger. "See there? These good people want to see me send you to meet the angels."

Ridge Holloway took a step toward Vedic. "You're not in John Stranger's league, Duke! If you want to see tomorrow, put a clamp on your mouth and vamoose."

"You stay out of this, federal man! I wasn't talkin' *to* you or *about* you!"

"Hold on there, Duke!" Sheriff Worland said, pushing his way through the gathering crowd.

"I ain't breakin' no law, Sheriff, and you know it. Ain't no law against a fair fight."

"Get on your horse and ride, Duke," commanded Worland. "You're not wanted in this town."

Vedic ignored the sheriff and looked back at Stranger. "You gonna square off with me, or are you gonna let these good people think you're yella?"

"I told you to get on your horse and ride!" Worland shouted, stepping between Vedic and Stranger. "I mean it! All you want to do is make a name for yourself."

"That's right, Sheriff! I, Duke Vedic, have challenged the dude who took out the great gunfighter Tate Landry. Question is, does John Stranger have a yella streak down the middle of his back, or is he man enough to square off with me?"

Stranger shook his head and sighed. "The only place you're going to make a name for yourself, Duke, is on your tombstone. Now, use your head and ride!"

The crowd was growing. Wagons, buggies, and surreys were choked up in the middle of the street as people gawked from every direction.

"You're a coward, Stranger!" Vedic said. "That's what you are. You're spoutin' off 'cause the truth is, you're afraid to face me. That's it, folks! John Stranger has melted into a lily-livered coward now that he's lookin' at the great Duke Vedic!"

"All right, Duke," Stranger said. "You'll have your gunfight."

People quickly made room, looking on with breathless fascination.

Sheriff Worland said, "Stranger, I can run him in. Lock him up."

"No use," replied the tall man, turning to face Vedic squarely. "If I don't take care of this now...it'll have to be done later." Then to Holloway, "Take Ebony down the street so he won't be in the line of fire, will you, Ridge?"

"Sure," Holloway said, leading the big black away. Over his shoulder, he said, "You're a fool, Vedic."

Vedic gave him a hateful look, then turned his attention back to John Stranger. The crowd lined the boardwalks, clearing the street. The two combatants squared off some forty feet apart.

Duke Vedic was like a child who had just received a new toy. His chance to make it big had finally come. He took a theatrical pose, spreading his legs just right and going into a crouch. His right hand hovered over the butt of his revolver.

"Anytime you're ready, Duke," Stranger said in a low, level tone.

Vedic ran the sleeve of his left arm over his mouth and gave Stranger a wicked leer. "*I'll* pick the time," he said. "This is my show and—"

"The time's now, Duke! You already picked it. Draw!"

Vedic's gun hand snaked downward. His fingers had barely closed on the grips of his gun when a .45 slug ripped into the bicep of his right arm. Another shot came so fast, they almost sounded as one. The second slug slammed into Vedic's left arm at the elbow. The double impact staggered him, and the gun slipped from his fingers. His legs gave way, and he fell in a heap, his teeth clenched in pain.

The crowd stood like statues, unable to believe their eyes. As Stranger holstered his smoking gun and strode toward his fallen opponent, one man said, "Didn't even see him draw that gun—and I was lookin' right at him!"

"I've never seen the like!" breathed another.

Stranger examined Vedic's wounds and said, "Both arms have the bones shattered, Duke. You'll never fast-draw a gun again. You'll live longer, now. You can thank me later for not killing you."

Vedic, teeth gritted, sucked in air and let it out, but did not reply.

Stranger turned to Sheriff Worland and said, "Better get him to a doctor, Sheriff, or he'll bleed to death."

Worland called on four men to carry Vedic to the town's doctor. As they carried him away, Worland looked at Stranger, eyes wide. "Never saw a draw that fast. Never."

The tall man grinned, wheeled about, and said to Ridge Holloway, "Let's head for the stable."

Came the morning of October 26.

High in the Elk Mountains at the hideout, Jack Slattery paced back and forth in the log cabin, swearing under his breath.

"Tomorrow morning," he said in a quivering voice. "Tomorrow morning, Frank dies at the end of a rope!" Tears filmed his eyes. He drew a shuddering breath and slammed fist into palm. "It's your fault, Ord! He dies in the morning, and it's your fault!"

But Ord Grabow was not there to hear Jack's accusation. He and Treg Taggart had left the cabin an hour earlier to hunt small game for food.

Jack's wrath had been building toward Grabow ever since they arrived at the hideout. He had nightmares in which he saw his brother plunge through the trap door of the gallows with the noose around his neck. Each time, he awoke with a start just as Frank hit the length of the rope with a snap.

Out in the forest, light snow fell under a heavy sky. A moderate wind rustled the tops of the tall pines and plucked the last leaves from the long-fingered limbs of the white-skinned birch.

Grabow and Taggart carried their rifles at the ready, expecting to see a rabbit or a squirrel dart across their path. Provisions in the cabin were holding out, but they needed fresh meat.

"I think he'll come apart tomorrow, Ord," Taggart said. "I can see it in his eyes. He's takin' Frank's hangin' awful hard."

"And blamin' me," Grabow said.

"Yeah. I don't think you ever really got it across to him how utterly useless Frank is."

"He'll bear watchin' at dawn tomorrow when he knows Frank's takin' the long drop."

"Well, I'll be watchin' him with you."

They came upon a thick stand of pine and worked slowly around it. Moments later, they faced snow-covered layers of rock and skirted them to more passable ground. Each step became more difficult as the snow continued to fall. They rounded a jutting boulder and saw a shallow cave partially covered with snow-crusted brush. They stopped at the sound of a deep growl.

Grabow swore when he saw a female wolf near the mouth of the cave. Her hackles were up and her eyes blazed. Behind her were three small cubs, pawing at each other playfully.

Grabow raised his rifle.

"No!" Taggart said, touching his arm. "Be the mistake of your life to shoot her!"

Grabow eyed him with speculation. "Whatcha talkin' about?"

"Back up real slow," said Taggart, "and I'll tell you."

They kept their eyes on the growling mother wolf and moved carefully backward.

"You don't know much about wolves, do you?" Treg said.

"No. Never been around 'em. Have you?"

"Yep. We had 'em close by all my growin' up years."

"Vicious beasts, ain't they?"

"Not in the way you're thinkin'. Most people think of 'em as blood-hungry predators, prowlin' about lookin' for humans to rip to pieces, but that's not so."

"Really?"

"Wolves have a natural fear of humans and usually avoid them."

"Except, I suppose, when their young seem to be threatened," Grabow said.

"Right. And when they're near starvation. Then they gather in packs and go after almost anything that moves, including humans, for food…but they really gotta be hungry before they'll do it."

Grabow peered into the trees around them. "I hope there ain't any starvin' ones around here."

"They'll also attack if they smell human blood. It throws 'em into a frenzy. They'll attack a bleeding man and not quit till they've picked the bones clean."

Still backing slowly from the cave, Taggart said, "There are very few lone wolves. Most of 'em collect in packs. If there's a pack anywhere around here…and you'd shot that female…we'd be wolf meat."

They had retreated some twenty yards when Grabow suddenly saw movement amid the trees off to his left. "Treg! Wolves there to the left!" he whispered.

Taggart caught sight of others glaring at them from the deep shadows to their right and another group in the thick forest behind them. "Stand real still. We got 'em on three sides."

Ord looked around and drew a shuddering breath, eyes bulging with fear. He made ready to bolt.

Taggart grabbed his arm. "Don't even think about runnin'! It'd be suicide! The pack already knows that mother wolf is angry at our intrusion. And they know why. If we run, the whole pack'll be after us."

Grabow was trembling. "What are we gonna do?"

"Real slow like, we're gonna head for the cabin."

"But it's a mile away!"

"Just turn around...and keep pace with me."

"What if they attack?"

"Then take out as many as you can. But we'd better pray they don't. We ain't got enough ammunition to kill that many."

"I don't know how to pray," said Grabow.

"Me neither. Just a figure of speech. C'mon, let's go."

With their hearts in their mouths, the two outlaws walked cautiously toward the cabin. The wind-driven snow pelted their faces. The wolves were visible in the forest around them, slinking among the trees.

Grabow gripped his rifle, fear evident on his face. "They're followin' us, Treg. Do you suppose they're hungry?"

"Don't think so," Taggart said. "They're most hungry in late winter when small game has been hard to come by. When they get desperate, they'll form large packs and go after deer, elk, and moose. Humans are a last resort. Naw, they ain't followin' us 'cause they're hungry. I think they're keepin' an eye on us to prevent us from harmin' those pups."

"Okay, so they follow us all the way to the cabin," Grabow said. "If they hang around there, we won't be able to hunt for small game. There ain't enough food in the cabin to sustain us without daily meat."

"I don't think they'll hang around long," Taggart said. "Maybe a day or two. They'll soon figure we mean no harm to the pups and go away."

"I hope you're right. Bad enough the way Jack's gonna be for the next coupla days. We don't need those wolves to think about, too."

They paused on the porch of the cabin and studied the wolves, who waited at the edge of the trees.

"How many you figure there are?" asked Grabow.

"Hard to tell. I doubt we're seein' all of 'em. They're smart. They'll not show you the whole pack. Looks like about fifteen, but there are probably more like twenty to twenty-five."

Grabow pushed the door open and went inside. Taggart followed, closing the door. Slattery was seated at the crude table near the fireplace, his features dull and pasty. Both men eyed him without speaking and shook snow on the floor as they removed their hats and coats.

"Where's the meat?" Jack said.

"Didn't get any," Grabow growled, irritated at Jack's tone.

Slattery had refused to go hunting with them, saying he was too upset about Frank. His mood worsened at the news. "Whattya mean, ya didn't get any? Ya been gone long enough to bring in a half-dozen rabbits or squirrels!"

"Well, if you'd gone with us, you'd know why we didn't get any!" Grabow yelled.

"And if you'd brought my brother along when we escaped, I'd have felt like goin' with ya!" Jack rose from the chair as he spoke.

Taggart felt the threat of violence in the air. He moved between Grabow and Slattery and said, "Ease up, Jack. We didn't get a single shot at a squirrel or rabbit because we ran into a pack of wolves. They followed us all the way back here. Take a look for yourself, they're right outside."

Slattery, skeptical, walked across the room and looked out a front window.

"That satisfy you?" snapped Grabow.

Slattery whirled about and glared at Grabow. "Yeah, that satisfies me. And it'd satisfy me more if you were hangin' tomorrow instead of Frank."

"You shut up about Frank's hangin', y'hear me? We've hashed this thing over plenty of times, and I don't wanna talk about it any more!"

Slattery started toward Grabow. "You don't wanna talk about it!" he said, mocking. "Well, that's just too bad. It ain't your brother hangin' tomorrow, pal, it's mine!"

Taggart jumped between them again, placing his hands on Slattery's shoulders. "Jack, it ain't helpin' Frank none with you two at each other's throats. Fighting amongst ourselves ain't gonna accomplish nothin'. Now, calm down."

"Wouldn't be no reason for trouble here if Ord'd brought Frank along like he said he was gonna do!"

"Don't you ever listen to anything I say?" Grabow boomed, his features going dark. "That brother of yours got us caught in the first place…and he'd be nothin' but a hindrance if he was here now. I got you out, Jack! You owe me plenty for that, and don't you forget it! If it weren't for me, you'd be takin' that last plunge in the mornin' yourself!"

Taggart saw the fire go out of Slattery's eyes and sighed with relief. "Okay. Let's play a game of cards."

"You two play," said Jack. "I ain't in the mood."

Through the rest of the day, Slattery paced nervously, muttering to himself. Grabow and Taggart left their card game from time to time to look out the windows. The wolves were still there, watching from the surrounding trees.

CHAPTER

TEN

J ack Slattery lay awake on his bunk, staring into the darkness and hating Ord Grabow. Grabow and Taggart were snoring, but Jack paid them no mind. His thoughts were solely on his condemned brother, whom he believed would be hanged at dawn.

Jack sat up. There would be no sleep for him tonight. He made his way to one of the front windows of the cabin and looked out on the snow-laden land. The air was cold, and goosebumps rose on his skin. He saw the moon shining and realized the snow had stopped. At the edge of the trees, he could see four or five wolves lying in the fresh snow. The rest of the pack, he knew, were in the shadows.

Jack rubbed his chilled arms and went back to the cot and crawled between the covers. His mind went again to Frank, and he wept silently. When he saw the bleak light of dawn touch the cabin windows, he broke into sobs. He pictured his brother walking up the gallows steps, his hands tied behind his back. He saw a black hood over Frank's head and a noose cinched tight around his neck. The lever was thrown and Frank shot downward.

Jack sat bolt upright on the bunk, his eyes bulging. He felt his heartbeat pounding in his eyes and in his throat. His chest was seized in spasms, and he struggled in a wild effort to breathe. Suddenly he got a gulp of air and filled the cabin with a grief-stricken wail.

Grabow and Taggart were yanked from their sleep and sat up, bewildered. They struggled to their feet and headed for Slattery. Taggart reached him first and seized him by the shoulders. "Jack!" he shouted, shaking him. "Get a grip on yourself!"

It did no good. Jack only looked at him with wild eyes and wailed Frank's name over and over.

"Let me handle him!" Grabow said.

Ord swore and stung Jack with five or six backhanded blows. Jack stopped screaming and looked at both men, as if seeing them for the first time. "It's your fault! It's your fault! Frank's dead because of you! He's dead!"

Ord slapped Jack again, and his head whipped sideways. Wrath contorted Jack's countenance, and he sprang like a cougar, grabbing Grabow by the neck. Both men hit the floor with Jack on top. Grabow tried to fight him off, but Jack was a man possessed. Grabow couldn't break his hold.

Taggart grasped Slattery's shoulders, shouting, "Jack! Jack, let go of him! You'll kill him!"

He tried to pull him off, but couldn't. He swore and dashed to the cookstove and picked up a heavy iron skillet. He hurried back and swung the skillet in a wild arc. Iron met skull, and Jack collapsed unconscious on top of Grabow.

Taggart dropped the skillet and rolled Slattery off of Grabow. Grabow coughed and sucked hard for air, then sat up, eyeing Slattery with hatred and revulsion. He rubbed his neck and swung his fiery eyes on Taggart. "I...I'm gonna kill that dirty rat!"

"No, Ord!" Taggart said. "We need each other! He's out of his mind with grief. He'll be all right once he gets over Frank bein' hanged."

Grabow went to a window and looked outside and saw that the wolves were still at the edge of the trees. He grinned to himself, hurried to the cupboard, and took from there a long-bladed hunting knife that lay next to the water bucket.

Taggart blocked Grabow's path, holding out pleading hands. "No, Ord! Don't kill him!"

Grabow pushed past him and rammed the sharp blade into Slattery's right arm. He howled and tried to avoid the knife, which lashed out again, this time at his other arm.

Taggart looked on in horror but did not intervene out of fear for his own well-being. Slattery cried out as Grabow stabbed him twice more, once in each thigh. Blood ran from all four wounds.

Grabow tossed the knife across the room, stepped to the door, and opened it.

"What're you doin'?" cried Taggart.

"Gonna teach this dirty scum a lesson!"

Taggart looked on wide-eyed as Grabow grabbed Slattery by the collar and dragged him through the door onto the porch. Slattery was breathing hard and trying to fight Grabow off, but his wounds made it impossible.

Taggart stood in the open door and saw the wolves lift their heads and look toward the cabin as Grabow dragged Slattery off the porch and dumped him in the three-inch deep snow.

"Hey, you beasts, come get him!" Grabow shouted, then turned and headed for the door.

Slattery struggled to get up. Two dozen wolves bounded toward him, eyes wild. He heard the cabin door slam shut as he pulled his knees under him and crawled to the edge of the porch. He grabbed hold of one of the posts and pulled himself to a standing position. He looked back. The wolves came in swiftly, snarling and growling. Some eight or nine of them hit him at once, knocking him down.

Inside the cabin, Grabow and Taggart watched from separate windows, listening to Slattery's screams above the snarling of the savage beasts.

Grabow threw his head back, laughing wickedly. "See what you get for tryin' to kill me, you rotten ingrate! I broke you outta prison, and you thank me by tryin' to strangle me!"

Taggart watched the wild scene as if hypnotized.

When the wolves had satisfied themselves, they slinked across the snow and disappeared into the forest.

Grabow opened the door and stepped onto the porch. "Got what you deserved, Jack. Should've known better than to cross ol' Ord."

Taggart came out and stood beside him, eyeing the bloody scene. "Tell you what, Ord. Think I'll saddle my horse and head south. It's time to go see my family."

"You go ridin' outta here right now, them wolves may decide to get hungry again real quick. Maybe they'll want to eat both you and your horse."

"No," Treg said, "they're headed on back to their lair. Vengeance has been exacted. I won't be in any danger from them."

"Well, you know more about 'em than I do. Still, I think it's too early for us to go traipsin' out in the open. Who knows how many lawmen might be out there lookin' for us?"

"Yeah, I know the risks, Ord. But I ain't seen my pa and my brothers and sister for a long stretch. I'll be real careful. Ain't no lawmen gonna get me."

"Well, I ain't gonna hog-tie you, Treg, but I think it'd be better if you waited another week or so."

"Can't do it. By now, Pa and the others have heard about us escapin'. I want 'em to know I'm okay."

Ord was behind him, closing the door. "So you're gonna leave right away?"

"I'll help you bury what's left of Jack, then I'll be on my way."

"Okay. I'll probably stick around here for another week... maybe two. Then I'll head for Cheyenne City."

"Cheyenne City? What's there?"

"I know a gang—train, stagecoach, and bank robbers—who've got a hideout near there. Headed up by an old pal of mine, Dyar Lynch. He told me one time if I ever wanted in his gang, I'd be more than welcome. If you wanna meet me there, I'm sure I can talk him into takin' you in, too. We'll do real good money-wise. I can guarantee it. Dyar will treat us right."

"Sounds good to me," grinned Taggart. "Draw me up a map, showin' where the hideout is, and I'll meet you there in about three weeks or so."

Treg stood over him and watched as Ord sketched out the map at the table, explaining details as he drew. When it was done, Treg said, "Well, let's go bury Jack's remains, and I'll be on my way."

It was three o'clock in the morning of October 25 when Lulu Taggart jerked awake and sat straight up in her bed. She had just dreamed that she died and went to hell, and the horror of it had torn her from her sleep.

Lulu's heart pounded like a wild thing in her chest. The effect of the awful nightmare held her in its grip. The black, soot-covered gates that had enfolded her seemed to still be there, wanting to seal her in hell's dark, fiery chasms forever. She had felt the unbearable heat of the flames and had heard the cries of hell's captives.

Lulu threw back the covers and made her way to the dresser by the moonlight that filled the room. The hard wooden floor was like ice to her bare feet. She filled a tin cup half full from the pitcher that sat next to it on the dresser and drank it down.

She returned to the bed and slid between the covers, then lay back on the pillow and struggled to get the nightmare out of her mind. It had been all too real. She was afraid to go back to sleep, lest the nightmare return.

She soon found her mind haunted by the Scriptures Autumn Lynne had quoted to her during their many conversations. She thought of Calvary, and pictured Jesus on the cross, dying for her sins.

"No!" she gasped in a hoarse whisper, rolling her head on the pillow. "No! It's all a myth, just like Pa taught me! There isn't any hell!" She turned on her left side and pulled the covers over her head. "It's all a myth!"

But Lulu Taggart knew better. Autumn Lynne's recent words reverberated through her mind: *Down deep in your heart, you know what your father taught you is not true, don't you?*

Lulu tossed and turned for the rest of the night, wanting to sleep, but fearful of slipping back into the horrid nightmare.

Morning finally came.

Lulu fixed breakfast for her father and brothers. She concealed her sleepiness, and no one was the wiser as she sat with them at the table.

"We need a few things at the general store, Pa," Lulu said. "Want I should go to town with Van and pick 'em up?"

Van had an appointment with Dr. Eldon Faulkner to change the dressing on the gash in his forehead. Faulkner had taken twenty stitches to close the gash, and told Van he would have an ugly scar for the rest of his life.

"Naw," grunted Otis. "I'm sendin' all the boys to town with Van. They've got to get a load of grain sacks for the horses. Just tell 'em what you need. I want you to stay here and clean house."

"Don't you worry none, little brother," Wick said to Van. "I'm gonna see to it Aaron pays for what he did to you."

"How you gonna make 'im pay, Wick?" Cliff asked.

"By plantin' him six feet in the ground. That's how."

Otis Taggart set steady eyes on his second oldest son. "Wick, you be careful. I don't want you hangin' for killin' Aaron Lynne. Don't you be killin' him unless you're dead sure you can do it without gettin' caught."

Wick grinned. "Don't worry, Pa. Nobody'll know who killed 'im."

Lulu had heard this kind of talk before, and it had never bothered her. Somehow this time it did. She wanted to say something, but she knew better than to argue with Wick when his mind was made up.

Van had his own plans but kept them to himself. There was no way he was going to allow Wick to take out the man who split his head open. That privilege would be his. While Wick was figuring out how to kill Aaron, Van would do it his way.

The morning sun was making its way upward in a clear, brisk Colorado sky as the Taggart brothers arrived in Delta. Wick drove the wagon with Van beside him. Nate, Cliff, and Jeb were on horseback.

Wick guided the wagon to a halt in front of Dr. Eldon Faulkner's office and said, "We'll be back in an hour or so, little brother. Just sit down in the waitin' room. I'll come in and get you when we're ready to go."

Van nodded and climbed out of the wagon. Wick clucked to the horses and moved on down the street with Nate, Cliff, and Jeb riding behind him. They picked up the items Lulu had asked for at the general store, then moved on.

They spent some twenty-five minutes at Grand Mesa Feed and Supply, purchasing several sacks of oats and barley, then crossed the street and entered the Delta Hardware and Gun Shop.

Doug Price was in the store alone when the Taggart brothers filed through the door. Price felt a jolt of fear when he saw them coming in. He tried to remain calm but felt a tightness in his stomach.

"Howdy, Doug," said Wick, drawing up to the counter ahead of his brothers.

Doug tried to smile, but did a poor job of it. "Hello, Wick. What can I do for you?"

"Need six boxes of .44s and a box of 45s."

"Coming up," nodded Doug, turning toward the shelves of ammunition behind him. Over his shoulder, he said, "Guess it's about time to be hunting deer and elk, huh?"

"Yep," said Wick, noting that his brothers were looking over some new rifles and revolvers on display.

Doug laid the boxes of ammunition on the counter. "Van didn't come to town with you?" he asked.

"Yeah, he's in town. At Doc Faulkner's office."

"Something happen to him?"

"Yeah, don't you remember? That dirty future brother-in-law of yours put a gash in his head."

"Oh. Yes, of course."

"Aaron *is* your future brother-in-law, ain't he?"

Doug cleared his throat. "Well, Autumn and I have discussed marriage a time or two…but there's nothing definite at this point."

"You oughtta be ashamed of yourself for even considerin' marryin' into that no-good family."

Doug Price's face tinted. "Well, like I said—"

"Yeah, I know. There's nothin' definite at this point. How much for the ammunition?"

The Taggarts paid for the cartridges and returned to the street. Wick climbed into the wagon, and his brothers mounted their horses. As they moved down the street toward Dr. Faulkner's office, they saw Van standing on the boardwalk in front of the office in a heated discussion with Aaron Lynne. People on the street gawked at them as they railed at each other, their noses almost touching. Van was hatless and a fresh white bandage was wrapped around his head.

As the Taggarts hauled up, Aaron blared, "You got a bad memory, Van! It was you Taggarts who rode onto Lynne property with trouble in mind! If the whole bunch of you had stayed home that night, you wouldn't have an ugly scar on your face the rest of your life!"

"Well, let me tell you somethin'!" Van lashed back. "We Taggarts wouldn't have been on Lynne property that night if your dumb sister wasn't always tryin' to make a Christian outta Lulu!"

"Nobody talks that way about my sister!" Aaron shouted as he bulled into Van, striking him with a left to the mouth and a right to the jaw. The blows sent Van backpedaling. He slammed hard against the clinic wall and slid limply down to the boardwalk.

Aaron heard Wick Taggart swear at him, and suddenly all four brothers jumped him, their fists swinging. Aaron fought back, knocking Jeb down and doubling Cliff over with a blow to the stomach. But his success was brief; the brothers soon overpowered him and began to beat him hard.

Van looked up trying to make out what was happening, but his vision was clouded. The nerves in his mouth and jaw seemed to have gone dead, and the fresh bandage on his head had come loose.

Suddenly, Aaron had help. Barber Clyde Arthur dashed out of his shop two doors down and began swinging at any Taggart he could target. Local ranchers Hector Peale and George Bancroft were quickly off their horses and plowed into the Taggarts, fists flying.

Cliff took another blow to the stomach and went to his knees. Wick downed the barber with a hard blow, but received two in return from Bancroft, a big, husky man. Wick found himself on his back with his legs on the boardwalk and his head in the dusty street. The whole town seemed to be going in circles.

Jeb cracked Peale a good one on the mouth, staggering him. Then Aaron flattened Jeb with a blow to the jaw. Aaron turned around just in time to see Nate aiming a haymaker at his face. Aaron ducked it and retaliated with a punch to the chin. Nate staggered and dropped to one knee, shaking his head.

Cliff groped his way to the space between two buildings and gave up his breakfast. Wick scrambled to his feet, and Bancroft was ready to deal him some more punishment when Sheriff Luke Prisk came running and hollered, "Hold it! Everybody hold it!"

The combatants froze in place, looking at Prisk. Nate stood to his feet.

"What's this all about?" Prisk demanded.

"Aaron started it, Sheriff!" Nate said. "He punched Van, and just after he came outta the doctor's office from gettin' a new bandage on his head."

"That right, Aaron? You punch him?"

"Yeah," nodded Aaron, breathing hard. "But I had good reason. He opened his big mouth and insulted my sister. Nobody's gonna talk about Autumn like he did and get away with it."

A crowd had gathered, looking on eagerly. Prisk swung an arm at them and said, "Go on about your business, folks. The excitement's over." Then he looked down at Van and said, "You'd better go back and have Doc work on that bandage. It's about to come off."

Nate and Jeb helped Van to his feet and guided him through the clinic door. "It was Aaron who put the gash on Van's head in the first place, Sheriff," Wick said.

"When was this?" Prisk asked.

"Couple nights ago."

"Where?"

"At the Lynne place. We rode over there with Pa to have a peaceful talk with Roy about Autumn pushing her religion on Lulu. What was supposed to be a friendly talk turned violent when Aaron got mad for no reason and slammed Van's head into the edge of the porch. Some Christian! And now this good Christian has become violent again and picked a fight."

Prisk turned to Aaron and said, "All right, let me hear your side of it."

Aaron explained why he slammed Van's head into the porch...and why he had just punched him.

The sheriff listened intently, then said to Wick, "Can't say as I blame Aaron for what he did to your little brother...either time.

Seems to me, Wick, you Taggarts oughtta stay away from the Lynnes."

"Yeah? Well how about Autumn stayin' away from Lulu?"

"Funny," said Prisk, rubbing the back of his neck, "I've seen Autumn and Lulu talking many times, and Lulu always seemed perfectly willing to talk. But I'll tell you what. You tell Lulu that next time she's in town I'd like to talk to her. Let's see what she says about it."

"Uh...yeah. Okay." Wick turned to Cliff and said, "Let's go see about Van."

When Wick and Cliff had entered the clinic, Aaron thanked Hector Peale, George Bancroft, and Clyde Arthur for helping him. They said they were glad to get a chance to get in a few licks at the Taggarts.

When those three had gone, Prisk looked at Aaron and said, "I'd say you better watch yourself. Those Taggarts are born trouble-makers. They may try to get you alone and work you over."

"I'll be careful, Sheriff."

A half hour later, the Taggart brothers were on their way home. Van had another bandage on his head, and his upper lip carried three stitches. It was bright red with iodine. Nate, Jeb, and Cliff rode close to the wagon. As before, Van sat beside Nick, who held the reins.

Wick was seething. He cast a glance at Van's puffy mouth and hissed, "I'm gonna kill that skunk! Don't you fret, Van. All I need is a little time to work it out so's no blame can fall on me."

"Somebody else needs a lesson, too, boys," Nate said. "Arthur, Peale, and Bancroft."

"Yeah," agreed Jeb. "We was givin' Aaron what he deserved when those dudes interfered."

"We'll tell Pa about it," said Cliff. "He'll figure out a way to get even."

When they arrived back at the ranch, Otis told Van to go to his room and lie down until suppertime. He assigned fence work to the others and told them he would talk about the incident in town later.

Van's room was on the second floor of the ranch house. When he moved inside and shut the door, he went immediately to the closet and pulled out his Remington .44 repeater rifle. He made sure it was fully loaded, then sneaked out of the house and headed for the barn. His father was in the kitchen with Lulu, and his brothers were all out mending fence.

As he rode away unnoticed, Van whispered, "You ain't never gonna see home again, Aaron. And you ain't never gonna lay a hand on me again, neither. Aaron Lynne...you're a dead man."

CHAPTER

ELEVEN

———◆◆———

Van Taggart rode to a spot halfway between Delta and the Lynne ranch where a giant rock formation loomed over the level ground reaching a height of fifty feet. The road ran close, along the base of the rocks.

Van knew Aaron Lynne would come riding down the road on his way home, and he dismounted and led his horse amid huge boulders and towering monolith pillars to a secluded spot and tied it to a naked-limb bush.

He pulled the rifle from its saddle scabbard and climbed up the backside of the massive rock jumble to a high spot that overlooked the road. He lowered himself into a shallow pocket between two weather-pitted rocks and scanned the road both directions. It was perfect. All he had to be concerned about now was that no one else be in sight when Aaron rode toward him.

Van removed his hat and levered a cartridge into the magazine and waited. A cold wind whipped down from the Rocky Mountains to the east, causing him to pull the collar up on his sheepskin jacket. The sky was cloudless and deep blue. He could see pure whiteness sweep away on the lofty shoulders above him under the late October sun, rising fold on fold to the higher elevations. Up there a ragged row of snow-capped peaks lifted sharp spires to the sky. The peaks above timberline had tasted snow several times since late September.

The raw wind bit hard, and he put his hat back on. He would watch for Aaron to come around the bend of the road past a thick stand of trees almost a half-mile away, then take the hat off so as to get a good bead on his victim without being seen.

After about an hour, Van felt the cold from the wind even more. The temperature seemed to be dropping. He laid the rifle on a smooth rock and breathed on his hands and rubbed them together. He cursed himself for not bringing gloves. He could feel his cheeks reddening from the bite of the wind.

Van told himself a hard winter was in the making. He had noticed the last few days that ground squirrels and prairie dogs were putting on extra-heavy coats. *Probably have some real blizzards in the high country this winter*, he told himself.

Van looked up the road toward Delta. The trees at the bend swayed in the wind. Soon Aaron Lynne would come riding around that bend and into the gunsights of the man he had dared to rough up.

Hatred burned within Otis Taggart's youngest son. Killing Aaron would be a pleasure. It would feel good. Not only would Aaron be paying for what he did to Van, but his death would also cause untold grief to the Lynne family. The pious Bible-thumpers deserved some misery. Especially Autumn. Try to convert Lulu, would she? Well, now she'd pay for it.

Van had just checked his pocket watch to find that it was three minutes past four when his eye caught movement on the road to the west. It was a lone rider. Van's heart quickened pace. Was it his intended victim?

Three more minutes confirmed that it was.

He removed his hat in spite of the cold wind, adjusted the bandage that encircled his head, and made ready. He breathed on his hands to warm them one more time, then picked up the rifle.

Carefully, lovingly, he ran his fingers along the walnut stock, caressing the smooth wood. He touched the blue-steel barrel, then kissed it and said, "You and me together, sweetheart. We're gonna rid the world of Aaron Lynne."

Aaron was now close enough for Taggart to draw a bead. He brought the stock to his shoulder, laid the barrel on the smooth roundness of the rock in front of him, and rested his right forefinger on the trigger. He could feel his heart pumping with excitement.

Van let Aaron come within seventy yards, then lined up the sights on the center of his chest. He would let his victim come toward him another forty yards. Once he was that close, there was no way he could miss.

The ranches of Hector Peale and George Bancroft both lay northeast from Delta, the same direction as the Roy Lynne ranch. The two men, having spent the better part of the day doing business in town, mounted up and rode for home at about twenty minutes before four.

They walked their animals at a leisurely pace and chatted about cattle and such things that interested them most. After riding a few minutes, Peale said to Bancroft, "I think that's Aaron Lynne up there ahead of us."

"Looks like it. Good kid. I like to see a fella who'll defend his sister...or mother or wife or daughter. Any female, you know."

"Yes, sir. Me, too."

Bancroft chuckled. "Aaron wasn't doin' too bad for himself when we jumped in. I don't think there's a Taggart who could whip him one-on-one."

"For sure. Not even Wick."

"Wick's the worst of the lot, barrin' Treg, of course. Felt good to give him what he had comin'."

"Why don't we pick up the pace and catch up to Aaron?" Peale said. "Might as well be neighborly."

"Let's do it," Bancroft nodded, putting his horse to a gallop.

At the same time, Aaron Lynne and his horse disappeared around the bend of the road, which was lined with trees.

High up in the rocks, Van Taggart followed Aaron Lynne's movement through his gunsights. He took a deep breath, let a little out, and held it. The .44 cartridge exploded in thunder. He saw the fleeting amazement on Aaron's face as the bullet tore through his chest. Then Aaron jerked in the saddle and fell to the ground. So elated was Van that he rose to his feet, shouting and waving the rifle in triumph.

Suddenly he was aware of two riders galloping toward him. They were close enough for him to recognize. It was Hec Peale and George Bancroft!

Peale and Bancroft watched Aaron Lynne peel out of the saddle at the same time they saw the puff of smoke from atop the rocks. The sound of the shot reached their ears as they bore down on the spot where Aaron lay in a heap.

Suddenly their attention was drawn to the rifleman as he stood and waved the rifle above his head.

Bancroft turned to Peale and called above the thunder of hooves, "Van Taggart!"

Peale nodded. "It's Van, all right!"

Abruptly, Van disappeared.

The two ranchers skidded their mounts to a halt and slid from their saddles. Both knelt beside Aaron Lynne's crumpled form and saw the ragged hole in his jacket where the bullet had come out his back.

Bancroft carefully turned him over and let out a sigh. "He's dead, Hec. Slug went right through his heart. He never knew what hit him."

Just then they heard pounding hooves and looked up to see Van riding away at a full gallop. Within seconds, horse and rider vanished from sight on the far side of the rocks. Bancroft rose to his feet, and his bulky form shook.

"Shall we go after him?" Peale asked.

"We could ride after him. Possibly catch him. But we don't have the authority to arrest him. Let's do this. I'll take the body to the Lynne ranch, and you ride to town and bring the sheriff."

"Okay."

"Make sure Luke understands that both of us saw it happen, and both of us recognized Van Taggart."

"Will do," said Peale, heading for his horse. "Luke and I will see you at the Lynne ranch shortly."

Hector Peale thundered away toward town, and George Bancroft hoisted Aaron Lynne's lifeless form onto the back of his horse, draping him face-down over the saddle. He mounted his own animal and led Aaron's horse northeastward toward the Lynne ranch.

Panic gripped Van Taggart as he galloped across the valley floor, and he swore out loud. "Why did Peale and Bancroft have to be comin' down the road just now? If I could recognize them, they could recognize me!"

He came upon a thick stand of cottonwoods and plunged his horse amid them and reined in. His mind was spinning. What should he do? The ranchers would tell Sheriff Prisk what they saw.

The first place Prisk would look for him would be the Taggart ranch.

Van would have to hide out somewhere. The only place he could think of was the top of Grand Mesa to the north. It was thick with forests amid dozens of ponds and lakes. He would take refuge from the cold in somebody's barn or shed. He spurred his horse northward.

John Stranger and Deputy U. S. Marshal Ridge Holloway rode south toward Delta Valley on Colorado's western slope. They talked as they rode, and Stranger learned that Holloway was a new Christian. Ridge found the mysterious man easy to talk to, so he brought up the problem he faced with Marlene Daniels and her attitude about his occupation. He asked Stranger what he thought and was pleased that he held the same opinion Nurse Breanna Baylor had, even quoted the same Scriptures.

"That makes me feel a whole lot better, John," Ridge said, smiling.

"Well, the truth is the truth."

"You're as emphatic about it as a Christian lady I talked to in Denver. She said exactly what you did about it, and she even quoted the same Bible passages you did."

"Well, she's got to be a very intelligent lady."

"Oh, she is. She's a nurse—C.M.N."

"I see." John's mind went immediately to the woman he loved.

"You may have met her, since you come to Denver a lot. She works out of Dr. Lyle Goodwin's office. Sometimes works right there in the office. Small. Blond. Pretty as a picture. Name's Breanna Baylor."

The sound of that name lanced a thrill through John Stranger's heart. "Oh. Yes. Miss Baylor. I've met her. Lovely lady."

"I've often wondered about her," said Ridge. "I mean, why isn't she married? With her looks and sweet personality, you'd think the men would be knockin' on her door by the dozens. Tell you this much...if I was a few years older, I'd be beatin' the door down myself."

Stranger smiled. "Wouldn't do you any good, Ridge. Miss Baylor was jilted one time by a man she dearly loved. They were engaged, and it was almost time for the wedding when he left her for another woman. She's vowed never to let herself fall in love again. She won't even let a man get close enough to be a good friend."

"That's too bad."

"Yeah. My sentiments exactly. But we were talking about Marlene's attitude about your wearing a badge, Ridge..."

"Yes, sir, we were."

"Are you aware that as a lawman you're actually considered in Scripture a minister of God?"

"Really?"

"I wouldn't kid you."

"Well, I've done a little speaking from the Bible since I became a Christian."

"That's not what I mean. The Bible actually says that the men who enforce society's laws are ministers of God."

"Even if they're not Christians?"

"Even if they're not Christians. They're ministers of God in the sense that God recognizes and approves the laws established by society for its protection against criminals and lawbreakers...and they are the ones who enforce those laws."

Stranger noted a small stream running underneath the road ahead of them. "Tell you what, Ridge," he said. "Let's stop up there at that stream and let the horses have a drink. We'll take a few minutes and I'll show you what I'm talking about."

"I'd like that," grinned Ridge, "seein' as how I'm a lawman."

They hauled up at the edge of the stream and left their saddles. John produced his big black Bible from the left saddlebag, then led Ebony to the water and said, "Have yourself a good drink." He patted the horse's rump and received a nicker.

Ridge left his horse to drink beside Ebony and moved close to the tall dark man. They settled under a large tree and read from Romans 13 about the important place of civil authorities for promoting good and maintaining order.

They talked for several minutes, then Stranger said, "So when you're forced to use your gun to execute wrath on outlaws and killers, you're a minister of God...a protector of the people and a revenger against the evil doers."

Ridge paused a few seconds, then said, "You know, the thought of being the other kind of minister—a preacher of the gospel—is intriguing. I really admire my pastor in Denver, and I've often thought of what it would be like to be in the ministry."

Stranger grinned. "Well, Ridge, the ministry isn't something a man just chooses for himself. If he's a Bible man, he has a special calling from the Lord to be a preacher."

Ridge grinned back. "I didn't mean that I was *considering* it. I just meant that the thought had passed through my mind a few times that it must be a wonderful thing to be called of God and to preach His Word. I'm...I'm quite happy being this other kind of minister. Speaking of preaching," Ridge continued, clearing his throat, "I've heard that you're quite a preacher yourself."

"Oh, I make a stab at it now and then...when a church needs somebody to fill the pulpit."

"But you don't feel the call of God to preach?"

"Not in the way we've been talking. I have a special calling from the Lord to do a special work. Sometimes it involves preaching, but it involves a lot of other things, too."

"I see. But you've never felt like you should be a pastor or an evangelist?"

"No."

"Tell me about this special call you have from the Lord, John. I'd like to hear about it."

"I think it's time we moved on," Stranger said. He got up and walked toward Ebony and placed his Bible in the saddlebag. He swung into the saddle and said, "Ready?"

"Yep," Ridge said, grinning, and mounted up.

As they moved out at a leisurely pace, Stranger said, "You said earlier that you've done a little speaking from the Bible since you became a Christian."

"A little."

"At church, or what?"

"At church. A few weeks ago my pastor asked me to bring a devotional message at a church social function. Afterward he said I did real good. Said I have a way with words. Most of the people took the time to come up and tell me how much they enjoyed it. Pastor liked it so well, he had me bring another message at men's prayer breakfast the very next week."

"That go over as good?"

"Sure did. Pastor's already asked me to prepare some more messages for other special occasions. I'm to give them when I'm in Denver between assignments."

"Wonderful," nodded Stranger. He looked furtively toward heaven and grinned.

CHAPTER

TWELVE

———◆———

The sun was almost out of sight on the western horizon as Nelda and Autumn Lynne prepared supper on the Lynne ranch. Roy and Adam were in the tool shed near the barn, repairing a well-worn saddle. The air was quite cool, and the door of the shed was closed.

The saddle was astride two sawhorses, with Roy on his knees beside it, wrapping the saddle horn with new leather. Adam was on his feet, holding it steady.

The latch rattled and the door squeaked open. Father and son turned to see Nelda, wearing a shawl over her shoulders and holding it tight at her throat. There was a hint of worry in her eyes as she asked, "Roy, did Aaron say anything to you about stopping off somewhere?"

"No, darlin'."

"It isn't like him to be this late."

"You're right. If he doesn't show up pretty soon, Adam and I'll saddle up and ride for town."

"Autumn and I have supper started," Nelda said. "It'll be ready in about forty, forty-five minutes. Maybe you should go now."

Adam had a view of the yard through a window from where he stood. There was movement out there, and peering through the glass, he caught a glimpse of a horse and rider. "No need," he said, pointing toward the window. "Here he comes n— Oh! No, it's Mr. Bancroft. He's leading Aaron's horse, and—"

Nelda adjusted herself so she could see through the window. A gasp escaped her lips. "Roy!"

Roy Lynne was on his feet in a flash. He bolted out the door with Nelda and Adam on his heels. George Bancroft saw the three of them running toward him and drew rein. He started to speak, but Nelda's wail cut him off. "He's dead! He's dead!"

Roy grimly examined the hole where the bullet had exited Aaron's back. Adam put an arm around his mother's shoulder and squeezed hard. Autumn came bounding off the back porch of the house, her long auburn hair flying.

Roy turned and moved up on Nelda's other side. He slipped an arm around her waist while he looked up and asked, "Where did you find him, George?"

George slid from his saddle at the same time Autumn drew up, face white. "Aaron!" she screamed, dashing to the lifeless form.

Adam left his mother with his father and went to Autumn, wrapping his arms around her. They wept together and listened to George as he said, "I'm sorry, Roy. Truly sorry. I didn't just find him, though. Hec Peale and I saw him shot down."

Eyes wide, Roy said, "You saw who did it?"

"Yeah. We saw who did it, all right."

Jaw set firm, Roy looked at his neighbor through tear-dimmed eyes. "Let me guess—the Taggarts."

"One of 'em. Van."

"So where's Hec? Did you two let Van get away?"

Bancroft explained how the incident happened, and that Hec was on his way to town to bring Sheriff Prisk to the Lynne ranch.

Nelda stood frozen to the spot, unable to take her eyes off the body of her son.

Roy squeezed her shoulder and said, "Let's take Aaron inside, honey. We'll put him on his bed for now. We'll…we'll have to take him to the undertaker tomorrow."

The Lynne's huddled together for a long moment, weeping and trying to console one another. Then Nelda and her two remaining offspring followed as Roy and George carried Aaron's lifeless form into the house.

When Aaron's body was on his bed and covered over with a sheet, the family gathered in the kitchen and waited for Sheriff Prisk. Eating supper was out of the question. No one was hungry.

They wiped tears and talked about Aaron. At times they gave voice to their questions as to why the Lord would allow such a thing to happen. Adam asked why God let people like the Taggarts come into the world in the first place.

Roy was trying to come up with an answer for Adam when the sound of riders coming into the yard caught everyone's attention. Roy crossed the kitchen and opened the door.

Sheriff Prisk had come with Hector Peale and had brought Clyde Arthur along. The three men spoke their condolences to the Lynnes, then Prisk said, "George, I'm making a posse of Clyde and Hec. I'm hoping you'll join us."

"Of course," Bancroft nodded. "I'll want to stop by my place and let Sylvia know what's happened and what we're doin'."

"Sure," Prisk said. "Then, I suggest we get going."

"Wait a minute," Roy said. "I want in on this posse, too."

"Wouldn't be wise, Roy," Prisk said. "I think you'd better stay here. Your family needs you."

"They also need to see Aaron's killer caught. There are six Taggarts, Luke, not including Lulu. Only four of you. My coming along will help even the odds."

"Can't let you go with us, Roy," Prisk said, shaking his head.

"It was my son that…that skunk killed, Luke! I've got a right—"

"Roy, listen to me!" cut in Prisk, taking hold of the rancher's shoulders. "You're too emotionally involved. The situation at the Taggart place could get real tight. Shape you're in right now, it could erupt into something really bloody. You stay here with Nelda and the kids."

Roy took a deep breath and forced calm into his voice. "I'm not going to go out of my head, Luke. I promise. You need another man, and I'm the only one available."

Prisk studied Roy Lynne's eyes. He took a deep breath, sighed, and asked, "You really think you can stay cool when you lay eyes on Van?"

"Yes."

"You sure? Seems to me your first inclination will be to shoot him down like the mangy coyote that he is."

Roy shook his head. "No, Luke. I wouldn't murder Van Taggart if I had him cornered all by myself. But I do want justice done. I want to help bring in the man who killed my son in cold blood."

Prisk sighed again. "All right. I'm trusting you to keep your word."

Roy looked down at Nelda. "I hate to leave you and the kids, sweetheart, but—"

"I understand," she said, reaching up to stroke his cheek. "You go with Sheriff Prisk and these men. Autumn and Adam and I will be all right. We have the Lord with us."

Sheriff Prisk deputized the four men. Roy strapped on his gunbelt and shouldered into his sheepskin jacket. He kissed and embraced Nelda and Autumn, then hugged Adam, telling him to stay close to his mother and sister.

Five minutes later, Roy had saddled his horse and led it out of the corral. He mounted, waved to his family—who looked on from the kitchen window—and rode away with the posse.

✴ ✴ ✴ ✴ ✴

Twilight was on the land as the Taggarts ate supper. One chair was empty, and the family discussed where Van might have gone.

"I've got a hunch Van's gone after Aaron Lynne," Wick said.

"You'd think he'd know to leave Aaron alone," Lulu said.

"I don't think Wick meant Van means to get into another fight," Otis said. "If he's gone after Aaron, it's to do him in like Wick said he was plannin' to do. Wouldn't doubt it if Van decided to beat Wick to it."

"So what're you gonna do, Pa?" asked Cliff.

"Nothin' I can do. We can't very well go ridin' onto Lynne property lookin' for 'im. We'll just have to wait till he comes home."

"But what if he tried and failed...and got himself shot or somethin'?" Nate asked.

"Well, I hope nothin' like that has happened," Otis said, "but what's done is done. We'll just have to wait and see what turns up. If Van's done got hisself shot, we'll hear from somebody."

"Unless the Lynnes killed him and decided to bury the body," Jeb said. "Then we'll never know—"

They heard a horse out in the yard, and they all jumped to their feet.

"I'll see who it is," said Otis, picking up a burning lantern off the cupboard. "Just stay alert if there's trouble."

He opened the door that led to the back porch and stepped outside. Five riders, horses snorting and breathing heavy, hauled up to the porch. Luke Prisk was out of his saddle and moving toward Otis while the others dismounted. Prisk halted at the porch steps and said, "We're looking for Van, Otis. Is he here?"

"No, he's not. What do you want with him?"

"Where is he?"

"I don't know. What do you want with him?"

"When did you see him last?" pressed the sheriff.

"Several hours ago. 'Bout one o'clock or so. I ast you a question, Luke. What do you want with him?"

"He shot Aaron Lynne from ambush and killed him," came Prisk's cold, level words. "These men with me have been deputized, and we're after Van to arrest him and take him to trial for murder."

Otis feigned surprise and asked, "How do you know Van's the one who killed Aaron?"

Prisk turned and said, "George...Hec...tell him."

"Happened at the big rocks on the road toward our ranches," Bancroft said. "Hec and I were a short distance behind Aaron, headin' for home late this afternoon. We both saw a puff of smoke, heard a shot, and saw Aaron fall off his horse. And we saw Van up in the rocks with a rifle in his hands. When he saw us, he made a quick disappearance. We were off our mounts and checkin' on Aaron when we saw Van ridin' away like the devil was after him."

Otis's sons filed through the door onto the porch as he scowled and snapped, "It's a put-up job, Luke! These guys have it in for us Taggarts so they made up a fancy story!"

"Aaron's dead!" Prisk said. "Shot through the heart!"

"I ain't doubtin' that, but these two birds are lyin' through their teeth about Van 'cause they detest him and the rest of us Taggarts!"

Bancroft started for Otis, but Prisk extended an arm to stop him. "Cool down, George," he said, keeping his eyes on the Taggarts. "I want to know where Van is, Otis. If you're hiding him and you don't turn him over to me this instant, you're looking at a long prison term. And so are your sons and daughter."

"We ain't hidin' him," Otis said.

"Then you won't mind if we make a search, will you?"

Wick Taggart moved up beside his father, eyes blazing. "You ain't doin' nothin' of the kind, Luke! You're on private property, and you ain't got no right nosin' around here!"

"You try to stop us, and we'll take you to jail tonight, Wick. Now, you just back off and stay out of the way." Then to Otis, "I'll need some more lanterns."

Wick was seething. Otis touched his arm and said, "We ain't got nothin' to hide, son. Let 'em go ahead."

Under the Taggart's close scrutiny, Sheriff Prisk and his posse made a thorough search of the house, barn, and outbuildings. When they finished and returned to their horses, Prisk said, "All right, Otis, I'm convinced Van isn't here."

"Well, that just makes me real happy. Now, take your little posse and get off my property."

Prisk fixed Otis with a hard glare and said, "Where is he?"

"I ain't got the slightest idea. He left here early this afternoon, and we ain't seen him since."

"I don't need to tell you that if he shows up here and you harbor him, I'll arrest the whole bunch of you."

"You can't hang Van on the testimony of these two, Luke! I still say they made up seein' Van shoot Aaron just to get at us Taggarts!"

"The law will hang a man on the testimony of two witnesses, Otis, especially when those witnesses are upstanding citizens in the community like George and Hec are. They're telling the truth, and you know it."

"So what're you gonna do now?" Wick asked.

"We're going to hunt him down and let the judge and jury take it from there."

"Ain't right havin' Roy in the posse, Luke," Otis said. "If you guys catch up to Van, Roy'll shoot him on sight and not give him a chance to surrender."

"Don't judge me by what you'd do if the tables were turned, Otis!" snapped Roy. "If that murdering son of yours doesn't resist arrest, he'll be brought in alive."

"Well, let me tell you somethin', Mr. Pious Christian. I wouldn't trust a hypocrite like you no matter what he said. I know what you'll do! You'll shoot Van down, then say he resisted arrest!"

"No such thing!" Prisk said. "Now you do some cooling down, Otis. I assure you Van will be taken alive if possible. Come on," he said, turning to his posse. "Let's get out of here."

The Taggarts stood in the cold night air and watched the posse ride away. When they were out of sight, they returned to the kitchen and shut the door. Otis swore, slamming a fist on the cupboard. "Van shoulda been more careful!" he boomed.

"Where do you suppose he went, Pa?" asked Cliff.

"I have no idea."

"At least he was smart enough to stay away from here," Nate said.

"We shoulda gunned the whole bunch down while we had 'em here," Wick said. "They're gonna kill Van. Can't go no other way with Roy Lynne in the pack."

"You're right, Wick," Jeb said. "If they catch up to Van, he's a dead man."

A dark hopelessness assailed Lulu. She had no doubt that Roy Lynne and Sheriff Prisk were being honest when they said they would take Van alive if possible, but she knew Van. He would resist arrest. She feared she would never see her hotheaded brother alive again.

When the posse reached the road, Prisk called for a halt and said, "Gentlemen, there's nothing we can do till morning. Let's meet at dawn at the big rocks where Van gunned Aaron down. We'll track him from there."

Everyone agreed and rode their separate ways for home.

Roy Lynne returned to his grieving family. They spent a sleepless night, taking their grief to the Lord in prayer and reading the

Bible together to find comfort and strength. Though they did not pretend to understand God's ways, by faith they agreed it was God's time to take Aaron home.

Van Taggart lay in pitch black darkness inside a woodshed atop Grand Mesa. It was very cold, and he was tired and hungry. Lantern lights had shone through the windows of the house in front of the woodshed when he arrived there just after dark, but he had resisted the urge to knock on the door and ask for refuge. He dare not be seen by anyone who could put the law on his trail. There was nothing to do but lead his horse deep into the woods and leave it tied there, then move into the shelter of the woodshed for the night.

Van lay on a floor of sawdust in the dark and shivered, his teeth chattering. There was still panic in him. He could not think clearly enough to make any plans. Van knew Prisk would form a posse and come after him. All he could do was try to elude them until they gave up the search. Once he knew they were no longer trying to track him, he would make his way off Grand Mesa and come up with a plan. He would like to return home, but he knew he wouldn't be safe there.

Van thought of his older brother. If only he knew where Treg was hiding, he would go to him. Treg would keep the law from finding him. If he got caught, he would hang. George Bancroft and Hector Peale were well-respected in Delta Valley. Their testimony would convince any jury of his guilt. Van swore in a low whisper. If only Bancroft and Peale hadn't been on the road when he shot Aaron Lynne.

But what if he hadn't actually killed Aaron? What if he were still alive? No. Aaron had to be dead. Van was a crack shot, and he had Aaron's heart in his sights. Aaron was dead, all right. The charge he would face if caught would be *murder*. He would hang. The thought of dying at the end of a rope was more than he could stand. Van Taggart must elude the law and make good his escape.

At dawn, Luke Prisk and his posse met at the rock formation. George Bancroft and Hector Peale led the others to the spot where Van Taggart had ridden his horse out of the rocks and onto the road. They found that the horse's shoe on the left rear hoof left a peculiar mark in the soft earth. It was apparently damaged, and Van was unaware of it.

Within half an hour, it was evident that the fugitive was heading for Grand Mesa. The posse rode hard and soon was atop the mesa, following Van's trail. By eight-thirty, they had located the spot in the woods where his horse had spent the night. They tracked Van's bootprints and found the woodshed where he had spent the night.

Prisk checked to see if the residents in the house were all right. He found them unharmed and unaware that they had sheltered a killer in their woodshed.

The search continued.

At midmorning, Lulu Taggart drove the family wagon toward Delta to buy groceries and supplies. Her father wanted his sons to stay on the ranch in case Van should show up in need of help.

Lulu's heart was heavy for Van, but she was glad to have some time alone. She looked toward the sky and said, "God, I think You're up there. Even though Pa says You ain't, I think You are. If I'm right, I want to know it. And…and if the Bible's really true—like Autumn says it is—I want to know that, too. Pa says it's just fairy tales, but if You really exist and the Bible is Your Word, please show me. I want to know what's true."

Lulu arrived in town and parked the wagon at the hitch rail in front of Mauldin's General Store. She climbed down, hitching up her Levis, and made her way across the boardwalk and entered the store.

George Mauldin was behind the counter tending to a couple of elderly women when he heard the bell above the door. He looked past the ladies and said, "Good morning, Lulu."

The two women looked over their shoulders and gave Lulu a look of disgust.

"Mornin', Mr. Mauldin," Lulu nodded, noting the eyes of the women on her. She knew what they were thinking.

"Be with you shortly," Mauldin said.

"No hurry. I'll just look around a bit."

While Lulu browsed about the store, she could hear the whispers of the two women. Though she couldn't make out what they said, she was sure the conversation was about her.

Lulu's eyes fell on a shelf bearing many books. She had seen the shelf before, but had never paid it any mind. This time it captured her attention, for among the books she saw three black Bibles. Her fingers trembled as she reached out to touch the spines of the Bibles. There was an irresistible urge to take one off the shelf and look at it.

Lulu looked around to make sure she wasn't being watched, then took the middle Bible from the shelf. Licking dry lips, she opened it and felt a stab of guilt. She thought of what her father would do if he knew she held a Bible in her hands. Her heart pounded as she let the Bible fall open where it would. The words seized her attention:

The fool hath said in his heart, There is no God. Corrupt are they, and have done abominable iniquity: There is none that doeth good. God looked down from heaven upon the children of men—

Lulu's heart seemed to leap into her throat. She swallowed hard and closed the Bible. Then, with trembling fingers, she let it fall open again. This time the book of Isaiah appeared, and her eyes locked on the last two verses of the fifty-seventh chapter:

But the wicked are like the troubled sea, when it cannot rest, whose waters cast up mire and dirt. There is no peace, saith my God, to the wicked.

Suddenly Lulu recalled a conversation she had with Autumn: "When you know the Lord, everything in life takes on a new meaning, and you can face the hard times with joy and peace of mind." Lulu had no peace of mind, and the Bible in her hands told her *the wicked have no peace.*

Lulu didn't understand all about "the wicked," but she was sure she qualified before God…God, whom she now had no doubt existed. He had put a Bible in her hands and spoken to her as clearly as if He had shouted from the sky. Lulu Taggart had to have a Bible. She must know more.

She waited until she heard the women leave, then made her way to the counter. She was the only customer in the store. Mauldin smiled at her, then noted what she had in her hand. He tried not to show his surprise.

"What's the price on this, Mr. Mauldin?" Lulu asked, laying the Bible on the counter.

"Three dollars."

"All right," she said, pulling a man's wallet from the hip pocket of her Levis. "I need to ask a favor of you."

"Yes?"

"I'm paying for the Bible with my own money, Mr. Mauldin, so it won't go on my father's bill."

"I see," Mauldin nodded.

"I don't want Pa to know I'm buying it. You understand?"

"Of course, Lulu."

"You won't tell him?"

"Of course not."

"He'd beat me good if he found out, Mr. Mauldin."

"I understand, Lulu. He won't find it out from me. But I would suggest you be real careful where you keep it at home."

"I will," she said, returning the wallet to its place. She pulled a slip of paper from her shirt pocket and handed it to him. "Here's the list of things I need."

Soon Lulu was on her way home. She kept the Bible on the wagon seat next to her and stopped occasionally to read for a few minutes. She looked especially for the verses Autumn Lynne had quoted to her.

As Lulu drew within sight of the Taggart ranch, she placed the Bible in a paper bag, then put it in a box with groceries. No one ever helped her carry the boxes into the house. She would hide the Bible in her dresser and read it every chance she got.

THIRTEEN

A t mid-morning, Van Taggart worked his way north across Grand Mesa, skirting the ponds and lakes and threading his way amongst the heavy underbrush and thick clusters of pine and aspen.

He had to know if he was being followed. He climbed a towering pillar of rock and scanned the mesa to the south. When he saw five riders coming his direction, skirting a lake, he swore. It was the sheriff, all right...and four men with him.

In a panic, Taggart scurried off the rock, vaulted into the saddle, and aimed his horse due north through the rugged terrain. Prisk and his posse were no more than two miles behind. The thought of dying at the end of a rope was more than he could stand. For a half hour, he pushed the horse as hard as he could, then stopped and climbed a tree. He caught sight of the sheriff and posse once more, and they were gaining on him.

He came down from the tree and saw clearly the horse's prints etched in the soft earth. He swore and jerked the rifle from its scabbard. He checked the loads in both his rifle and revolver, then took off in a mad dash for life and freedom. He cut around the edge of a lake and plunged into heavy timber, breathing heavily. He ran for all he was worth, threading his way through the dense trees in deep shade.

Moments later, Luke Prisk and his four possemen came upon Van's horse. Prisk left his saddle to examine the horse for injury. "Nothing wrong with this horse," he said. "I think Van finally figured out he was leaving a trail a blind man could follow."

"We know how good you are at trackin', Sheriff," George Bancroft said. "You ain't about to lose his trail."

"Not when I'm this close," Prisk replied, swinging back into the saddle. "How about bringing his horse along, George? We'll need it when we capture him."

After another hour, Van's legs were giving out and his lungs burned. He climbed another tree and took a look at his back trail. To his dismay, the posse was pressing closer, with one of them leading the horse he had abandoned.

He dropped to the ground and ran north in blind panic. His lungs felt as though they would burst, but on he ran. His mouth was dry as a sand pit, but on he ran. His legs felt as if they would drop off, but on he ran. He heard only his huffing breath, his thundering heartbeat, his boots crunching pine cones and snapping twigs.

He tripped and felt his back slam the ground. He rolled onto all fours and forced himself to stand. He summoned all his strength and ran on.

Suddenly he emerged from the trees and found himself staring into a jagged rupture of the earth. It was a hundred feet deep in dark shade and forty feet across. There was no way he could jump it. The narrow canyon ran both ways as far as he could see. He looked behind him. Through the dense trees, he could make out the approaching posse.

He staggered back into the woods and planted himself behind a rough-barked ponderosa and leaned hard against it. He jacked a cartridge into the chamber of the rifle and cocked the hammer of the revolver. He waited for the posse to draw near.

He could hear the horses blowing and braced his back against the tree on the opposite side of the posse's approach. He would get off only one shot with the rifle, but he would give them six shots from the revolver.

The possemen were talking in low tones. He heard Luke Prisk say something about being so close, they were breathing down his neck.

Taggart waited until they were within a few feet of the tree. He took a deep breath and swung around the trunk, keeping his back braced against it, and blazed away.

The bullet from the Remington .44 ripped through Prisk's left arm, but the possemen unleashed a barrage of hot lead that tore into Taggart's body. He slid down the side of the tree and slumped over on the ground. Luke Prisk bent over in the saddle and gripped his wounded arm. While the other three left their horses to move in on Taggart, Roy Lynne stepped up to Prisk and said, "Here, Luke. Let me help you down."

Lynne helped the lawman sit against a tree, then removed Prisk's jacket and tore the bloody sleeve so he could examine the wound. "Doesn't look like it touched the bone, Luke. I'll wrap it with my bandanna, and we'll get you back to town to Doc Faulkner."

Luke nodded, then glanced toward the others, who were standing over the lifeless form of Van Taggart. Bancroft had Van's rifle, and Peale had his revolver. Arthur looked at Prisk and said, "He's dead, Sheriff. How are you?"

"Just a flesh wound," Prisk replied through clenched teeth. "I'll be all right. Roy's fixing me up till I can get to Doc Faulkner."

Bancroft was bent over the dead man. Straightening up, he said, "Sheriff, we put a dozen bullets in him."

"Guess that ought to do it," Prisk replied.

"You know what Otis is gonna say, don't you?" Arthur said. "He'll swear Roy cut loose on him without givin' him a chance to surrender, and we joined in."

"I don't rightly care what Otis says," Prisk said. "We all know the truth, and the truth is, we had no choice but to take him out."

Roy finished wrapping the sheriff's arm while the other three carried Van Taggart's body to his horse and draped him over the saddle. They tied his hands to his ankles underneath the horse's belly so he wouldn't slip off while they descended the steep slopes of the mesa to the valley.

Lynne hoisted the sheriff onto his mount and said, "I'll take you to the doctor, Luke. These boys can deliver Van's body to Otis."

Prisk shook his head. "Nope. I'm sheriff, and I led this posse. It's my duty to deliver the corpse to the family."

"But that arm will continue to bleed until Doc puts some stitches in it," argued Lynne. "You really need to get to him as soon as possible."

"I'll be okay. We have to go by the Taggart place to get to town anyway, so there's no reason for me not to do my duty and deliver Van's body to his pa."

It was nearing eleven o'clock when the posse rode onto the Taggart place and headed for the ranch house.

"Now, you gentlemen be ready for anything," Prisk said.

"You're sure you want to ride in there, Sheriff?" Clyde Arthur asked. "If we do have trouble, you won't be a hundred percent."

"I can still use my gun," Prisk assured him. "I hope it won't be necessary, but you never know with the Taggarts."

They were in sight of the house, and all except Lulu were in the yard, watching the posse's approach. By now they could see Van's horse with the body limply draped over its back. No one spoke, but the tension in the air was tight.

Prisk could feel the pressure of their eyes as he slid from the saddle, and he left his gun hand near the butt of his revolver. The rest of the posse left their saddles at the same time.

Otis Taggart took two steps forward and glowered at Roy Lynne. Prisk saw it and said, "It wasn't Roy, Otis. It was all of us. Van didn't give us any choice. He surprised us and opened fire with his rifle and revolver. We had to take him out. As it was, he got me in the arm with the first shot."

Otis couldn't find his voice. Wick moved up beside him and exploded. "We knew it would be like this, Prisk! Pa told you not to take Lynne with you! I'd lay my life on it that Van tried to surrender, but Lynne and all the rest of you joined in and cut him down!"

Nate and Jeb moved to the body and began undoing the ropes.

Cliff sided his father and growled, "You're lyin', Sheriff! You didn't want to take Van alive. None of you did! Especially Lynne! The bunch of you murdered him!"

Otis finally got control of his tongue and shouted, "Justice will be done, Luke!"

"Justice *has* been done, Otis. If you and your sons have retaliation in mind, you'd best forget it. Van murdered Aaron Lynne in front of two witnesses. Whether you believe it or not, this posse and I went after him with full intention of taking him alive. As I told you, he wouldn't let us. Man opens up on us like he did will be shot dead. Now, you'd better just bury Van and let his foolishness be a lesson to the rest of you. If Roy or anyone else in this posse has any hint of trouble from you and your clan, you'll rue the day any of you were born. Do I make myself clear?"

"Yeah. Real clear. Now get off our property and let us bury our dead."

"Heed my warning, Otis, or you'll be burying more of your dead."

Prisk mounted up and rode away with the posse trailing behind. When they were out of earshot, Otis Taggart hissed through his teeth, "They're gonna be the sorriest bloody skunks you ever saw, boys!"

Lulu stood at the door, looking on. A shudder ran through her. She knew what her father meant.

"Everybody get a shovel," Otis commanded. "You, too, Lulu. Let's bury your brother."

While the grave was being dug at the side of the house, Otis stood close by and said, "I make a solemn vow to each of you—Wick...Nate...Cliff...Jeb...Lulu. Every man who was in that posse will die."

"They got it comin', Pa!" said Wick, fire in his eyes. "And I'm gonna enjoy havin' my part in it. Especially when it comes to Roy Lynne."

"As soon as it gets dark," said Otis, "we're goin' for a ride, and we're gonna start with the sheriff. With him out of the way, the rest won't be so dangerous. We'll get Clyde Arthur next, since he lives right there in town. Then we'll ride to the Peale and Bancroft ranches. We'll save Lynne till last. Bullets will do for the others, but Roy Lynne is gonna hang while his family watches."

There was a silent cry of anguish deep in Lulu's soul. She had to find a way to stop the killings. Somehow she must get off the ranch and warn the sheriff, the barber, and the ranchers what her father and brothers were planning. She would have to do it before dark.

Van Taggart was buried without ceremony. Otis would allow no tears. When the last shovelful of dirt was tossed on the mound, the elder Taggart reminded them that Van no longer existed and weeping would not bring him back. He announced that he and his sons would ride into town, do a little drinking, and buy some more ammunition. He wanted to have plenty of cartridges.

"So let's get goin', boys," Otis said. "Gun shop closes at five. We'll buy the ammunition first, then put a few drinks under our belts. We'll leave in 'bout half an hour. Lulu can have supper ready for us when we get home."

It was now just after three o'clock. Lulu hurried to her room. She planned to saddle her horse and ride to the Lynne ranch as soon as her father and brothers headed for town. The Lynnes would not only be warned, but they would also help her get the warning to the others.

Lulu closed the door and crossed the room to her dresser. Her heart was heavy as she opened a drawer, reached under some articles of underclothing, and pulled out her new Bible. She sat on the edge of the bed and began flipping pages until she found passages on heaven...and on hell. When she read the story Jesus told of the rich man who died and went to hell, she began to weep. Her whole body shuddered. She thought of Van and wiped tears, knowing her father was wrong. Van was not out of existence. He was in the same place as the rich man, and he was begging for someone to come back to earth and tell his father, brothers, and sister that there really is a hell.

Lulu did not hear the footsteps in the hall. Otis Taggart was heading for his bedroom and heard Lulu weeping. He had not heard her weep since the day of her mother's funeral, years before, when he had angrily told her to stop crying. He figured she was mourning over Van, and it angered him. He grabbed the door knob and flung open the door.

Lulu's head jerked up at the unexpected intrusion, and her eyes bulged with fear when she looked into the wrathful face of her father. His eyes were fixed on the Bible before her. Otis spewed saliva as he swore at his disobedient daughter. "You wicked wench!" he bellowed, lunging for the Bible and snatching it up. "You know not to bring this vile trash into my house!"

Lulu's heart was racing, pounding so hard she could feel a throbbing in her temples. Her father's eyes were hellish and fearsome. He began ripping pages out and throwing them on the floor. Lulu could barely breathe. She hugged herself and sat on the bed, frozen in terror.

Wick and Jeb appeared at the door, looking in. When the madman had torn out the last page, he threw the leather cover against the wall and ejected another string of vile words. Then turning to his two sons, he said breathlessly, "You boys go to town and get the ammunition. I'm stayin' here with your sister."

Wick glanced at Lulu, who was still affixed to the bed, then he and Jeb hurried down the hall.

Otis whipped off his belt and doubled it, pinning his rebellious daughter with smoldering eyes. "It seems Father must teach his daughter a much-needed lesson."

Lulu Taggart had her back to her brothers when they entered the kitchen. She busied herself at the stove. Otis had worked on hooded masks while his sons were gone and had them laid out on a small table in a corner of the large kitchen.

While her father showed her brothers the masks, Lulu made plans to ride to the Lynne ranch when the rest of the family headed toward town. If she couldn't save Sheriff Prisk and Clyde Arthur, she would at least warn the Lynnes and hope they could help her warn the Bancrofts and Peales.

Wick admired the masks and said, "They'll work real good, Pa. But how come you made six? There are only five of us now."

"I made one for Lulu, too. She's goin' with us."

Lulu turned, eyes wide with surprise. The Taggart sons saw their sister's face for the first time since entering the kitchen. Her eyes were puffy, and the left one was almost closed. There were various cuts and bruises, and her lips were swollen.

The Taggart brothers exchanged glances. Lulu had been beaten before, as had they when they were younger, but never this badly.

Otis noticed them staring and said, "I think your sister has learned her lesson about this Bible stuff. I don't think she'll ever touch another Bible or listen to people like Autumn Lynne. I want you to wear your sidearm when we go, too," Otis said to her. "When we gun those dudes down, I want your weapon used on 'em, too. You got that?"

Lulu nodded weakly. She wanted to pray that God would somehow spare the intended victims from the fate her father had planned for them, but she wasn't sure how.

As darkness fell over Delta Valley, John Stranger and Deputy U. S. Marshal Ridge Holloway rode into Delta. A cold wind whipped through the valley.

They stopped at a café to eat and learned from the waitress where Sheriff Luke Prisk lived. After the meal, they rode through the dark streets to the sheriff's house.

Their knock was answered by Delia Prisk, the sheriff's wife. When they told her who they were, she invited them to step inside and called her husband from the back of the house. Stranger and Holloway introduced themselves to Prisk and explained that they were there under orders from Marshal Solomon Duvall in Denver to observe the Taggart ranch in anticipation that Treg Taggart would show up there.

Prisk led them into the parlor to sit down and told them he had made a thorough search of the Taggart place and found no sign of Treg. But he believed Treg would show up there sooner or later. Prisk told them he was glad they were there because he had little time to observe the Taggart ranch.

Luke Prisk then told John Stranger he had heard many things about him—exciting stories of Stranger's exploits in capturing out-laws, out-shooting famous gunfighters, and helping people in trouble. He wanted to ask about some particular incidents and get the stories from Stranger himself.

Smiling, Stranger told him he would answer his questions in brief.

Otis Taggart, his sons, and his daughter left their horses in the alley behind Sheriff Prisk's house and crept through the yard toward the front porch. Beneath their hats, they wore white hooded masks. The raw wind lashed at them as they gathered at the front corner of the house and saw two horses at the hitching posts near the porch.

"They got company," Otis said. "Wick, the parlor's on the other side of the house. Sneak over there and see what you can find out." The rest of the Taggarts stood against the wall and waited while Wick ducked low and dashed to the other side.

Lulu was sick to her stomach. If her father did not see her fire her gun, she would face his wrath. So she would fire, but she would miss. She didn't want the murder of Sheriff Luke Prisk on her conscience.

Some three or four minutes later, Wick returned. "Two men," he said. "Their backs are to the window, so I couldn't see their faces, but I heard Delia call one of them Marshal. I figure they're federal men. Don't make sense that two town marshals would be ridin' together."

"You're prob'ly right about that," Otis nodded. "We sure don't need that kind of trouble." He paused a moment. "We'll have to make a change of plan, here. I'd like to get Prisk outta the way first, but it ain't gonna work out that way. We'll take care of him later."

"We goin' after Clyde Arthur next, then pa?" asked Cliff.

Otis thought on it, then said, "Wouldn't be too smart, either, with these two extra lawmen in town. Best thing is to take out Prisk and Arthur after them guys are gone."

Lulu let out a quiet sigh of relief. At least the sheriff and the barber were spared for the time being.

"Okay," said Otis, turning toward the rear of the house. "Hector Peale is next. Let's go."

CHAPTER

FOURTEEN

———◆———

A t the Peale ranch, Hector and his wife Marla were seated in the parlor, their hearts filled with joy. They had been surprised in late afternoon by the arrival of their four sons, all army officers. The oldest son, Don, was a major, stationed at Fort Laramie. The next oldest was Chet, who was a captain, stationed at Fort Collins. And the twins, Larry and Barry, were lieutenants stationed at Fort Bridger. Since the forts were relatively close, the brothers kept contact with each other and planned their surprise visit a few weeks earlier.

The Peale sons had enjoyed their mother's excellent cooking for the first time in over a year, and still dressed in their uniforms and wearing their service revolvers, sat in the parlor with their happy parents. Their horses were in the barn, which left no clue to anyone approaching the ranch house that there were four extra men inside.

The twins were seated on a small couch with their mother between them. Chet sat on the other side of the room near the fireplace. Don was in an overstuffed chair with his back to the front window, and Hector stood behind the chair, leaning on its back.

The Taggarts rode up and dismounted behind some bushes about forty yards from the house. Otis spoke to Lulu through the slit in his mask. "I'll give you a little reprieve for now. Since we've stashed the horses so far from the house, I need you to stay with 'em. Your brothers and I will make short work of Hector and be right back. You keep these horses ready. Got it?"

"Yes, Pa," Lulu replied, relieved that she would not have to watch. "Can I take my mask off, then?"

"I suppose you don't need it, bein' all the way out here."

Lulu lifted her hat, removed the hooded mask, and tucked it under her belt. She placed the hat back on her head and peered through the darkness at the shadows of her father and brothers as they skulked toward the house. Lantern light glowed from the windows closest to the front of the house.

Otis and his sons drew up to the cottonwood trees that fringed the Peale yard some sixty feet from the front of the house and saw their intended victim directly in front of them at the window. "Looks like he's standin' there talkin' to someone in that chair he's leanin' on," Wick said.

"Gotta be Marla," said Otis.

"Should we get closer, Pa?" Jeb asked.

"No need to. He's makin' hisself a perfect target. I wanna take the first shot, then you boys fill him full of lead like he and his pals did to Van."

Otis cocked his revolver, leaned it against the tree in front of him, and drew a bead on Hector's back. He steadied himself by placing one foot on a protruding root at the base of the tree. The rest of the Taggarts cocked their hammers and waited.

Otis held his breath. Just as he pressed the trigger, his boot slipped on the curved root. His gun fired, but the bullet veered to the left and hit Hector in the upper left shoulder. The impact of the bullet spun him halfway around and dropped him a split second before the Taggart brothers began their volley. Guns roared and glass shattered. Bullets chewed into the chair, but Major Don Peale was already on the floor, pulling his revolver.

His brothers reacted just as quickly. Barry seized his mother, taking her to the floor with him, and dragged her into the hallway. By the time he crawled back into the parlor, his brothers had flung the door open and were returning fire from there and the shattered window.

The Taggarts were stunned to suddenly find themselves under fire. Bullets hissed at them and splintered bark from the trees around them.

"Pa, what happened?" Cliff cried.

"Don't know!"

"S'pose somebody somehow got word what we were plannin', Pa?" Nate asked. "Holed up in there to blast us?"

"If Hector knew we were comin', he wouldn't have been makin' such a good target of hisself! Way they're shootin', they know how to handle guns."

"You s'pose it's their sons?" Jeb asked, ducking his head as a slug chewed bark above him.

"Reckon it could be," Otis said. "We gotta git outta here. That's all I know!"

"But there's open space between us and the horses," Wick said.

"We gotta keep shootin' till they run outta ammunition!" Otis said.

"What if we run out before they do?"

"Then we'll have to run for the horses in spite of flyin' bullets!"

Lulu could hear the voices of her father and brothers amid the barking guns. They were pinned down and would be for a while. She pulled the hooded mask from under her belt and dropped it on

the ground. Then she climbed aboard her horse and galloped away
in the dark, unnoticed by her father and brothers.

The George Bancroft ranch was closest. Lulu rode hard with
the cold wind in her face, letting her gelding pick its way on the
rugged terrain in the darkness.

She found the Bancrofts reading in the library. Quickly, she
told them of her father's plan and what was going on at the Peale
ranch. Both George and Sylvia Bancroft mounted horses and rode
for town to get the sheriff. Lulu headed for the Lynne ranch as fast
as her horse could carry her.

The Peale brothers were reluctant to charge into the darkness
when they didn't know how many gunmen they were facing. Three
of them kept shooting from the door and the window while Barry
dragged their father into the hallway where Marla could check on
him. Once he had his wounded father safely in the hall, Barry
returned to the parlor to help his brothers.

Marla was pleased to find that her husband's wound was not
serious. He had been winged on the left shoulder, and she packed
the wound and bandaged it.

The Peale guns were suddenly silent. Outside in the cottonwoods, Cliff Taggart's left ear was bleeding. A bullet had chewed off
the top of it, and the warm fluid ran down the side of his face as he
pressed his bandanna against it.

Noting the silent guns, Otis said, "C'mon, boys! They're
prob'ly reloadin'. Let's get outta here!"

"I'm bleedin' bad, Pa!" Cliff cried as they dashed for the spot
where they had left Lulu and the horses. "A bullet tore up my left
ear!"

"Really bad?" the older man asked as they ran.

"Yeah. I gotta do somethin' to stop the bleedin'!"

"Maybe you'd better go on home and take care of it, Cliff,"

Otis said. "Your brothers and I will take care of Roy Lynne. We'll decide after that what to do about Prisk and Arthur."

"Okay, Pa," Cliff said, taking the bandanna from his ear long enough to mount his horse.

"Pa!" Wick gasped. "Lulu's gone!"

"She can't be!"

"She is, Pa," Nate said. "Here's her mask."

Otis swore. "Where could she have gone to?"

"I know where she went," said Wick. "She's gone to tell Bancrofts and Lynnes our plan, Pa!"

Otis swore again and mounted his horse. "Let's go. We gotta stop her."

"Would you rather I stayed with you, Pa?" Cliff asked as his brothers swung into their saddles.

"No. You go on home and get that bleedin' stopped. We'll see you there whenever we get this chore done."

"What're you gonna do to Lulu when you catch her, Pa?" Cliff asked.

"I'm not sure. I may break her neck. Go on home."

Without another word, Cliff spurred his horse and galloped away.

Otis said, "All right, boys, let's ride. Bancroft place first. If Lulu's warned 'em, we'll find out when we get there."

Ten minutes later, the four Taggarts skidded their mounts to a halt in front of the Bancroft house, which was totally dark.

The horses blew and snorted as Otis said, "Looks like Lulu got here, all right. Place is deserted. Leastwise it appears that way. Wick, you and Jeb go check the barn and corral. See if their horses are here."

Wick and Jeb made a quick examination of the barn and corral, striking matches to provide light. Returning to their father, they reported that by the looks of things, two horses, along with bridles and saddles, were missing.

More profanity exploded from Otis's mouth. "That girl's in deep trouble. I mean *deep* trouble."

"She's changed, Pa," said Wick. "She's been actin' funny of late."

"I know what it is, and so do you," Otis clipped.

"Yeah. Autumn Lynne."

"Well, let's go take care of her pa."

Lulu Taggart was within a mile of the Lynne place when her horse stumbled and fell. She flew out of the saddle and hit the ground rolling. She lost her hat, and the .44 Colt slipped out of its holster and landed in the grass.

The animal made a pitiful whinny and struggled to a standing position. Barely able to see, Lulu checked its legs and found that the right foreleg was painful. She patted its neck and said, "You'll have to wait here, ol' boy. I'll go warn the Lynnes, then be back for you."

Suddenly she heard rumbling hooves and realized riders were coming her direction. "It's Pa!" she gasped, and led the limping horse deep into a nearby stand of trees.

Lulu held her hand over the horse's muzzle as her father and three of her brothers rode by. She could see well enough to identify a couple of the horses, but could not make out who was missing. One of the Taggarts was not with them, but there was no question where they were headed.

Lulu's heart pounded. She felt around in the grass and found her gun, holstered it, and headed for the Lynne ranch on foot, leaving the horse amongst the trees.

In Delta, Luke and Delia Prisk stood in their parlor with John Stranger and Ridge Holloway and listened as George and Sylvia

Bancroft told them of Lulu Taggart coming to their house.

"Hard to believe that Lulu would turn on her family, but it looks like she has," Prisk said. "We've got to move fast, men. First place we'll go is Peale's."

Delia and Sylvia stood at the door and watched the four men gallop away into the night.

At the Peale ranch, they found that Marla had bandaged Hector and decided they could wait till morning to take him to the doctor. The Peale brothers had decided not to pursue the men who had fired on them. By the time they could get their horses saddled, it would be too late. They were going to report it to Sheriff Prisk when they took Hector to the doctor in the morning. They were not surprised to learn that their assailants were the Taggarts.

The Peales were pleased to hear that Lulu had turned on her father and brothers. Marla expressed her fear that Lulu would face reprisal from the family for what she had done. Prisk assured her that when this was over, Otis and the rest of them would be in jail where they could enact no reprisal.

Don asked if he and his brothers could ride with Prisk, Holloway, and Stranger to help catch the Taggarts. Prisk was glad to have them and deputized them on the spot. Then he asked Stranger to take George Bancroft and Larry and Barry Peale with him to the Taggart ranch. Prisk would take Ridge Holloway and the other two Peale brothers with him to the Lynne ranch. Both groups would have to play it by ear since they didn't know what the Taggarts would do next.

Light snow fell from the heavy night sky, driven by the cutting wind, as they galloped away.

The wind whipped the falling snow into their faces as Otis Taggart and his sons arrived at the Lynne place. They donned their masks, left their horses a good distance from the house amid some trees, and crept up to the house on foot. Otis had a long rope looped over his shoulder.

They halted at some bushes a few yards from the porch and saw lantern light burning brightly through the windows of the parlor. "Nate," Otis whispered, "go take a look in the window. I wanna know if Lulu's been here."

Nate crept up to the parlor window, studied the situation for a moment, then hurried back.

"Everything looks normal, Pa," he said. "Roy and Adam are sittin' together on the couch lookin' at some book. Nelda and Autumn are in the dinin' room sewin' on somethin'. Lulu ain't been here, that's for sure."

"Where you suppose she went, Pa?" asked Jeb.

Otis swore, shaking his head. "Only thing I can think of is she decided to go straight to town and get the sheriff. We ain't got no time to waste. We gotta hang Roy quick and get outta here." He lifted his hat and removed his mask. "Don't need these things anymore. Lulu's gonna tell Prisk the whole story."

"Maybe we oughtta just stop the whole thing right now, Pa," Jeb said. "Since Prisk'll know what we're doin', he can't get too tough on us unless we've already hanged Roy."

"You're forgettin' somethin', Jeb," Otis said. "We shot Hector. If he's dead, Prisk'll already have a murder charge on us."

"Maybe Hector ain't dead, Pa. The charge will be less if that's the case."

"Yeah, attempted murder. Still would mean prison. No thanks. We'll be on the dodge anyway, so let's do what we came here to do. We hang Roy, at least we've got a piece of revenge for what that posse did to Van."

"Let's get it done," said Wick, taking off his mask.

The boys followed their father onto the front porch of the Lynne house. The howl of the wind covered the squeaking of the floorboards as they moved up to the door. Otis ran his gaze over the faces of his sons and whispered, "Wick, you're the biggest. Hit that door hard. We're goin' in."

Wick gathered himself and hit the door with all his weight. It splintered and flew open, and the Taggarts bowled in, guns ready.

Roy and Adam looked up from the couch, surprise in their eyes. "Don't move or you're dead!" Otis barked, pointing his gun at them.

Wick hurried to the dining room door, waved his gun at the two women, and rasped, "Into the parlor! Right now!"

"What's going on here?" Nelda asked.

"Jist you and Autumn get into the parlor!"

Roy Lynne sat on the couch, looking into the muzzles of three guns, and noticed the rope Otis carried on his shoulder. "What do you want, Otis?" he demanded.

"Vengeance," the elder Taggart said coldly, holstering his gun. While the Lynnes looked on, he quickly fashioned a hangman's noose.

Nelda and Autumn stood near the couch, eyes filled with fear. Adam licked his lips nervously.

"Stand up!" Otis snapped.

Roy stood slowly to his feet. When Otis dropped the noose over Roy's head and cinched it tight around his neck, Autumn sprang forward, screaming, "No-o!" Her fingernails bit into Otis's face as she wailed, "You leave my pa alone!"

Wick seized Autumn and threw her against a wall. She slammed the wall hard and fell to the floor, gasping for breath.

Roy yanked the rope from Otis's hand and was about to punch him when Nate grabbed Nelda, put the muzzle of his gun to her head, and blared, "Hold it, Roy, or I'll blow her head off!"

Roy froze, a look of despair claiming his features.

Otis grabbed the rope back and said, "Listen to me! We're gonna hang this dude for killin' Van! Any more resistance and we'll shoot the rest of you like mangy dogs!"

The Taggarts took two lanterns from the house and shoved Nelda, Autumn, and Adam through the door and off the porch toward a large cottonwood tree that stood in the yard. Otis dragged Roy Lynne toward the tree with the rope around his neck.

Horror filled Nelda's mind. Fighting nausea and panic, she screamed, "Otis, you can't do this! My husband was only in the posse to bring Van in for murdering our son, and you know it!"

Otis tossed the rope over the lowest limb of the tree. "You religious hypocrites make me sick! You ruined my daughter, and for that, you paid with Aaron. Now it's time to pay for Van bein' riddled with bullets! Your husband put some of them bullets in Van...and now I get my revenge!" He pulled the end of the rope down tight and laughed hysterically, maniacally.

Nelda lost control. She wailed and lunged for Otis, but Wick rushed up and grabbed her. She screamed at him to let go of her. Cursing, Wick threw her against the tree. Her right leg made a loud cracking sound, and she fell to the ground, crying out in pain.

Young Adam saw red and bolted for Wick, who whirled and met the boy with a savage blow to the jaw. Adam went down, unconscious.

Roy's rage was almost more than he could handle. Only the fear that the Taggarts would shoot his family kept him from trying to get his hands on Otis.

Jeb Taggart moved up, removed Roy's belt, and used it to bind his hands behind his back. "Now, he can't grab the rope when we hoist him up, Pa," he grinned.

"You're a good boy, Jeb," Otis remarked with conviction. Then he said to Nate, "Wake that kid up. I want 'im to watch this."

"Otis, you'll hang for this," warned Roy.

"Shut up!" Otis growled. Then to Wick, "I want you to make sure that woman watches. Y'hear me?"

"Yes, Pa." Wick bent down to lift Nelda to her feet.

She could barely stand on her injured leg. Her hair was disheveled, and her body quivered from the cold and the horror.

Autumn Lynne stood like a statue, trembling. Her heart seemed frozen within her.

Nate slapped Adam's face with several stinging blows to revive him, then jerked him to his feet. "I want you to watch your old man die, kid."

"All right," Otis said. "Wick, you and Nate keep your guns trained on the woman and the brats. If they close their eyes or turn their heads, shoot 'em! I want 'em to watch! Jeb, c'mere and help me hoist this dude so's he can dance on air."

Roy Lynne's heart was a triphammer in his chest. He started to tell his family he would meet them in heaven, but he never got the words out. Otis and Jeb yanked on the rope and lifted his feet off the ground. They hoisted him higher, stopping when he was some five feet off the snow-flecked ground. His rasping efforts to draw air into his lungs grew louder and louder.

Nelda and Adam looked on in abject terror. Autumn was rigid with horrified amazement. As she watched her father kick and gag, struggling for his last ounce of life, her head began to swim. Then her legs gave way, and she crumpled to the ground in a dead faint.

At the same instant, Lulu bolted into the circle of light with her gun pointed at Otis. "Let him down, Pa!" she roared.

Startled, the old man's head whipped around. His eyes widened. "Lulu, put that gun away!"

Lulu aimed the black muzzle at his face and rasped, "Let him down *now*, or I pull the trigger!"

"Lulu!" Wick yelled. "That's your pa you're aimin' that gun at!"

"Shut up, Wick! *Now*, Pa...or you die!"

"Let him down, Jeb," the old man gasped.

Roy Lynne was still gasping when his body touched earth.

Lulu moved up behind her father and jammed the gun against the base of his skull. "Don't move!" she blared. "Wick, throw your gun down and take that rope off him!"

When Lulu saw Wick hesitate, she snarled, "I mean it! I'll kill this old man unless you do what I say!"

The look in Lulu's eyes told Wick she meant what she said. He threw his gun down and went to Roy Lynne and began removing the noose.

"Nate! Jeb! Throw your guns down, too!"

Both brothers obeyed.

"All right," said Lulu. "Jeb, you take that belt off Mr. Lynne's wrists. Nate, you stay put!"

"Lulu, you're a dirty traitor!" Otis railed. "I'm your father!"

"Don't remind me, you murderer!" Lulu said.

"Lulu, we'll get you for this!" Nate hissed.

Lulu ignored him and kept her eyes on Otis. "Mr. Lynne, are you all right?"

Roy Lynne was now in a sitting position, his head between his knees. He tried to speak, but could not.

Nelda stumbled, sobbing, toward her husband. The rumble of galloping hooves filled the night. Lulu pressed the muzzle firmly against the base of her father's skull and turned to see the dark forms of four horses and riders closing in.

FIFTEEN

The four riders thundered into the Lynne yard and saw Lulu Taggart standing behind her father, holding the revolver to his head.

"Am I glad to see you, Sheriff!" Lulu said, relief evident in her voice.

Luke Prisk's attention was drawn to the rope lying on the ground with a hangman's noose on one end. He looked at Roy Lynne, who was kneeling beside Nelda. Adam had dashed into the house, put a coat on himself, then hurried back with coats for his parents and a heavy blanket to cover his unconscious sister.

"Roy, I understand Lulu told George Bancroft that Otis was planning on hanging you."

"Well, he did," replied Lynne, shouldering into his coat. His voice had a gravelly sound. "I'd have been dead in another minute if Lulu hadn't shown up and put a stop to it."

Prisk frowned. "You all right?"

"Pretty bad rope burns on my neck," Roy said, putting a hand to his throat. "And my voice is hoarse. Other than that, I'm okay."

"You're to be commended, Lulu," Prisk said. "Took a lot of courage to do what you did."

Lulu kept the gun pressed to the back of her father's head. "Thank you, sir."

Prisk looked back at Roy Lynne, who had his arms wrapped around Nelda. "She hurt?"

"Yes. Wick threw her against that tree. I'm sure her leg's broken."

Prisk then turned toward Adam, who was kneeling over Autumn, tucking the blanket close around her. "What's the matter with your sister, Adam?"

"They roughed her up, Sheriff," replied the youth, "but that was before they hanged Pa. When she saw Pa swinging by his neck, it was too much for her. She passed out."

"You and your boys did it this time, Otis," Prisk said. "You'll face two charges of attempted murder—Hec Peale and Roy Lynne. With all these witnesses, you Taggarts won't stand a chance in court. You're going behind bars for a long, long time."

Jeb Taggart's brain went into a whirl. "Whattya mean two counts, Sheriff? You ain't got no proof that we shot Hector Peale!"

Prisk swung down from the saddle and moved up real close to Jeb. "I didn't say Hec was shot, Jeb. How did you know that?"

"Sure you did, Sheriff. You said Hec was shot."

"You're having hallucinations," Prisk said. "I never mentioned what happened to Hec. All I said was that I had you Taggarts on two counts of attempted murder."

"Well...I just naturally assumed—"

"Quit lying, Jeb!" Prisk blurted.

"Yeah, quit lyin'," Lulu said, still pressing the muzzle of her gun to the base of Otis's skull. "I'll testify in court that you, Pa, and these other two sneaked up to the Peale house and opened fire. Cliff, too."

"Lulu, you dirty traitor!" Wick roared. "You'll get yours!"

"Not by your hand, she won't!" Prisk said. "By the time you get out of prison, you'll be too old and feeble to raise a finger against her."

Otis was breathing hard, wanting to get his hands on Lulu, but he said nothing.

Prisk looked toward the three mounted men and said, "Okay, gentlemen. Let's use some of that rope to tie these birds up. Then we'll put them on their horses and take them to jail." To Lulu, he said, "You mentioned Cliff. He was in on this, too?"

"He was in on the attack at the Peales. I don't know where he went."

"Where'd Cliff go, Otis?" demanded the sheriff.

The old man jutted his jaw. "I ain't tellin' you nothin'!"

"Fine. My guess is that he went home for some reason. No matter. I've got men on their way there, anyhow."

While the Taggarts were being bound, Nelda looked at Adam and asked, "Is Autumn coming around yet, son?"

"Well, sort of, Mom. But she looks real strange."

Roy left Nelda's side, asking, "What do you mean?"

"Her eyes are open, but it's like…she's in some kind of daze."

Roy knelt beside his daughter and found her lying perfectly still, eyes staring vacantly.

"What is it, Roy?" asked Nelda, wincing from the pain in her leg.

Roy waved a hand in front of Autumn's face, but she did not move her eyes or even blink. "I don't know," Roy replied. "She's looking at me, but she's *not* looking at me."

"She's breathing, isn't she?" Nelda asked.

"Yes, but she's awfully pale."

"Come help me over there. I want to look at her."

Roy went to his wife and lifted her to her feet. Nelda winced when she put her weight on the leg, sucking air sharply through her teeth.

"Here, honey," Roy said. "Let me carry you."

Roy hoisted Nelda into his arms and carried her to Autumn. "See what I mean? Her eyes are open, but they're not focusing. It's like she's really not there."

Nelda waved a hand in front of her daughter's eyes and got no response. She leaned close and stroked her cheek. "Autumn… Autumn, it's your mother. Can you hear me, honey?"

Otis was now in the hands of Sheriff Prisk with his wrists lashed behind him. Lulu dashed to where Autumn lay and knelt down beside Nelda. "We'd better get her to Dr. Faulkner, Mrs. Lynne. Somethin's wrong."

"Very wrong, Lulu," Nelda said, still tenderly stroking Autumn's cheek. Then to Roy, "Honey, I know you've been through a lot tonight, but I think we'd better get her to Dr. Faulkner right away."

"We need to get both of you to him," Roy said.

Adam rose to his feet. "I'll harness the team and hook 'em to the buggy, Pa."

"Fine, son. Take one of these lanterns…and hurry." Adam ran toward the barn, lantern in hand.

Luke Prisk stepped up and said, "We've got 'em ready to take to town. I'll need a statement from both of you and Adam… Autumn, too, when she's back with us."

"Of course," said Roy.

"If you need me for any reason when you get to town, you know where I live," Prisk said.

"Sure," Roy grinned weakly. "And thanks."

"Mr. and Mrs. Lynne, how about letting me drive you into town?" Ridge Holloway said. "Sheriff Prisk and the Peale brothers can take the Taggarts in. I know you folks have been through a lot tonight, and I'd like to help."

"That'd be wonderful, Deputy," Roy said. "That way I can ride in the bed of the wagon with both my girls."

"I'll go along, too, Mrs. Lynne, if it's okay," Lulu said.

"Of course," Nelda responded, trying to smile.

"Lulu," said Roy, "I don't know how to thank you for saving my life. There aren't words in the English language to express—"

"You don't need to, Mr. Lynne. I just did what had to be done."

"You did more than that, Lulu," said Nelda. "You alienated yourself from your family by saving my husband's life. We can never thank you enough. Can you go home once they've arrested Cliff?"

"No, ma'am. There's always the chance Treg will show up, and I don't want to be there if he does. He'd probably beat me to death once he found out what happened."

Nelda looked at her husband. "Roy, can we take Lulu into our home until things are settled for her?"

"Most assuredly. You're more than welcome to stay with us as long as you want, Lulu."

"Thank you, Mr. Lynne. That's very kind of you both."

Adam pulled up with the wagon.

"Run into the house and bring some extra blankets, son," Roy said. Then he picked Nelda up and placed her in the bed of the wagon.

Ridge Holloway bent down and gathered Autumn into his arms. She was limp as a rag doll. As he tenderly laid her beside her mother, Ridge said, "Beautiful girl, Mr. and Mrs. Lynne. I sure hope she'll be all right."

"Thank you," Nelda replied. "She underwent an awful shock tonight." She stroked her daughter's cheeks again and said, "Autumn...honey, can you hear me?"

Autumn's eyes were still blank and unfocused. Suddenly her mouth opened slightly and she made a tiny mewing sound.

"That's it, baby!" Roy exclaimed. "That's it! Talk to us!"

There was another mewing sound, followed by a weak groan, but Autumn neither moved her eyes nor blinked.

"Let's get going," Roy said. "We've got to get her to Doc Faulkner."

✱ ✱ ✱ ✱ ✱

The wind plucked at Treg Taggart's wide-brimmed hat and whipped snow into his face as he rode up to the ranch house and dismounted at the back porch. He expected to see lantern light glowing in the windows and smoke billowing from the large chimney, but the place was dark, and there was no fire in the fireplace.

He entered the house and found a lantern, lit it and carried it outside and led his horse to the barn. He removed saddle and bridle and pitched hay from the loft into the feed trough.

He returned to the house and stomped snow from his boots on the back porch, then went inside and lit more lanterns. He built a fire in the fireplace. When the parlor began to warm, he hung his coat on a peg by the front door, placed his hat over it, and stood in front of the fire.

After getting the chill out of his body, he went to the kitchen and opened the pantry and found enough food to satisfy his hunger. He returned to the parlor and sat in an overstuffed chair near the fire, figuring his father, brothers, and sister would be home soon.

He eased back in the chair and let his mind stray to Ord Grabow and the Dyar Lynch gang Ord was going to get him into at Cheyenne City. He had great confidence in Ord. The man knew what he was doing.

He had the map showing the location of the Lynch hideout, so— Suddenly Treg sat up straight in the chair. His hand went to the shirt pocket where he always carried small items he deemed important. The map was not there. He closed his eyes and swore at himself. He had left the map in the cabin. He could still picture it lying on the bench where he had sat the last time he put on his boots.

He swung a fist through the air and cursed his stupidity, then eased back in the chair. "Okay, okay," he said out loud. "So you pulled a stupid stunt, Treg. It ain't the end of the world. You get to

Cheyenne City, you remember enough about the map...you can nose around a bit and find the hideout."

He closed his eyes and listened to the wind thump the side of the house and whine around the eaves. Suddenly he heard footsteps echoing through the house from the back porch. He heard the back door come open with a loud wail of wind, then close. Springing from the chair, he headed for the kitchen. "Hey, it's about time!" he said. "Where *is* everybody?"

Treg was shocked to see Cliff with blood all over the left side of his face and a bandanna wrapped around his head.

"Hello, big brother," Cliff said, shivering. "I saw your horse in the barn. When I first rode up and saw the lights, I thought Pa and the others had come back."

"Come back from where?"

"Long story. I need to get this ear bandaged properly. Will you help me?"

"Sure. You can tell me the story while I take care of it. I guess you heard I'd broken outta prison."

"Yeah. You, Ord, and Jack. Pa figured you'd show up here once't you felt it was safe." Cliff paused, then asked, "Where are Ord and Jack?"

"Another long story. We'll get 'em both told while we fix you up."

The wind was dying down to a slight breeze, and it had stopped snowing as John Stranger, George Bancroft, and Larry and Barry Peale rode onto the Taggart ranch. "Looks like we've got somebody home," Bancroft said as they drew near the house.

"We'll stash our horses some distance from the house so there won't be a chance of tipping them off that we're out here," Stranger said. "Before we close in, I want to check the barn to see who all's here."

The four men moved in stealthily from the spot where they had left the horses. They entered the barn and Larry Peale struck a match. There were only two horses in the barn and none in the corral.

"Let's move up to the house and see what we find," Stranger said.

Guns drawn and ready for action, the four men crept up to the side of the house, where light glowed from a snow-flecked window.

"That's the parlor," Bancroft whispered.

When they reached the window, they could hear male voices inside. Bancroft peered in and got a look at both men. "Stranger!" he whispered, turning to the tall man. "Cliff Taggart's in there... and Treg!"

Stranger pushed his face close to the glass and asked, "Which is which?"

"Treg's the one without the bandage on his head."

"Well, let's just listen for a few minutes before we go in. We might learn something."

Both Taggart brothers had loud voices. Every word they said could be heard clearly by the four men at the window.

Treg was telling the story of the prison break, explaining why Ord had refused to take Frank Slattery with them. He explained about the trouble between Ord and Jack, and about Ord stabbing Jack and throwing him to the wolves.

"So is Ord still at the hideout?" Cliff asked.

"Yeah."

"Where is it, anyhow?"

"In the Elk Mountains."

"Oh. Straight north of here."

"Yeah. He's gonna stay there for a week or two, then he's plannin' to join up with the Dyar Lynch gang over at—"

Barry Peale's feet slipped on a wet, snow-covered board, and he slammed into the wall with all his weight. Treg and Cliff looked quickly toward the window.

"Somebody's out there," Cliff said, pulling his gun and dashing across the room. Treg followed, removing his gun from its holster and cocking the hammer.

The four men outside headed for the front door, guns drawn.

From the window, Cliff saw the shadowed figures heading for the front porch, but was unsure how many there might be. He turned to Treg, eyes wild, and gasped, "It's the law! Looks like a bunch of 'em!"

Without a word, Treg made a dash toward the back of the house.

Cliff knew the lawmen would come through the front door, and he swung his gun toward the door and fired. The door was not locked. Suddenly it burst open, but the tall, dark man who appeared first was bent low. The bullet had chewed through the door higher up.

Cliff fired at him, but John Stranger hit the floor and the slug plowed into the wall behind him. Cliff leaped into the hall that led to the kitchen in time to avoid Stranger's shot, which clawed into the door casing, sending splinters every direction.

George Bancroft and the Peale twins rushed inside as Stranger sprang to his feet in pursuit of Cliff. Stranger saw him heading toward the kitchen. He lined his gun on Cliff's back and shouted, "Stop right there, or I'll shoot!"

Cliff whirled and fired.

The bullet hissed past Stranger's ear as he dropped the hammer of his bone-handled Colt .45. The slug ripped through Cliff's upper chest near his left shoulder. He staggered, cursed, and fell to his knees. Stranger kicked the gun out of his hand, sending it across the kitchen floor.

✹ ✹ ✹ ✹ ✹

Treg Taggart bolted through the back door, leaped across the porch, and ran for the barn. The snow caused him to slip and slide, but he made it to the barn and hurried inside. He swung onto his horse's back, sank his fingers deep into the thick mane, and urged the horse out of the barn into the corral. Guiding it by the mane to a far gate, he leaned over, threw the latch, and swung the gate open. He put the horse to a gallop and headed west. The horse's hooves threw snow high into the air as it carried him away from the Taggart house at full speed.

When Stranger's partners entered the kitchen, he was on his way toward the back door, which was standing open. Over his shoulder, he said, "One of you see to Cliff. The other two come with me!"

Larry Peale volunteered to stay, and Barry hurried out the door behind George Bancroft.

Cliff's horse nickered at Stranger when he entered the barn. He saw the door to the corral was swinging loose, and when he stepped into the corral, he could vaguely make out that the wide gate at the far corner was standing open.

George and Barry hurried up behind Stranger as he made his way toward the open gate. When they reached it, Stranger eyed the hoofprints that trailed off to the west. "He got away, gentlemen. Be senseless to try to catch up to him now. Let's get Cliff on his horse and take him to the doctor."

As the men rode away from the Taggart ranch, Stranger knew he would have to ride hard for Canon City tomorrow. Somehow he had to squeeze out of Frank Slattery the location of the hideout in the Elk Mountains. Ord Grabow would be his responsibility. He hoped Grabow would stay at the cabin hideout long enough for him to get there.

Four lanterns burned in the clinic as Dr. Eldon Faulkner, Delta's middle-aged physician, finished setting Nelda Lynne's broken leg. Nelda was under the influence of ether. Roy and Adam Lynne, along with Ridge Holloway, stood close, looking on.

Autumn Lynne lay on a cot in a corner of the room, unmoving, still in a daze. Eva Faulkner, the doctor's wife and nurse, stood over her. Lulu Taggart sat in a chair beside Autumn, holding her hand.

"Honey, I'll need your help now," Dr. Faulkner said to his wife. "It's time to put the splint on."

Eva moved to the examining table to assist her husband. They had barely started when Autumn groaned and moved her head.

Faulkner paused, looked that way, and asked, "What's she doing, Lulu?"

"I...I think she's coming out of it, Doctor."

"We can't stop what we're doing here," Faulkner said. "Roy, talk to me. Tell me what she's doing."

"She's moving her head back and forth and blinking her eyes," Roy said.

"Good! Anything else?"

"Yes. She's licking her lips."

"Give her some water."

Lulu hurried to a counter next to the medicine cabinet and dipped water from a bucket into a tin cup. She rushed back and put the cup to Autumn's lips. "Here," she said. "I have some water for you." Lulu could tell Autumn did not recognize her.

Autumn had lost the vacant look in her eyes, though they were a bit glassy. She nodded slightly and took the water a tiny sip at a time.

"She's taking the water, Doc," Roy called across the room.

"Wonderful! Don't let her get too much. No more than what you have in the cup. A few sips intermittently. Talk to her, Roy. See if you can get some response."

Lulu paused with the cup in hand and asked, "Would you like to sit here in the chair, Mr. Lynne?"

"No, it's all right. You stay there and keep giving her the water."

Roy knelt beside the cot and took hold of his daughter's hand. Slowly, she brought her line of sight to his face. It took a few seconds for her to focus on him, but when she did, her eyes widened and filled with tears. She tried to speak, but no words would come.

Roy squeezed her hand and tears filled his own eyes. "Yes, honey, I'm alive! It's all right. Everything's going to be all right."

Autumn tried desperately to speak, but her tongue seemed numb and immobile. Her widened, tear-filled eyes ran to Lulu.

"Hi, Autumn," Lulu smiled. "Remember me?"

Autumn was surprised to see Lulu and wondered at her friendliness and warmth. Lulu reached over and thumbed the tears from Autumn's cheeks.

Adam brushed up next to his father and leaned over her. "Hello, Sis," he smiled. "Come on. Let me hear you say something."

Autumn worked her jaw again, trying desperately to speak, but to no avail.

Roy patted her shoulder. "It's okay, sweetie. You've been through an awful ordeal. Give it a little time, and you'll be able to talk."

Autumn looked hard at her father, then ran her gaze all around the cot, frantically, making the mewing sound again.

"I think she's looking for Ma," Adam said.

Roy leaned close, squeezing her hand. "Your mother's leg is broken, honey. Dr. Faulkner is putting a splint on it right now. She'll be fine."

Autumn smiled and her countenance relaxed. She then looked up at the man who stood just behind her father.

Roy saw her looking at the young lawman and said, "Autumn, this is Marshal Ridge Holloway. He's here in the valley to try to catch Treg Taggart."

Autumn smiled at Ridge, nodded, then looked at Lulu.

"I hope he does catch him, Autumn," Lulu said.

Autumn nodded again, then looked back at Holloway. She smiled, and he smiled back.

Dr. Faulkner came into her view. "You're going to be fine, Autumn," he said. "And your mother's leg will heal nicely, I'm sure. I need to put some salve on your daddy's neck, then I'm going to take a look at you. Everything's going to be all right. You're with people who love you."

Autumn blinked and smiled at the doctor, but inwardly she was fearful. She could not feel her legs nor her feet. It was as if they had been cut off.

CHAPTER

SIXTEEN

———◆———

D r. Eldon Faulkner attended to Roy Lynne's rope-burned neck, then moved to the cot and leaned over Autumn. Still under the effects of the ether, Nelda lay on another cot, with Eva Faulkner watching over her.

Lulu stood up with the empty cup in her hand and stepped out of the way.

"Okay, Autumn," said Faulkner, taking her by the hand, "let's get you over to the examining table."

Autumn bit her lips and shook her head, fear evident in her expressive eyes.

"Come on, honey," Faulkner said. "I need you on the examining table."

Autumn made a piteous whine, shaking her head.

Roy leaned over her and said, "Autumn, come on. Dr. Faulkner won't hurt you."

Pleading with her eyes, Autumn mewed and shook her head again.

Impatience showed in Roy's eyes. "Autumn, what's wrong with you? You need to—"

"Wait a minute, Roy," Faulkner said. "I think there's something strange going on here. Autumn...are you trying to tell us you can't stand up and walk?"

Autumn nodded, running her eyes between the doctor and her father.

Faulkner reached down and took hold of Autumn's ankles. Squeezing hard, he asked, "Can you feel this?"

She shook her head no.

Roy Lynne's face blanched. Adam was stunned.

"Doc, is she...could she be paralyzed?" Roy asked.

"I don't know. Help me carry her to the table."

Nelda began to roll her head back and forth on the pillow where she lay on the cot. Eva took hold of her hand and began to speak soothing words to her.

Faulkner spoke to the men. "Eva will remain here with me, gentlemen, but I'm going to ask that you sit out in the waiting room while I do this examination."

As they moved toward the door, Roy said, "Eva, if Nelda needs me, just call, okay?"

"Of course," she smiled.

Nearly half an hour had passed when Eva Faulkner opened the waiting room door and said, "You can come back in now. Doctor is finished with the examination, and Nelda's awake. I told her about Autumn's paralysis."

Once they were in the room, Dr. Faulkner said, "Roy, you and Adam spend a couple minutes with Nelda, then we'll talk about our girl, here."

Roy let Adam lean over and hug his mother, then did the same. Nelda assured them she was feeling very little pain. Her concern now was for Autumn.

Father and son, along with Ridge Holloway, moved up close to the table where Autumn lay. She managed a weak smile for them, then looked to Dr. Faulkner.

"Well?" said Roy.

Faulkner rubbed the back of his neck and said, "Autumn has no physical injuries. Her collision with the wall did no damage at all. Her spine is normal, as are her legs."

"Thank you, Lord," Roy breathed, closing his eyes for a brief moment.

"There is no physical reason she should be paralyzed. Nor is there any reason, physically, why she should not be able to speak."

"Then what's causing it, Doctor?" Nelda asked.

"This little gal has suffered a severe trauma. She was watching you die, Roy, and it was too much for her."

The eyes of father and daughter met. Tears welled up in Autumn's eyes, and her lips trembled. Roy reached down and took her hand. Autumn squeezed down hard. He was glad she had the use of her hands.

"So what now?" Roy asked.

"I don't think it'll hang on long. She should snap out of it shortly—a day or two, maybe a week. She's already shown improvement since you brought her in here."

Autumn looked up at her father, shaking her head. With her eyes she tried to say she would not be over it soon…if ever.

Dr. Faulkner picked up on it and said, "Now, Autumn, you've got to take a positive attitude on this. It's all psychological, dear."

Autumn still shook her head.

"Now, honey," Faulkner said with a firm voice, "I want you to listen to me. You can talk when you really want to talk…and you can walk when you really want to walk."

Autumn began to weep, still shaking her head. In her mind, she would never talk nor walk again.

The sound of heavy boots entering the waiting room met the ears of those in the clinic. Dr. Faulkner hurried to the door and pulled it open. He recognized the two men carrying an unconscious Cliff Taggart, and he recognized George Bancroft, who preceded them. The tall, dark man was a stranger to him.

Setting his gaze on Cliff, Faulkner said, "He looks pretty bad."

"He's definitely in bad shape, Doc," Bancroft said. "We went to your house, and when we couldn't rouse anyone, we figured you might be over here."

John Stranger looked at Ridge and said, "When we got there, Treg had shown up and was talking with his brother, here. Treg got away. We tried to take Cliff without shooting him, but he made a fight of it."

Lulu appeared, took one look at her brother, and said, "This is all my father's fault."

Dr. Faulkner had Roy place Autumn back on her cot and directed the Peale twins to put Cliff on the examining table. He asked for Eva's assistance and said to the others, "You can move Autumn over next to her mother and sit down with them. I have a free-standing partition that I can place between you and the table."

Two of the men quickly put the partition in position, and Roy and Adam moved Autumn next to her mother. Ridge Holloway told Stranger, Bancroft, and the Peale twins what had happened at the Lynne ranch, and that Sheriff Prisk and the others had taken the Taggarts to the county jail.

Bancroft and the Peale twins excused themselves, saying they would go to the jail. Stranger thanked them for their help, then sat down to wait out the fate of Cliff Taggart.

While the doctor labored to save Cliff's life, Ridge Holloway introduced John Stranger to the Lynnes and Lulu. Stranger commended Lulu for what she had done to save Roy's life even though she knew it would sever her from her family. He asked about Nelda's broken leg, and when he was told that it would be as good as new, he turned his attention to Autumn. Roy explained what had happened.

Stranger smiled at Autumn and said, "All you need to free your tongue is something to stimulate your earnest desire to speak again. The same thing is true with your legs. When the proper circumstance occurs, your legs will work."

Autumn stared intently into the iron-gray eyes of the man, wondering who he really was. For the moment, she did not shake her head in disagreement.

"Do you have some medical training, Mr. Stranger?" Roy asked.

"Not formally, but I've had to deal with a lot of medical problems in my travels, and I've learned a great deal. I've seen cases like Autumn's, and I know what Dr. Faulkner has told you is true. This paralysis could just wear off in time, but my experience says it won't. It'll take some special circumstance to stimulate her desire to talk and walk."

They heard Mrs. Faulkner say something to her husband in a low voice. A few seconds passed, then both of them came around the partition. The physician's features were grim as he looked at Lulu and said, "I'm sorry, but I couldn't save your brother. The bullet punctured a lung. He was hemorrhaging badly when they brought him in, and it was just too late for me to be able to save him."

"I understand, Doctor," Lulu said softly. "I know you did all that you could."

"I tried to take him down without killing him, Doctor," Stranger said, "but there wasn't much time to take aim. He was bringing his gun to bear on me, and I had to act fast."

"Nobody could put any blame on you, sir," Faulkner said. "The blame lies with Otis Taggart and the way he brought up those boys. I'm sorry, Lulu, but it's the truth."

"You don't need to apologize to me," Lulu said, tears misting her eyes. "My brothers have all turned bad since my mother died. Pa seems to want his children to be menaces to society. And now...both Van and Cliff are dead. It must be God's justice bein' meted out." Lulu trembled at the thought of where Van and Cliff had gone when they died.

Autumn was pleased to hear Lulu speak of God. Had her labors not been in vain after all? She wished she could speak tender words to Lulu, but her tongue was lifeless in her mouth.

"John, there's been a lot of strain here tonight," Ridge Holloway said. "Since you're a preacher, how about some words of comfort and encouragement for these people?"

"You're a preacher?" Roy asked.

Stranger grinned. "Well, not in the sense that I'm a pastor or an evangelist. I just fill some pulpits now and then when I'm needed. My main work in life involves a lot more than preaching."

"But you preach the Bible as the Word of God, and the Lord Jesus Christ as the only way of salvation, Mr. Stranger?" Nelda asked.

"Sure do, ma'am. The way of the cross leads home, and there isn't any other way."

"Oh, praise the Lord!" Nelda said, clapping her hands. "Maybe the Lord will direct you to come and be our pastor. Several families have been praying that God would send us the man of His choice. We need a church in Delta."

"Now, hold on, ma'am. I just said that my work in life involves more than preaching."

"Yes, but the Lord can change that, and—"

"Nelda," cut in her husband, "we have to let the Lord pick the man of His choice, as you just said. We can't hurry Him."

Nelda smiled at Stranger and said, "I'm sorry. It's just that we've prayed so hard for a church and a pastor...I just thought maybe God was about to bring it to pass."

"He will in His own good time, Mrs. Lynne," Stranger said. "Ridge, you've been doing some speaking in your church in Denver. Maybe you have some words of encouragement for these people."

"Well, I..."

"Ridge has known the Lord only a short time, folks," Stranger said, "but from what I hear, his pastor says he has a way with words. Come on, Ridge."

"Well, all right. I'll get my Bible out of my saddlebags."

"No need, son," said Dr. Faulkner. "I keep a Bible in the desk out in the waiting room. I'll get it."

Autumn was thrilled to learn that Ridge was a Christian, though it was not a complete surprise. She had suspected as much.

Faulkner returned and handed the Bible to the deputy. Ridge opened it and read several comforting passages. With each one, he pointed out that only born-again believers could claim the promises and draw strength from them. Stranger picked it up and explained the gospel, making sure the unbelievers in the group understood that Jesus Christ is the only way of salvation.

The words of John Stranger and Ridge Holloway were taking effect in the minds of the Faulkners, but even more in the mind and heart of Lulu Taggart. What both men said backed up what Autumn Lynne had spoken to her on many occasions.

The Faulkners excused themselves to clean up the examining table. Lulu sat in silence as the Lynnes discussed with Stranger and Holloway the joy of knowing the Lord. The discussion soon led to Autumn's paralysis, and the ability of the Lord to take it away.

John Stranger suggested they ask God to give Autumn her speech back, along with the use of her legs, then he led them in the prayer. When he was finished, Ridge leaned over Autumn and said, "Young lady, I believe the Lord is going to answer our prayers. He may not do it as quickly as we'd like, nor in the way we would want to see it happen, but He is a prayer-hearing and a prayer-answering God."

Autumn smiled warmly and tried to speak. The look in her chocolate-brown eyes told Ridge she liked him very much. His heart seemed to grow warmer in his chest.

Dr. Faulkner and his wife returned to the group, and Faulkner said, "Well, folks, the night is far spent, but Eva and I are going home to get what little sleep we can squeeze in before morning. Cliff's body is covered. I'll have the undertaker pick it up first thing tomorrow."

Dr. Faulkner granted Lulu's request to stay with Nelda and Autumn for the night. There was another cot she could use. The Faulkners invited Roy and Adam to come to their house, saying they had plenty of room. Stranger said he and Ridge would head to their hotel rooms.

Before leaving, Stranger and Ridge spoke encouraging words to Autumn. Then the two of them led their horses down the street toward the stable. While they walked, Stranger gave Holloway the details about Treg Taggart's escape. He was sure Sheriff Prisk would guide Ridge to the Taggart ranch so he could pick up the trail.

Ridge agreed he would see Prisk early and go from there. Stranger would head for Canon City at dawn. They would see each other again someday in Denver.

Dr. Faulkner gave Nelda a sedative and a small dose of laudanum to relieve the pain in her leg. Within a few minutes, she was asleep.

Lulu prepared her cot for sleeping, then stood over Autumn and asked, "Anything I can get you?"

Autumn smiled and motioned that she was thirsty. Lulu brought her a cup of water and stood looking down at her. Strong emotions churned in her heart. She was overwhelmed with her guilt as a sinner and wanted to be saved. She also was worried about Autumn's paralysis, and was going over in her mind what Dr. Faulkner and John Stranger had said about Autumn being able to talk if her desire was strong enough.

Autumn looked up, noticed the strange expression in Lulu's eyes, and gave her a quizzical look.

Lulu sat down in the chair beside Autumn's cot and said, "You want to know if somethin's wrong?"

Autumn nodded.

"Well, somethin's been wrong for a long time, and I want it made right. I want to be saved, Autumn. I want to be saved *now*."

Autumn's eyes were suddenly swimming in tears and her lips quivered. This was what she had prayed for, and now God was answering her prayers. Lulu was ready to become a child of God! Autumn's heart pounded with excitement.

Ridge Holloway had laid Dr. Faulkner's Bible on a small table nearby. Autumn raised herself on one elbow and pointed to the Bible, motioning for Lulu to get it.

Lulu left her chair, picked up the Bible, and sat back down. Autumn wiped tears from her cheeks and motioned for Lulu to open it.

Lulu shook her head and said, "No, honey. My reading it won't do it."

Autumn nodded vigorously that it would.

"No. I had a Bible for a short time until Pa caught me with it and tore it up. But before he did, I read about Philip the evangelist and the Ethiopian eunuch. The eunuch told Philip he couldn't understand the Scriptures unless someone guided him. I need you to lead me to Jesus."

Autumn wept. She wanted to lead her friend to the Lord, but her tongue and her voice were frozen.

Lulu saw Autumn's struggle. "Please," she said, extending the Bible toward her. "Guide me to Jesus."

Autumn's body quivered. She moaned, and her head shook and her face reddened as she tried to free her tongue.

"C'mon, Autumn!" Lulu cheered her. "C'mon! I want to know Jesus. I want to be saved and know I'm going to heaven! Help me!"

Autumn made a whine that started low and began rising in pitch. Suddenly her voice was there. "Yes!" she gasped. "Yes, Lulu! I will lead you to the Lord!"

Lulu burst into tears, fell to her knees, and wrapped her husky arms around Autumn. "I knew you could do it!" she cried. "I knew you could! Doc and that other man said you could speak if you wanted to bad enough. And you do, don't you."

"Yes, I do! I sure do," Autumn sobbed, hugging her. "Let me see that Bible!"

With Lulu kneeling beside her, Autumn guided her to passage after passage that dealt with salvation, explaining them carefully. She took her to the cross, and like Paul of old, preached to her "repentance toward God, and faith toward our Lord Jesus Christ."

With tears streaming down her cheeks, Lulu Taggart called on Jesus to save her and make her a child of God. Autumn then prayed for her, asking the Lord to help her grow in grace and in her knowledge of Him.

Lulu sat back down on the chair and thanked her friend for not giving up on her and for the many times she had talked to her about the Lord. Autumn's cup of joy was bubbling over.

Nelda Lynne's sleep was so deep, she didn't awaken during the entire time. The two young women talked for an hour, then Lulu finally turned the lanterns low, and they settled down to get some sleep.

Before they dropped off, Lulu said, "I've been havin' nightmares about goin' to hell, Autumn."

"Well, you won't have any more of those now that you belong to Jesus."

Lulu was quiet for a moment, then said, "You'll walk again, too, Autumn. When you want to bad enough, like you wanted to talk to me about Jesus tonight."

"I'm afraid that using my legs will be much harder than using my voice."

"Well, now that God is *my* Heavenly Father, I can pray about those legs workin' again."

"Yes...yes you can, Lulu. And I'd appreciate it a whole lot."

Early the next morning, Ridge Holloway entered the clinic to check on Autumn and her mother, and found all the Lynnes and Lulu Taggart eating breakfast together and rejoicing in two marvelous things—Lulu Taggart had become a child of God, and Autumn's voice was back.

Not being Christians, the Faulkners were a bit off balance with it all, but stood by and listened as Autumn gave Ridge the details of how it came about.

Ridge thumbed tears from his eyes and rejoiced with them. He added his encouragement to Autumn, saying she would walk again when she had the same type of desire that caused her to speak.

Autumn looked up at him with undisguised admiration and said, "Thank you, Ridge. You pray for me, okay?"

"I will," he grinned. "Well, I've got to go after Lulu's oldest brother." Turning to her, he said, "I wish it wasn't your brother I have to track down and take back to the hangman."

"No fault of yours," Lulu said. "I love Treg, but he's a killer. You have no choice but to hunt him down and take him in."

Ridge spoke for a moment with Roy and Nelda, then turned and looked down at Autumn. "Miss Autumn?"

"Yes?" she replied, giving him a warm smile.

"Would…ah…would it be all right if I come back and see you again some time?"

"Why…yes, of course. I'd love to see you again."

"Thank you!" Ridge said, grinning from ear to ear. "I don't know when it might be, but I'll make it as soon as possible."

"I hope it's very soon," Autumn said as Ridge headed out the door.

When Ridge was gone, Nelda said, "What a fine young man. He'll make some young woman a real good husband."

"Yeah," Adam said. "I'd like to have him for a brother-in-law."

"Really, Adam!" Autumn gasped. "Ridge Holloway is a nice young man…and friendly enough that he wants to come see me again, but that doesn't mean he wants to marry me!"

"Maybe not yet," Adam chuckled, "but I'll bet it comes to that."

"Well, I'm sure Doug will have something to say about that," Roy said.

Autumn felt a tinge of guilt. She was promised to Doug Price, and though there was no official engagement, there was an understanding between them. She loved Doug, but she couldn't deny there was a special feeling in her heart toward Ridge Holloway.

SEVENTEEN

---◆---

Dr. Eldon Faulkner examined Nelda Lynne's splinted leg and told the family she could go home in another day. He showed concern about the paralysis of Autumn's lower body, but told her she could go home at the same time as her mother. He wanted to know immediately if she started getting feeling in her legs.

Roy and Adam were about to leave for the ranch when there was a knock at the door between the clinic and the waiting room. Eva Faulkner hurried to the door. Opening it, she found Doug Price with a worried look on his face. "Hello, Mrs. Faulkner," he said. "I understand Autumn Lynne is here."

"Yes," smiled Eva. "The rest of the family is too."

"May I see her?"

Everyone in the clinic looked at Doug as Eva turned and said to her husband, "Doug would like to see Autumn, Doctor. Is that all right?"

"Of course," replied Faulkner, who was restocking his medicine cabinet from a box that had arrived on the afternoon stage.

Everyone smiled at Doug as he removed his hat and stepped up to Autumn's cot. "Hello, Autumn," he said, face drawn. "Word got to me this morning about what happened at your place last night. I know you can't talk, but—"

"Oh, but I can," Autumn countered.

Doug's jaw slacked. "Well, they're telling it wrong, then."

"She couldn't talk when we first brought her in here, Doug," Roy said. "Her speech has been restored."

"Great!" he smiled. "And your legs?"

"I still can't use them," Autumn said.

"What exactly is wrong?"

Dr. Faulkner left his medicine cabinet and stood before Doug Price to explain Autumn's situation.

"Will she ever get the use of her legs back?" Doug asked.

"She will when she's put in a position where she wants to walk bad enough."

"What if that situation never comes?" Doug asked, frowning.

"Well, the paralysis could wear off in time. I was hoping it would start to wear off by this morning, but so far it hasn't."

"What if it doesn't wear off, and no situation occurs to make her want to walk bad enough?"

"Possibly psychological therapy would work. If not, she will never walk again."

Doug looked down at Autumn and his face drained of its color.

"We're asking the Lord to take the paralysis away," Adam said.

Doug nodded and slowly made his way to the door. He glanced back at Autumn, then put his hat on and entered the waiting room, pulling the door shut behind him.

Adam hurried after Doug and caught up with him just outside the doctor's office. "I need to talk to you for a minute," he said.

"All right," nodded Doug, face grim.

"I think you hurt my sister's feelings just now. You seemed to grow cool toward her after Dr. Faulkner explained she might never have the use of her legs again."

Price cleared his throat. "Well, I didn't mean to be cool, Adam. It's all such a jolt to me. I just can't stand to see Autumn in that condition."

"But we've prayed about it, and we believe the Lord will answer."

"But what if He doesn't?" Doug asked.

"You love her, don't you?"

"Well, yes...of course. But—"

"But what? Don't you still want to marry her?"

Price's features were pale. "Adam, I'm awfully upset right now. Can we talk some other time?"

"All I can say is, if you wouldn't still want Autumn for your wife if she never recovers, you don't really love her."

Doug scrubbed a shaky hand over his face. "I don't want to talk about it right now." With that, he turned and walked away.

Adam stared after him, muttering something uncomplimentary under his breath, and went back inside.

"What was that all about, son?" Roy asked.

"I'd prefer not to say just now. Maybe we can talk about it later."

The next day, Roy and Adam took Nelda, Autumn, and Lulu home in the wagon. Lulu rode in the bed with Nelda and Autumn, and Roy and Adam were in the seat.

Lulu took the women's hands in hers, thanked them for taking her in, and said, "I...I'm going to ask a very special favor of you."

"What's that, honey?" Nelda asked.

Lulu cleared her throat. "Well...now that I'm a Christian, I want to change some things about myself. I want both of you to help me work on developing the feminine qualities I ought to have. I want to let my hair grow out, and I'll need you to teach me how to style it. And...I want to get some dresses and learn to be a lady. Will you help me?"

Nelda and Autumn looked at each other and smiled. "Of course we will, Lulu," Autumn said.

Five days later, Dr. Faulkner went to the Lynne ranch to check on his two patients. Nelda was doing as well as could be expected. Faulkner told her he would let her start using crutches within another week or so.

But Autumn had him worried. Her lower body was still without feeling. He had hoped by now that she would be showing signs of getting over the paralysis.

Faulkner sat beside Autumn's bed with Nelda, Roy, and Adam close by. He looked at the pretty redhead and said, "Autumn, I'm getting more concerned about your paralysis. The longer you go without using your legs, the less chance there is that you will ever use them again. You need to see a doctor who is trained in psychological therapy...and time is of the essence."

"What do you suggest we do?" Roy asked.

"I know a doctor in Denver who is an excellent therapist. His name is Dr. Lyle Goodwin. If anybody can help her, he'll be the man. He's quite reasonable when it comes to charges for his services, too."

"The cost doesn't matter," Roy said. "All that matters is that my girl walks again."

"Yes," Nelda said. "We would spare no expense to see that happen."

Roy looked at Autumn. "What do you think, honey? You want to go to Denver and see what Dr. Goodwin can do?"

"Of course, but I feel guilty about it."

"What do you mean?"

"Well, Dr. Faulkner said if I really wanted to, I could walk. I do want to, but my legs won't move. They're like two dead things attached to my body. I could save whatever the cost is going to be if I could just make them move!"

"I still believe if you had the right stimulus, you would be able to move your legs again, Autumn," Faulkner said. "And one of these days, that stimulus might come along. But as I said, the longer you go without using your legs, the less chance you ever will. We can't wait any longer. You need to get help soon."

"Then let's do it, Doc," Roy said. "Since you know Dr. Goodwin, would you wire him for us? I'll pay for it. Explain the situation to him. Tell him we'll bring Autumn to Denver. We'll ride the Butterfield stage from Delta to Grand Junction and take the train from there to Denver."

Faulkner cleared his throat. "Well, I...ah...I already took the liberty of wiring Dr. Goodwin. Explained the whole situation. He wired me back and said he believes he can help her. I'm to let him know when you can make the trip."

"Right away," Nelda said.

Faulkner pulled at an ear and said, "I'm afraid you'll have to stay here, Nelda. Let Roy take her."

"Stay here?"

"Yes. You won't be strong enough to travel for at least another ten days. You really shouldn't try traveling until you've learned to use crutches. Be so much better for you...easier, too."

"Doctor, I'm not letting my daughter go to Denver without me."

Faulkner shook his head, rubbing his chin. "Nelda, you've been through some major trauma. You really aren't up to that long, tiring trip. Believe me. I sure don't want you getting worse on me."

"None of us want her getting worse, Doc," Roy said. "Ten days, you say?"

"At the very earliest."

"Will it hurt Autumn to wait that long?"

Faulkner thought on it for a moment. "It won't help her any…but I guess it's the lesser of two evils. It would probably be best for her if she could have her mother along." He headed for the door. "I'll wire Dr. Goodwin as soon as I get back to town. You planning on being in town today, Roy?"

"Hadn't planned on it, but I sure can be."

"Okay. Give me till three o'clock. Physicians are hard to get ahold of. I should hear back from him by then."

At precisely three o'clock, Roy and Adam Lynne entered the doctor's office. They found Faulkner sitting at the desk in the waiting room, making notes for a patient's file.

Faulkner looked up at them and smiled. "Howdy, gents."

"Doctor," nodded Roy. "How goes the communication between you and Dr. Goodwin?"

"Just fine," Faulkner replied, closing the folder and rising to his feet. "We've kept the wires hot. Here's the situation. Dr. Goodwin says because of Autumn's problem, it would be best that Nelda come along. He also understands about Nelda's broken leg, so here's what we've worked out. Dr. Goodwin insists that Autumn's paralysis is serious and wants her under special care until he can see her."

"Special care?"

"He has a visiting nurse who works out of his office. She's a C.M.N. and has some experience in dealing with psychological disorders. He's putting her on the Grand Junction train tomorrow. She'll arrive in Delta on the last Butterfield stage tomorrow evening and help prepare Autumn for the treatment Dr. Goodwin will give her when she arrives in Denver. She can also help Nelda learn to get around on crutches, and she can check the splint every day."

"Sounds good to me," Roy said. "So exactly when is Dr. Goodwin expecting us to be in Denver?"

"On the fifteenth. Well, your appointment is actually on the morning of the sixteenth, but since the train leaves Grand Junction late in the afternoon, you'll arrive in Denver about an hour before midnight on the fifteenth. That'll give Nelda a full ten days before she has to make the trip."

"Okay," Roy nodded, reaching for his wallet. "Now, what do I owe you for the telegrams?"

"You don't owe me a thing."

"Now, wait a minute, Doc. I don't want the cost of those wires coming out of your pocket."

"Oh, don't worry," chuckled the physician. "Just wait'll you see my bill!"

The two men laughed together, and Adam joined in. Then Roy said, "I'll need to know the nurse's fee."

"From what Dr. Goodwin said, Miss Baylor sets no price on her medical services. Her patients or their families just pay her whatever they figure her work was worth."

"I see. Fine. I'll see she's treated right."

"I don't doubt it."

As father and son rode the family wagon toward home, Adam said, "Dad, am I gonna get to go along?"

"To Denver?"

"Uh-huh."

"Of course. We wouldn't leave you at home."

A smile broke over Adam's face. "Great!"

"Of course, you'll have to take your school books along and keep up your lessons."

The smile quickly drained away.

"I figure we'll take Lulu, too, since she's part of the family now."

"Yeah. Be good for Autumn to have her along, too."

"That's the way I look at it."

✹ ✹ ✹ ✹ ✹

Ridge Holloway followed Treg Taggart's trail westward to the Utah border. He figured the convicted murderer wanted to get as far from Canon City as possible.

As he tracked Treg across snow-covered fields and through thick forests, his mind was almost constantly on Autumn Lynne. He prayed earnestly, asking the God of heaven to give her back the use of her legs.

On November 4, Lulu Taggart rode her horse into town. The mare was back to normal, having recovered from her fall.

Lulu entered Mauldin's General Store and bought another Bible. The Lynne family had let her use one of theirs for Bible study and Sunday services, but she wanted one of her own.

She left Mauldin's with the new Bible in her hand and led the mare down the street to the sheriff's office. Entering the office, she found Sheriff Luke Prisk at his desk, reading his mail. Prisk was stunned to see her in a dress.

"Why, hello, Lulu. What can I do for you?" His eyes also found the Bible she carried in her hand.

"I'd like to see my father and my brothers, Sheriff," Lulu replied nervously.

Prisk stood and stroked his chin. "I'll be glad to let you in the cell block, but from the way I've heard them talking about you, I doubt seriously they'll want to see you."

"I know how they feel, but I'd like to try."

Prisk shrugged and rounded the desk toward the door that led to the cells.

"I got word that they're all going to the prison in Canon City," Lulu said. "That they'd been sentenced."

"Circuit judge gave them twenty-five years for attempted murder. Couple of deputy U. S. marshals are coming in a few days to take them to Canon City."

They entered the cell block. There were four cells. Otis and Wick shared one, and Jeb and Nate another. One man who was sleeping off a drunk occupied the third cell, and the fourth was empty.

Otis and Wick were stretched out on their cots, each with an arm laid across his eyes. Jeb and Nate sat on a cot, facing each other, playing cards. Nate's back was to the corridor. When Jeb looked through the bars and saw his sister, he swore and snapped, "Get her outta here, Sheriff! We ain't interested in talkin' to no traitor!"

Nate pivoted on the cot and scowled at Lulu. Both Otis and Wick sat up to see what was going on.

Otis jumped off his cot, looking at Lulu with cold, hostile eyes. He released a string of profane words and growled, "What're you doin' here? Get out!"

Lulu steeled herself, trying to keep a grip on her composure.

"We don't want you here, Lulu!" Nate said. "You're stinkin' up the place!"

"Good thing these bars are between us, you low-down female Benedict Arnold, or I'd make you sorry you were ever born!" Wick said.

"Look what she's got, Pa," blurted Jeb, pointing to the Bible in her hand.

Otis eyed the black Book and swore. "Whatcha bringin' that thing in here for? Ya gonna preach to us, traitor?"

Tears moistened Lulu's eyes, loosening the tenuous grip she had on her composure. Her lower lip quivered slightly as she said, "Pa, I've become a Christian, and—"

"Yeah, and ya look dumb in that dress, too," the old man clipped.

"We don't wanna hear nothin' about your religion!" Wick said. "Get outta here and leave us alone!"

Luke Prisk had watched Lulu take the abuse long enough. "Shut your mouth, Wick! The rest of you, too! Can't you see Lulu's here because she cares about you?"

"Well, we don't care about her!" Nate growled. "And we don't wanna hear nothin' about that Bible!"

"Just get her outta here, Sheriff!" Otis said. "We ain't listenin' to no sermon!"

"Pa, I just want to talk to you about what I found in Jesus Christ," Lulu said, thumbing tears from her eyes. "I want you to go to heaven, so you'll be there with me."

"I'd rather go to hell!" Wick boomed. He paused, grinned, and looked around at his father and brothers. "If there was a hell, that is."

The others laughed.

Lulu opened her Bible and said, "Let me read somethin' to you."

Wick picked up a tin cup off a small table and began rattling it across the bars. His father and brothers followed suit, creating an ear-splitting din. They screamed for Prisk to get the traitor out of their sight.

"It's no use, Lulu! They're not going to listen to you!"

She nodded and closed her Bible. Prisk led the way out, and they returned to the office. The racket stopped the instant Prisk closed the door.

Prisk looked at her with compassion as she wept and said, "I'm sorry, Lulu."

"It's not your fault, Sheriff. Thank you for at least letting me try."

Dusk was settling over Colorado's western slope as Breanna Baylor sat alone in the Butterfield Stagelines office. The large window that faced the street offered a picturesque view of Grand Mesa to the north, reflecting the fading light of day from its lofty granite walls.

Breanna looked toward the window when she heard a wagon approaching, but eased back when it passed on by. The stage had arrived on schedule, and the other passengers had been met by family or friends, but so far none of the Lynne family had shown up. The Butterfield agent had excused himself, saying his wife had supper on the table upstairs. He left the lanterns burning for her.

A wagon rolled up in front of the office and rattled to a halt. Horses blew and snorted, followed by rapid footsteps on the boardwalk. The door came open, and a rather tall man entered with a teenage boy behind him.

"Miss Baylor?" said the man, removing his hat.

Breanna rose from the hard bench. "Yes."

"I'm Roy Lynne, ma'am, and this is my son, Adam."

"I'm happy to meet you, gentlemen."

"Please forgive our tardiness, Miss Baylor, but Adam and I were just ready to leave the ranch to come to town when my wife tried to use her crutches for the first time and took a tumble. As I'm sure you know, she's got a broken leg."

"Yes. Dr. Goodwin told me about it."

"Well, I couldn't leave her till I was sure she hadn't damaged the leg further. Seems to be all right, thank the Lord. We'll want you to look at it as soon as we get you there. Adam and I had a prayer meeting all the way into town. As you know, we're holding off taking our daughter to Denver because Nelda—that's my wife—"

"I know," Breanna smiled.

Roy's face tinted. "Of course you do. Anyway, if Nelda's hurt that leg some more, it could mean she'd have to stay home when Autumn goes to see your Dr. Goodwin. That would be devastating to her."

"I understand," said Breanna. "It hasn't hurt me to wait here for a while."

"Forgive me, Miss Baylor?"

"On one condition."

"What's that?"

"That you quit calling me Miss Baylor. I'm Breanna to my patients and their families."

"Even to teenagers?" Adam asked.

"Especially to teenagers," she laughed.

Roy noted the small trunk next to her with the black medical bag and purse on top. "These yours?"

"Yes."

Roy loaded the trunk into the wagon while young Adam helped Breanna aboard. She sat on the seat between them and pulled the collar of her coat up tight around her neck. They crossed a bridge over the dark Gunnison River, and soon were rolling across the open fields, patched with snow.

Breanna asked about the prayer meeting Roy said he and Adam had held while driving into town, and asked if he meant it literally. The discussion soon revealed that the Lynnes were Christians, for which Breanna was thankful. She told father and son about her own experience in coming to know the Lord, and there was an immediate bond between them. Roy said Nelda and Autumn would be happy to know their nurse was a Christian.

Breanna asked Roy to tell her all about his hanging, Autumn's trauma, and Nelda's broken leg. Roy gladly obliged, starting with Van Taggart murdering Aaron and all that had happened since then. He went on to tell her about Deputy U. S. Marshal Ridge Holloway and a tall, dark man named John Stranger arriving in the valley in pursuit of the oldest Taggart brother, Treg.

"John Stranger?" Breanna gasped. "He's here in Delta Valley?"

"You know him?" Roy asked.

Breanna's heart was pounding. "Why, yes. I know both of them. Deputy Holloway has been a patient of mine on occasion."

"And John Stranger? Very mysterious man. How well do you know him?"

Breanna cleared her throat nervously. "Well, quite well. We met in Kansas a year or so ago. I...haven't seen him for a while, though."

"Well, to answer your question, both Holloway and Stranger are gone now. Stranger killed Cliff Taggart in a shootout at the Taggart ranch, and Treg Taggart got away. Holloway is in pursuit of Treg, and I'm not exactly sure where John Stranger went."

"Oh," Breanna said with obvious disappointment in her voice. "I...I would love to have seen both of them."

Roy and Adam arrived home with Breanna Baylor, and she was given a warm welcome by Nelda, Autumn, and Lulu. Lulu had cooked supper while Roy and Adam went after Breanna. Her heart was still heavy over the treatment she received from her father and brothers, and over their refusal to listen to the gospel.

Around the supper table, Breanna learned how Autumn's tongue was loosed, and she showed elation that it had come as a result of Autumn's deep desire to lead her friend to Christ. Autumn was seated directly across the table from Breanna, who looked at her with compassion and said, "You'll walk again, too, honey. I'm sure of it."

CHAPTER

EIGHTEEN

———•◦•———

A heavy snowstorm in the Colorado Rockies slowed John Stranger's progress, but he rode up to the cabin hideout in the Elk Mountains at midday on November 9.

He had arrived in Canon City on November 4, and Warden Burl Hedge immediately put him in a private room with Frank Slattery. At first, Slattery refused to talk, but when Stranger told him he heard it from Treg Taggart's own mouth that Ord Grabow had fed Jack to a pack of wolves, Frank began to show interest.

Frank asked how he could be sure Stranger was telling him the truth. Stranger described in detail how he had stood at the window outside the Taggart house and listened as Treg told Cliff about the wolves eating Jack. He also heard Cliff ask where the hideout was.

"So what did Treg tell Cliff when he asked about the cabin's location?" Slattery asked.

"Let me ask you something before I tell you," Stranger said. "Outside of the gang, is there anyone who knows the location of the cabin?"

"No one. Nobody else even has the remotest idea where it is."

"All right. Then if I can tell you its approximate location, will you tell me its exact location so I can bring to justice the man who fed your brother to the wolves?"

"Wait a minute!" Frank said, shaking his head. "I don't understand what you're sayin'."

"I'm saying that in my hearing, Treg told Cliff Taggart two things—that Grabow had murdered your brother, and that the cabin is somewhere in the Elk Mountains. That's all he told him. No details on its exact location."

Frank nodded slowly. "Okay, I get it. You wouldn't know that the cabin was even in the Elk Mountains unless you heard it from a gang member."

"Correct. That's so, isn't it?"

"Sure is. So you're sayin' that in the same conversation, you overheard Treg tell Cliff about feedin' my brother to the wolves."

"Exactly."

"Well, you've convinced me. Of course I want to see Grabow pay for killin' Jack. I'll draw you a map."

Snow crunched under John Stranger's boots as he crossed the porch of the cabin. This was the place, all right, exactly as Frank had described it and precisely where his hand-drawn map showed it to be. There was only one thing wrong. There were no footprints in the snow anywhere around the cabin, nor was there any sign of a horse in the small corral a few yards away. Ord Grabow was gone.

Stranger tried the knob and found the door unlocked. He stepped inside and felt the chill of the large room as he glanced at the cold ashes in the fireplace. Ord Grabow indeed was gone—but where?

A sheet of paper caught his eye. It lay on a bench that stood against one wall, and he picked it up and saw that it was a map of the Cheyenne City area. Someone had marked a dark square on the map and indicated that it was five miles east of the town in a draw. The square was labeled *Dyar Lynch hideout.*

John Stranger knew who Dyar Lynch was—one of the most notorious gang leaders in the West. It didn't take Stranger long to guess that Ord Grabow was heading north to meet up with the Lynch gang. Perhaps he had left the map for Treg Taggart to follow at some later date.

Stranger aimed Ebony toward Cheyenne City and wondered if Ridge Holloway had tracked Treg down yet. He wound his way through the snow-covered mountain country with Grabow's map in his pocket and let his thoughts drift to the woman he loved.

The wintry wind howled and blew crusted snow across the Wyoming plains when Ord Grabow arrived at the Dyar Lynch hideout. Lynch welcomed him and introduced him to his nine gang members and to his uncle Webley Snipes. The grizzled old man stayed at the hideout and took care of the place while his nephew and the gang were out pulling robberies.

Uncle Webley was sharp for his age, and his hearing was excellent. When Grabow informed Lynch that Treg Taggart would be showing up in a few days, the old man remarked that Taggart had better hurry or he would miss the big haul.

Grabow listened as the gang leader told him of a big job they had planned. A large gold shipment was being sent on the train from Grand Junction to Denver on November 15. Lynch had a friend who had recently taken a job with the mining company, located in the mountains east of Grand Junction. His friend had sent him the information via another mutual friend, expecting a cut of the loot.

Lynch's friend reported that eight well-armed guards always rode in the baggage coach where the gold was kept, but Lynch told Grabow that before the train ever left Grand Junction, his men would overpower the guards and leave them bound and gagged in the depot woodshed.

While the men sat around the cabin drinking and joking, Dyar Lynch spread on the table a map of the Denver & Rio Grande Railroad route over the Rockies. It was 246 miles from Grand Junction to Denver. Lynch traced the line of tracks with his finger and showed Grabow where the train would cross the Continental Divide over Vail Pass at 10,666 feet.

Just west of the pass, where the incline was very steep, was an old line shack about two hundred yards south of the tracks. The train was scheduled to leave Grand Junction at 4:30 P.M. and to arrive in Denver just before midnight. It would be on the incline near the shack, chugging very slow, at about 8:00.

The group of men in the shack would include Grabow, Taggart (if he showed up in time to go with them), Errol Banning, and Lynch. They would build a barricade on the tracks and light a couple of fires to get the engineer's attention. With the train barely moving on such a steep incline, the engineer would not dare try to crash the barricade.

When the train came to a stop, half the gang would hold crew and passengers at gunpoint while the other half unloaded the gold onto a horse-drawn wagon. By the time the train could make it to Denver to report the robbery, the Lynch gang and the gold shipment would be long gone.

At the Lynne ranch, Breanna Baylor was winning the hearts of the family and Lulu Taggart. Each day, she spent several hours talking to Autumn, conditioning her for her therapy with Dr. Goodwin.

Breanna also took time to work with Nelda, teaching her simple techniques for using her crutches to the best advantage. She checked Nelda's leg daily and was confident she would be able to make the trip to Denver as scheduled.

When Treg Taggart rode his horse away from the ranch on that dark night, he soon found that the animal didn't take well to being guided by the mane. It kept balking when he tried to make it head northeast.

Treg finally gave up and gave the horse its head. It then carried him at a full gallop due west. His main desire was to get far from those lawmen as fast as possible. It mattered not which direction the horse decided to take him.

It was not until daylight the next morning that Taggart realized he had been carried across the Utah border. This was a long way from where he had planned to be by that time. He had hoped to be across the Wyoming border and heading due east toward Cheyenne City.

His horse was headed in a north-by-northwesterly direction when Treg spotted a small ranch up ahead. He decided he would steal bridle, saddle, and food there. If the rancher or his wife gave him any trouble, too bad for them.

When Taggart rode into the yard of the ranch, he was shocked to find the rancher and his wife lying dead near the porch. There were arrows in their bodies, and they had been scalped.

Fear gripped him as he rode away, thinking that the hostiles might be somewhere near. A quarter hour later, he came upon another ranch and found a family of five massacred—a couple in their late thirties and three children. This time he decided to stay long enough to take a bridle and saddle for his horse.

He entered the barn and found an elderly man lying on the floor with an arrow in his back. Like the others, he had been scalped, but he was still alive! He was lying face-down, but when he heard footsteps, he raised his head and stared with terror, as if he was expecting the Indians back.

Treg moved to him and bent down. The old man struggled to find his voice. "Did they...did they kill my family?"

"Yes," Treg nodded.

"You'd better be careful, mister. Utes...on the prowl. They're killing every white person they see. Best you don't be riding out in the open for a few days. Give them...a chance to settle down. They...they've done this before. Once they spill enough white men's blood...they're usually satisfied for a while."

As Treg started to turn away, the old man said, "Would you...break the arrow off? Help me into the house? I need water."

Treg decided the thing to do was leave the bodies lying in the yard and hole up in the house for a day or two. The Indians had already done their damage here. They probably wouldn't bother to come on the place again. He put his horse in the barn and headed for the house. The old man was still begging for water, but Treg ignored him.

At dawn on November 13, Treg rode off the ranch with his horse bridled and saddled. Watching for Utes, he continued north. Twice he saw army camps, but skirted them. He was glad the army was in the area, which meant the Indian trouble may have been quelled, but he wasn't interested in meeting up with any soldiers.

Taggart had run out of grain and hay for his horse the day before. Mid-morning he saw a small wagon train coming from the east, and he angled toward them. When he drew up to the wagon master and asked for grain, he was told they couldn't spare any. The wagon master told him there was a small town called Cottonwood Wash about twenty miles due north, on the road that ran between Green River, Utah, and Grand Junction, Colorado.

Taggart was angry that they wouldn't spare him some grain, but there were too many men in the wagon train for him to try to take it by force, so he rode on.

He had gone no more than seven or eight miles when he topped a high rise and stopped to give his hungry horse a breather. He happened to look back south and saw movement amid a stand of trees. Seconds later, he made out a lone rider coming his way. Could it be a lawman on his trail? If it was, the lawman had already spotted him. He spurred his horse and galloped full-speed, holding his northerly course.

Ridge Holloway knew he had spotted his man when the distant rider suddenly rode away at a gallop. He had almost given up the chase when a new snowstorm covered Taggart's trail the second day out. He had lost track of him, then suddenly found the tracks of a single rider leading away from a ranch where the Utes had left five corpses in the yard.

Most of the snow was melted off the ground again, except for small patches on the north side of heavy stands of trees, boulders, and hills. Holloway put his horse to a gallop and bounded after the fleeing outlaw.

Treg Taggart dipped into a shallow draw as he urged his horse to run faster. When he topped the rise on the opposite side, he looked back to see his pursuer coming at a full gallop. There was no question he had a faster steed. The lawman was gaining on him.

Taggart knew he would have to kill the man, and he began looking for a spot to set up an ambush. About a quarter-mile ahead was a dense stand of cottonwoods intermingled with tall pines. When he reached the patch of woods, he plunged his horse into the deep shadows and skidded to a halt. He left the heaving horse and ran back several yards in the direction he had come and hauled up behind a towering, naked-limbed cottonwood at the edge of the clearing. He would have a clear shot at the man when he drew near.

He pulled his revolver and eared back the hammer, leaned against the rough bark and waited. Seconds later he saw the lawman coming, but it looked as if he was going to ride on by. He must have been in a low spot when Taggart veered into the trees and had not seen him.

Suddenly the man pulled rein. He wheeled his horse and leaned from the saddle, studying the ground as he backtracked at a slow walk.

Taggart swore under his breath. Even at a gallop, the lawman had been able to tell that his man had suddenly changed course. The lawman straightened in the saddle, peered at the wooded area, and put his mount to a gallop.

Taggart rubbed a palm across his eyes and hugged the tree as he drew a bead with his revolver. "C'mon, tin star," he whispered. "Just a little closer. C'mon. That's it. That's it."

Ridge Holloway knew Treg Taggart could be waiting in ambush for him. On the other hand, he might be fleeing through the dense trees as fast as he could go. Ridge decided to get to the edge of the trees as quickly as possible, then go in on foot.

He was within thirty yards of the woods when a shot rang out, echoing across the open fields. His horse went down head-over-heels. Holloway somersaulted out of the saddle and scrambled out of the way.

He sprang to his feet and ran toward the first line of trees. A second shot clattered on the cold air. The bullet hummed past him, and before Treg could get off another shot, Holloway was safe behind a thick-trunked cottonwood.

Ridge heard rapid footsteps and realized Taggart was running deeper into the woods. Instantly he was after him. It took only seconds to catch sight of Taggart as he dashed for his horse.

Holloway slowed his pace, drew a bead, and fired. The bullet sped past the fleeing outlaw and chewed bark from a nearby tree, splattering bits of bark into the horse's eyes. Terrified, the animal pivoted and bolted away, threading quickly through the trees.

Taggart cursed and started after the horse.

Holloway's voice cut through the timber. "Taggart! Stop or I'll shoot!"

Treg kept running, but looked back to see sunlight flicker off the man's badge. He fired a shot, but it went wild, chewing into a lofty pine above Holloway's head.

Holloway fired back, and the slug plucked at Taggart's coat sleeve. He kept running, but Holloway was on his heels. Taggart stopped, and using a tree for a shield, blasted away at the elusive lawman until the hammer of his revolver snapped hollowly on an empty cartridge.

Ridge heard it and rushed up on him, gun ready. "End of the line, Taggart!"

Treg looked at the empty gun in his hand, then met the lawman's steady gaze.

"Deputy U. S. Marshal Ridge Holloway, Taggart. I'm taking you back to Canon City."

"Gonna be a long walk, Deputy. Seems my horse's done run away, and yours is dead."

"You and I are going to walk to Cottonwood Wash, about ten miles due north of here. We'll catch the next available stage to Grand Junction, then take the train to Denver. Won't take long to get you back to the prison."

"You'll never get me there, Holloway."

"Drop the gun, Taggart. Then turn around and put your hands behind your back."

Defiance danced in Taggart's ice-blue eyes.

Holloway growled, "We can do this the easy way or the hard way, pal. You choose."

"Whatcha gonna do? Shoot me in cold blood?"

"No, but it wouldn't bother me to put a dent in your skull. Drop the gun, turn around, and put your hands behind your back."

Taggart held Holloway's gaze for a few seconds, then let the empty revolver slip from his fingers.

"That was step number one. Number two is to turn around."

Taggart started to say something, but Holloway cut him off. "Do it!"

Taggart made a slow pivot, squaring his back with the lawman.

"Step number three—put those hands behind your back. And I mean *now*."

Holloway produced handcuffs from inside his coat and the ratchets snapped loudly as he tightened them on Taggart's wrists. "Okay, let's go to my dead horse first."

"What're we goin' to the horse for?" Taggart asked.

"I'm taking my saddlebags with me."

When they reached the lifeless animal, Ridge pointed to a spot a dozen feet away and said, "You stand right over there."

Taggart moved to the spot, glaring at his captor. Holloway kept an eye on his prisoner as he broke his gun open and punched out two empty cartridges. He gave Taggart a crooked grin as he slipped a fresh cartridge from his gunbelt and said, "Don't even think about it, Treg. You make a dash for me, I'll use this gun to crack your cranium."

Holloway replaced the second spent shell, snapped the cylinder shut, and slid the weapon home into its holster. He bent over and unbuckled the straps that held the leather bags to the saddle and pulled them free. He laid the saddlebags on the dead horse's hip, opened the right bag, and started to reach inside when he heard the shuffle of Taggart's feet. The outlaw was coming at him.

Ridge shifted his weight slightly and stuck a foot into the outlaw's legs. Taggart stumbled and fell, cursing Holloway profusely. The deputy stood over him as he struggled to his feet—off balance because his hands were cuffed behind him—and said, "One more little trick like that, and I promise you'll regret it."

Taggart licked his lips but did not respond.

The saddlebags had slid off the horse's hip and spilled their contents. Among packs of beef jerky and hardtack were two boxes of .45 cartridges and a black Bible.

Ridge laid the saddlebags on the horse's hip once again and stuffed the food packs in first. He then laid the Bible on the saddlebags and opened a cartridge box, pulling out two bullets to replace those he had just taken from his gunbelt.

Taggart eyed the Bible with disdain and said, "What're you doin' with that fairy-tale book?"

Ridge picked up the Bible and said, "This is no fairy-tale book, pal. This is the Word of God."

"Pf-f-f-t! Ain't a word of truth in it."

"No?"

"Of course not. Man's a fool who thinks there is, too."

"So you don't believe it's true, huh?" Ridge said, stepping closer to him.

"Not one word."

"Oh, how wrong you are, Treg. *Every* word is true."

"Yeah? Prove to me there's one statement in that Bible that's true. Go on. You can't do it!"

"If I do, will you believe the rest of it? I mean, either it's God's Word or it's not."

"But there ain't no God," Treg said.

"You know better than that. You just won't admit it to yourself. Because if you admit God exists, you also have to admit that you're responsible to Him for your deeds, and you don't like that."

"What are you...some kind of preacher?"

"No. Just a believer in the truth. You said I can't prove one statement in the Bible is true, right?"

"You can't do it. My pa said there ain't *one word* in the Bible that's true. It's all fairy tales."

"Well, pal," Holloway said, flipping pages, "I'm going to prove your father wrong."

When Ridge found the page he wanted, he laid the open Bible on top of the saddlebags, then surprised the outlaw by grabbing the back of Treg's neck with his left hand and his nose with his right.

Taggart tried to free himself from the lawman's grip, but he couldn't do it. It took only seconds for blood to bubble from his nostrils. As soon as it appeared, Holloway let go and stepped back.

Taggart swore at him, sniffed blood, and whined, "What'd you do that for!"

"I just proved the Bible to be true," Ridge said, wiping blood from his hand on the dead horse's coat. "You said I couldn't prove one word in the Bible to be true."

"What're you talkin' about?" Taggart said, sniffing more blood.

Holloway picked up the open Bible and asked, "Can you read, Treg?"

"Of course."

"Then read me Proverbs 30:33."

Taggart lanced him with a hot look.

"Go on. Read it!"

Treg sniffed blood again, focused on the verse, and read falteringly, "*Surely the churning of milk bringeth forth butter, and the wringing of the nose bringeth forth blood: so the forcing of wrath bringeth forth strife.*"

Holloway lowered the Bible and grinned crookedly. "Now tell me there isn't one true word in the Bible. Tell me, mister."

Taggart glowered at him but did not answer.

"The Bible does speak the truth, doesn't it, Treg?"

Taggart fixed the lawman with hate-filled eyes. "Yeah, I guess. There at least."

"Well, let me show you another true statement right here in the same book." Holloway flipped back a few pages to Proverbs 11.

He placed a finger on verse 5 and said, "See this, Treg. The first half of the verse says, *The righteousness of the perfect shall direct his way.* Now read me the last half."

Taggart frowned as he read aloud, "*But the wicked shall fall by his own wickedness.*"

"Think about it, Treg. Just as sure as the wringing of the nose brings forth blood, so shall the wicked fall by his own wickedness. Every unbeliever is called 'the wicked' in Scripture. That's you, pal. Unless you repent, turn to Christ, and let Him change your life, you will fall by your own wickedness. Understand? Your very own wickedness will bring you down."

"You wanna try to get me to Canon City, Holloway, go to it. But I don't wanna hear none of this Bible stuff, ya hear me! Don't preach to me! You wanna get goin', then let's go. Just shut up with that Bible stuff!"

"Well, mister outlaw, you'll find out that just as sure as you bled when I wrung your nose, 'the wicked shall fall by his own wickedness.' Better think it over."

A little over two hours later, Ridge Holloway and his prisoner arrived in Cottonwood Wash. Holloway checked at the way station and learned that the next stage to Grand Junction would come through Cottonwood Wash November 15, the day after tomorrow. It would get him and his prisoner into Grand Junction in plenty of time to catch the 4:30 train to Denver.

CHAPTER

NINETEEN

———◆———

J ohn Stranger followed the map Treg Taggart left behind in the
Elk Mountain cabin, and late in the day on November 12, he
passed through Cheyenne City and rode onto the plains east
of town. The wintry, gusting wind cut at him. Low pockets in the
prairie floor were white with snow, and the wind scooped up icy
particles, hurling them against horse and rider.

Stranger soon found the draw that held the Lynch hideout.
He drew rein at the crest and looked the place over. The corral near
the large log cabin contained only one horse, and smoke drifted
from the stove pipe that protruded from the flat sod roof.

He nudged his horse forward and said, "Well, Ebony, from
the looks of things I'd say there's only one person on the place. Let's
check it out."

Ebony nickered and carried his master down the gentle slope.
As they neared the cabin, the back door came open, and a grizzled
old man stepped out on the porch with a pan of dirty water. He
tossed the water on the frozen ground and caught sight of horse and
rider.

The old man grinned and motioned for him to move on in,
as if he had been expecting him.

"Howdy!" he called in a high, squeaky voice. "You must be Treg Taggart."

"Howdy, yourself," Stranger grinned as he swung from the saddle. "I see only one horse in the corral. I take it Lynch and Grabow aren't here."

"Nope. They've done headed out with the rest o' the gang to pull a big train robbery west o' here. I'm s'posed to give you a letter Ord wrote. C'mon inside where it's warm."

Stranger wrapped the reins around a hitch rail next to the porch and heard the horse in the corral whinny. Ebony whinnied back.

The warmth of the cabin felt good to John Stranger as he moved in behind the old man and closed the door. The wind whined around the eaves.

The old man placed the pan on the cupboard and offered his hand. "I'm Uncle Webley Snipes, Treg—Dyar's uncle. All the boys call me Uncle Webley. I'm eighty-two years young."

Stranger liked the old man. He had a captivating grin, nearly toothless, and a twinkle in his eyes. It had been some time since he had been near a barber, and it looked as if he hadn't shaved in about a week.

"Glad to meet you, Uncle Webley," Stranger grinned.

The old man went to a crude cabinet, opened a drawer, and pulled out a folded sheet of paper. "Ord said to give you this, but if you didn't git here in time to make it to Grand Junction by the fifteenth, jist to stay here. You'd be too late to be in on the robbery. They're gonna make a big haul, Treg. Gold."

"I see," Stranger nodded, unfolding the paper.

Uncle Webley went to the cookstove—which also heated the five-room cabin—and dropped a couple of logs onto the fire while Stranger read the letter. Grabow gave him the entire plan for the robbery, telling him how the eight guards would be overpowered and replaced by gang members, and that Lynch, Grabow, and Errol Banning would be holed up in the line shack near the crest of Vail

Pass. Taggart was to come to the line shack and help them build the barricade that would be used to stop the train on the steep slope. A map was included on the paper, showing him how to find the shack. On the last line, Grabow assured Treg that if he did not arrive in time to get in on the robbery, he would still share with him a small portion of his part of the gold.

Stranger folded the paper small enough to fit it into his shirt pocket and slipped his hand under his coat. "Well, Uncle Webley, I'd better be on the move. I'll have to hurry if I'm going to make it."

The old man squinted, cocked his head, and said, "You don't talk like a outlaw, Treg. Must have some refinement o' some kind, eh?"

"A little," Stranger grinned, and headed for the door.

Stranger decided to wire Mesa County's Sheriff Woody Worland from Cheyenne City. Sufficiently warned, Worland could step in and prevent the robbery. When Stranger reached the telegraph office in town, however, he was told that the lines were down all over southern Wyoming and northern Colorado because of the high winds. They would not be back in service for several days.

Stranger knew he must ride hard for Grand Junction in order to thwart the robbery before the train pulled out. Ebony was worn out from carrying him through the mountains all the way from Canon City. He would board Ebony at a stable and rent a fresh horse. And because it was going to be difficult to make it to Grand Junction in time, he improvised a back-up plan.

He went to a shop that sold women's paraphernalia, hurried from there to a used clothing store, then made a hasty purchase at the general store. Then he left Ebony at the stable and rode westward on a large gray roan with the north wind lashing him.

The Butterfield stage pulled into Cottonwood Wash at mid-morning, November 15, and hauled to a stop in front of the small way station. Driver Simeon Nickols and shotgunner Kent Morlan entered the station, rubbing their wind-turned faces, and closed the door. The potbellied stove in the room's corner put off welcome heat.

Butterfield agent Harry Sanders was on his feet talking with two men who sat on wooden chairs next to the far wall. When Sanders turned to greet them, Nickols and Morlan saw that one of the men was handcuffed to the chair. The other man rose to his feet and shouldered into a coat that bore a deputy U. S. marshal's badge.

Nickols whispered to Morlan, "From the looks of this, I'm glad we don't have any other passengers on this run."

Sanders grinned and said, "Well, boys, I drummed up a little business for you. Marshal Holloway and his prisoner, here, will be riding to Grand Junction with you."

"Fine," nodded the driver. "It ain't often we just haul a little freight. It'll be nice to have some warm bodies inside the coach, too."

"Even if one of 'em's an outlaw?" Treg Taggart asked as Holloway unlocked the handcuff attached to the arm of the chair.

"Don't bother me as long as the marshal's got you in cuffs," Nickols responded.

Holloway allowed Taggart to put on his coat, then attached the free cuff to his left wrist, shackling himself to his prisoner. Moments later, the stage was rolling eastward with the six-up team moving at a steady gallop.

Inside the coach, Taggart—who sat on Holloway's left side opposite his holstered gun—leered at the deputy and said, "It's still a long way to Canon City, Holloway. You ain't gonna get me there."

"Shut up," Ridge grunted. "I'm not intimidated by your threats."

Taggart let a minute pass, then chuckled to himself. Holloway looked at him and asked, "What's so funny?"

"You."

"Me?"

"Yeah. You and that holy stuff about 'the wicked shall fall by his own wickedness.'"

"It's the truth whether you believe it or not," Holloway said. "Plenty of examples to back it up. Happened to a wicked man named Cain and another named Haman. Classic example of all is Judas Iscariot. He sure went down by his own wickedness. All the way to his own place in hell."

"Aw, that ain't nothin' but fairy tales."

"You're wrong, but how about men outside the Bible—like Benedict Arnold, John Wilkes Booth, and Van and Cliff Taggart? Didn't their own wickedness bring them down?"

"Well, it ain't gonna happen to me."

"Yes it will. You just wait and see."

The stage was now just ten miles from Grand Junction. Taggart decided it was time to make the desperate move he had been planning ever since they boarded the stage. He poised himself, then sprang against the deputy, reaching around him and seizing the butt of the Colt .45. He had it out and the hammer cocked before the surprised lawman could react. Ridge grabbed Taggart's left wrist, and the two men were in a grave struggle.

They met each other strength for strength, and the struggle was awkward but fierce. Treg threw his weight hard against the deputy, trying to break his grip on his wrist, but it failed. Their shackled hands swung upward as Ridge fought to overcome his prisoner. Suddenly the hammer dropped and the gun roared. The bullet plowed through the thin wood of the stagecoach.

Up in the box, Simeon Nickols groaned as the .45 slug struck him in the back, drilling straight into his heart. He let go of the reins and fell forward, striking the rear legs of the two horses closest to the coach.

The sound of the shot was enough to startle the six-up team, but when the driver's body struck the two horses, they bolted forward. The lead horses felt the abrupt pressure and went into a wild gallop, taking the others with them.

The coach rocked and fishtailed, and Kent Morlan grasped the reins and tried to bring the frightened animals to a halt, but they only ran harder. In the coach, the battle for supremacy continued. Both men were amazed at the other's strength.

Morlan's eyes bulged when he saw the team veer off to the left of the road and thunder blindly toward a deep, sharp-edged ravine. "No!" he screamed as horses and stagecoach went over the edge. The coach landed on top of the horses, then cart-wheeled and came to rest on its top, the wheels still spinning.

Treg Taggart's head whirled and the muscles in his back were shooting pain, but he was fully aware of what had happened. He was lying partially on top of Ridge Holloway, who was unconscious.

Taggart worked one leg free and shoved a boot against the door, snapping it open. He fished in the pockets of Holloway's pants and coat, but could find no key. He swore at the unconscious lawman and rummaged through every pocket again. Still no key.

He searched for the revolver, and finally saw the tip of the barrel sticking out from under Holloway's body. It took him only a few seconds to work the weapon free. *One bullet, and the chain on the cuffs'll be cut in two. Another bullet in Holloway's head, and I'll be on my way!*

He was about to ear back the hammer when he heard voices. He inched his way to the open door and saw several cavalrymen standing at the edge of the ravine, looking down at the wreckage and the dead horses. The leader said, "Let's get down there. Could be somebody's still alive."

As the soldiers slowly made their way down the steep side of the ravine, Taggart worked furiously to remove Holloway's gunbelt and put it on himself. The cavalrymen were almost to the coach.

Taggart heard one of them say, "This one's dead, too." Taggart knew he had to be talking about the driver and shotgunner.

The footsteps were drawing close. Taggart snatched the badge from Holloway's coat and pinned it on his own.

"Hey!" said a sergeant, bending down to look through the open door. "We've got one alive, at least!"

A lieutenant drew up beside him and looked at Taggart. "You all right, Deputy?" he asked.

"Yeah, I think so," Taggart said.

"How about your prisoner?"

"He's out cold."

"I'm Lieutenant Gregory Ashton. This is Sergeant Bill Dahl. We're on patrol from an army camp about five miles north of here. We found the older man a ways back. Dead. Bullet in his back. All busted up, too. I assume he was the driver."

"Yeah," nodded Taggart. "Younger one's the shotgunner."

"He's dead, too. Broken neck. What happened?"

"Well, I'm Ridge Holloway, deputy U. S. marshal. My prisoner here escaped from the prison down in Canon City. I've been trailin' him, and finally caught him a couple days ago. Lost both of our horses. Utes took 'em while I was chasin' 'im on foot. We walked to Cottonwood Wash and caught this stage. He tried to take my gun, and it went off and apparently hit the driver."

"I assume you were heading for Grand Junction to catch the train for Denver," said Ashton.

"Uh…yeah. That's right." No sooner had the words come out of his mouth than he realized the last thing he wanted to do was get on that train with Holloway cuffed to him. But it was too late to change his story.

But any hope of eluding the train vanished when Lieutenant Ashton said they would carry both men to the depot in Grand Junction on separate horses. All the deputy had to do was unlock the cuffs. He could put them back on later.

"Good idea, Lieutenant," Taggart said, fishing in his pants pocket as if to locate the key. Ridge Holloway groaned and rolled his head.

"I can't find the key. It must've dropped out of my pocket when we crashed. Maybe your men could find it if you'd pull us outta here."

"Come over here, men," Ashton called. "Help us get these two out of the coach."

Holloway blinked awake and saw the badge on Taggart's coat and his gunbelt on Taggart's waist. He remembered the coach racing out of control just before it became airborne and the lights went out. When he saw the blue uniforms, the whole thing came together.

As strong hands began to drag both men through the door, Ridge said, "You men need to understand something. I'm the deputy U. S. marshal! My name's Ridge Holloway, and I work out of the chief U. S. marshal's office in Denver. This man is Treg Taggart, my prisoner."

"Oh, I see," Ashton chuckled. "That's why he's wearing the badge and the gun."

"Stupid trick, Taggart," Treg said. "You really don't think the lieutenant or his men are gonna believe you!"

"Lieutenant," Ridge said, "this man is lying! I tell you, I'm the lawman!"

The lieutenant ignored him and sent two men into the battered coach to hunt for the key. After several minutes, they emerged from the stage, saying they couldn't find it. Taggart and Holloway were put on the same horse with their wrists linked together, and the sergeant rode double with Lieutenant Ashton.

Again, Holloway tried to convince Ashton of the truth, but his words fell on deaf ears. They had gone four or five miles when Ridge realized his saddlebags had been left behind. He knew it would do no good to ask that they send a rider back to fetch them.

As they neared Grand Junction, Holloway said in a low tone, "This masquerade will backfire on you, Taggart. *The wicked shall fall by his own wickedness.*"

"Shut up, Taggart! I'm sick of listenin' to you! When will you outlaws learn the error of your ways?" The riders-in-blue gave them a casual glance but kept silent.

The sky was spitting snow when they arrived at the depot in Grand Junction. Taggart and Holloway were put on the train only minutes before it was scheduled to pull out of the station. The conductor ushered them to a seat at the rear of coach number three. The whistle blew and the train—coal car, baggage coach, three passengers coaches, and caboose—surged forward.

The conductor stood on the platform at the rear of passenger coach number three and noted a rawboned, stoop-shouldered Mexican running along the platform, dodging people who were waving to friends and loved ones. Wind-driven snowflakes stuck to the Mexican's sombrero and shabby coat as he strained to reach the coach before he ran out of platform. In the nick of time, he gripped the metal handle and swung himself aboard.

The conductor gripped an arm, helping him to steady himself, and said, "That was a close one, sir."

"Si, señor," said the stoop-shouldered Mexican, out of breath. "Are there any seats lef' in zees car?"

"Yes, sir. Up at the front."

The Mexican's long, shaggy black hair dangled to his shoulders. His white teeth stood out against a bushy mustache as he smiled and said, "Gracias."

The conductor opened the door and asked, "Do you have a ticket?"

"No, señor. I deed no have time to buy one. I can pay you, no?"

"Yes. I'll be by to collect from you in a little while."

The Mexican thanked him and moved into the swaying coach. He made his way to the front seat on the right side, which was unoccupied, and sat down. He looked out the window and saw that the snow was coming down heavier and sticking to the glass.

In car number two, Breanna Baylor sat near the aisle in the second seat from the rear, which faced backward. Next to her was Autumn Lynne, whose wheelchair was tied between two empty seats across the aisle. Lulu Taggart sat on Autumn's other side, next to the window, and Roy, Nelda, and Adam faced the three young women from the rear seat.

In the baggage coach, just behind the coal car, Dyar Lynch's eight men sat on wooden chairs around the potbellied stove, posing as guards. They laughed about how easy it had been to overcome the real guards and leave them bound and gagged in the depot's woodshed. By the time someone found them, it would be too late to stop the robbery. They looked around at the boxes that held the gold and chattered happily about their sudden riches.

Treg Taggart leaned close to the man shackled to him and said, "Holloway, if you've got that key on you, I want it."

Ridge eyed him with disdain. "I don't have it. I've already checked and double-checked the pocket where I carried it. The thing fell out when the stagecoach crashed. You're stuck with me all the way to Denver, Taggart, and your goose will be cooked when we get there. You lose, pal. You're goin' back to Canon City to hang."

"That's what you think! I'll get loose from you somehow!"

Ridge shook his head. "*The wicked shall fall by his own wickedness.* Proverbs 11:5."

The wind howled into the coach as the front door came open, and the conductor appeared, carrying a box loaded with small, tightly stuffed paper sacks. Taggart mumbled something indistinguishable and sat up straight.

The conductor handed out snacks in each coach as the train wound its way higher and higher into the Rockies. Darkness settled over the mountains, and the snow kept falling, whipped hard against the sides of the coaches by the wind.

As the evening grew older, passengers became sleepy with the steady rocking of the coaches and the clacking of the wheels.

Engineer Todd Bandy leaned his head against the window of the cab and studied the beam of the big headlight. Ice crystals slanted across the beam, and blue-black shadows danced over the broken white surface dotted with towering pines.

Dorsey Lowe was at the fire box, tossing logs into the flames. He slammed the big iron door of the fire box shut and pressed close to the window on his side of the cab. "Looks like we just might be buildin' up to a blizzard, Todd."

"That's what I was thinkin'," Bandy nodded.

The train was on the steep incline that would carry it up and over Vail Pass. Bandy pulled out his pocketwatch, slanted it toward the lantern that burned overhead, and noted that it was 7:53. "If we can get over the pass before it gets any worse, I'll feel better. I'd rather be headin' down through a blizzard than up."

"I'll say amen to that," the fireman said.

Dyar Lynch, Ord Grabow, and Errol Banning bent their heads into the fierce wind as they stood next to the tracks. They had piled up more than a dozen fallen trees to form a barricade and had three fires going to illuminate it. One fire was directly between the tracks. The shadows thrown by the fires made the barricade look larger than it really was.

Lynch peered through the driving snow toward the team and wagon that stood some fifty feet from the track. The horses fought their bits and tried to turn their rumps into the wind. "Sure hope that train's on time!" he shouted into the wind. "Horses are gettin' edgy!"

"I think we got us a full-fledged blizzard, boys!" Banning hollered. "It might slow the train some, but it oughtta be comin' along here any time!"

Grabow stomped his feet and worked his arms to help stay warm. He was thinking about Treg Taggart, still hoping he would get there in time for the robbery.

Less than five minutes passed when Banning pointed down the mountain and said, "There it is! See the headlight through the trees?"

Todd Bandy gave the engine full throttle as he always did at this point on the steep incline. Snow was piled up on the tracks, but the cow-catcher plowed it away from the wheels.

Something caught his eye as he peered through the window up the side of the mountain. "Look up there!" he said to the fireman.

Dorsey Lowe leaned tight against the window on his side and said, "Looks like somebody's built a fire on the tracks!"

"Somebody's built a barricade! They want the gold we're carryin' as sure as shootin'!"

"Maybe you oughtta ram through it."

"Don't dare. Can't tell how big it is. Besides I've got it to full throttle already. I've got to stop. If I don't, the barricade could derail us, and we'd really be in trouble!"

"Well, those guards in the baggage coach will earn their money tonight," said the fireman. "Hope they can hold the robbers off."

"Dorsey, hurry back and warn 'em," Bandy said, hand on the throttle. "We got about three minutes before I have to start slowin' down."

At the same time Dorsey Lowe left the engine and made his way along the catwalk on the coal car, the stoop-shouldered Mexican entered car number two. He knew they were getting close to the summit of Vail Pass. It was almost time to execute his plan. He moved into car number two and sat at the seat where Autumn Lynne's wheelchair was tied.

When Dorsey Lowe entered the baggage car, the guards immediately put guns on him. Lowe stared into six muzzles while two of the outlaws, Vic Cochran and Ervin Dill, tied him up and gagged him.

In the cab, Todd Bandy wondered where his fireman was as he eased the throttle back and let the train chug to a stop. The pile of trees and the fire in the center of the track were only inches from the tip of the cow-catcher.

Dyar Lynch and Ord Grabow climbed in the cab, guns pointed at Bandy. Errol Banning worked his way through the driving snow to the baggage coach. Just as he drew up, the door slid open and the outlaws came piling out.

Banning told them that Lynch said they were to take over the train until the storm was over. It would be too difficult to unload the gold into the wagon and make it to the line shack in such fierce weather. Todd Bandy was escorted quickly to the baggage coach and bound hand and foot.

Inside car number two, the Mexican remained in his seat across the aisle from Breanna while several passengers crowded at the windows, trying to see what was going on. Roy Lynne headed for the rear door of the coach, saying maybe he could find the conductor and get some answers. Suddenly the door flew open, and four men burst in, waving their guns in a threatening manner. The four outlaws were Les Hodge, Vic Cochran, Ray Sibley, and Marlon Kalbaugh.

Roy Lynne backed up and placed himself between the outlaws and his family. Kalbaugh barked at him, "Siddown, mister!"

Cochran waved his revolver at the twenty-three passengers in the car and yelled, "Ever'body sit still! Let me see every hand reach for the ceilin'! Now, we're gonna take ever'body's guns. Any resistance and you'll die!"

It galled the Mexican to have both of his .45s lifted, but there was nothing he could do about it. He had been in many a tight spot before. This would be just another challenge.

The conductor was also tied up in the baggage coach, leaving the entire crew helpless. Dyar Lynch assigned four men to coach number three, while he, Grabow, and Banning manned coach number one. In number three were Clarence Judd, Lionel Ruppert, Ervin Dill, and Merle McBroom. The entire train would be in the hands of the outlaws until the weather broke and they took off with the gold.

McBroom was a giant of a man, with sloping, bull-like shoulders and arms like tree trunks. There was a mean, demonic look in his dark eyes that were set unusually far apart.

He grinned at Ridge Holloway, showing dirty yellow teeth and said, "What did ya do, pal?"

"Let him get the advantage of me," Ridge replied.

Merle laughed. "No, I mean what's he takin' ya in for?"

"It's a trumped-up charge," Ridge said, pressing bitterness into his voice. "I'm innocent."

McBroom grinned. "Yeah. Me, too."

Treg Taggart's brain was spinning. Should he tell this outlaw who he really was? Would he believe him? He decided to wait and see how things developed.

Each car had a supply of wood, and the outlaws began barking orders to male passengers, making them feed the potbellied stoves to keep the cars warm. The passengers were told why the gang had taken over the train and that nobody would get hurt if they all cooperated.

In car number two, the Mexican watched the outlaws carefully. He felt Breanna's eyes on him and returned her gaze for a brief instant, then looked away. Suddenly Breanna was aware of one of the outlaws standing over her. Marlon Kalbaugh grinned down at Breanna and said, "My name's Marlon, honey. What's yours?"

"Leave her alone," Roy Lynne said.

Kalbaugh stabbed a stiff forefinger at the rancher and blurted, "You stay out of it, mister!"

"You want the gold in the baggage coach? Fine, take it. But don't bother the lady. She's a nurse, and she's caring for my daughter."

Kalbaugh's gaze went to Autumn. "What's the matter with her?"

"Her legs are paralyzed," Breanna said.

"I think maybe you're storyin' to me."

"That's her wheelchair across the aisle."

Kalbaugh turned and looked at the wheelchair. "Okay, so you told me the truth. I like healthy nurses better than cripples anyway."

"Get away from us!" Roy blurted.

The Mexican rose from his seat and leaned toward Roy. "Please, señor. Eet ees not wise to roffle zee feathers of thees man. I'm sure he weel not harm zee nurse." Turning to Kalbaugh, he added, "Ees that not correct, señor?"

"Of course, Pancho. I wouldn't hurt the little nurse. I might give her a great big kiss, but I wouldn't hurt her."

The front door of the car opened and Errol Banning called, "Hey, Marlon! Dyar wants to see ya in car number one!"

Kalbaugh leaned close to Breanna and said, "Later, sweetheart," and headed for the front of the coach.

The Mexican looked at Breanna and said, "I am sorry for zee way zee man talk to you, señorita. Let us hope he weel not bother you any more." Then to Roy, "Please forgive my butting een, señor. I know thees kind of man. He would keel you as quickly as he would swat a fly. I only wanted to keep you from being harmed."

"I appreciate that, sir," nodded Roy, who had an arm around a white-faced Nelda. "I've been known to lose my temper now and then. I'm sure you're right. These men are bad dudes."

"Hey, Mex!" snapped Cochran, who stood in the aisle a few feet away. "Siddown and shut your greasy trap!"

The Mexican nodded and took his seat next to the wheelchair.

Autumn looked at her father and said, "Pa, please be careful. The Mexican is right—these men are killers. I can see it in their eyes."

Roy leaned forward and patted his daughter's cheek. "I'll be careful, honey."

"We need to pray that this thing will end," Nelda said.

"I agree," said Roy. "I'd like to pray out loud, but I'm sure it would cause trouble. Let's each pray in our hearts and ask the Lord to take care of this outrage."

The blizzard grew worse as the wind howled around the stalled train. Few of the passengers could sleep. In car number one, Grabow and Banning made passes at two women while their husbands stoked the fire in the pot-bellied stove. The husbands lost their tempers and jumped the outlaws. Lynch joined in, and two more male passengers decided to try to subdue the outlaws.

The gang members in car number two heard the ruckus. Kalbaugh headed toward the front door, saying, "Ray! Les! You two come with me! Somebody's givin' the boss trouble! Vic, you stay here and keep an eye on these people!"

Hodge and Sibley followed Kalbaugh, slamming the door behind them. Cochran kept his revolver at the ready and said, "Don't nobody move. I got a itchy trigger finger."

Cochran moved slowly down the aisle and stopped beside Breanna. He leaned close to her and said, "I'm glad Marlon's gone for a while, honey. Gives me time to get to know you without him interferin'."

"Leave me alone. I'm not interested."

"Aw now, honey, that's no way to act. All I want is a little ol' kiss."

"Get away from me!" Breanna said.

The sounds of a fight were still coming from the first car. The Mexican stood up quietly behind Cochran and tapped him on the shoulder. "Señor…you wan' a kees, do you? Well, kees my feest!"

The Mexican's fist hit Cochran square on the mouth, whipping his head back. Another caught Cochran flush on the jaw, and he went down like a rotten tree in a high wind, hitting the floor hard. He was out cold.

"Please! Everyone seet still an' be quiet!" The Mexican picked up Cochran's gun and handed it to Breanna, butt first. "Take thees gon, señorita. Hide eet for future use!"

Breanna took the revolver and slipped it into her medical bag.

The Mexican picked up the unconscious outlaw and hoisted him over his shoulder. He carried Cochran out the rear door and pulled it shut behind him. The harsh wind hit him like a fist, taking his breath.

Wind-driven snow turned the scene around the train into a milky blur. He could barely make out a steep embankment on the right side of the train. He moved down the steps of the platform and carried Cochran to the edge of the precipice and tossed him into the yawning white chasm. Cochran sailed down in a flailing heap and disappeared.

The Mexican hastened back to the platform at the rear of the coach and stepped inside. The other outlaws had not yet returned.

"Hey, Mex!" a man said. "I saw you give the nurse that guy's gun. Let's use it to take out the rest of 'em!"

"There are too meeny of zem! One gon ees not enough! We weel wait for better opportunity."

He looked back at the group in the corner and asked if all of them knew how to use a gun in case one of them had to use the one he had given Breanna. Roy assured him that he and his family were well acquainted with handguns. "Autumn is so good, she could shoot a squirrel between the eyes at forty paces," he said with a wink.

"Daddy exaggerates, sir. I'm not that good."

Voices were heard at the coach's front door. The Mexican took his seat quickly. The door burst open, and Hodge, Sibley, and Kalbaugh filed in with blowing snow behind them.

"Hey!" Hodge exclaimed. "Where's Vic?"

Kalbaugh swore and said, "I told him to stay here! All right, you people! Where'd Vic go?"

A man seated next to his wife about midway in the car, said, "We have no idea where he went, mister. Couple minutes ago, he suddenly hurried out the back door."

"Les, he's got to be in the last car," Kalbaugh said. "Go see what he's doin'."

Hodge hurried out the back door and was back in less than half a minute. The gang members in car number three had not seen Cochran. Kalbaugh then sent both Hodge and Sibley to look in the caboose, the engine, and the coal car. When they returned ten minutes later without finding him, Kalbaugh said, "You guys stay here. I'll go tell Dyar."

Lynch was stunned to learn that Cochran was nowhere to be found. He stomped into car number three and demanded that the passengers tell him the truth. Something had happened to Cochran, and he wanted to know what it was. The people stuck together, insisting Cochran had left without saying where he was going.

Lynch swore, saying Cochran had to be somewhere on the train. When he showed up, he was going to have to explain why he left the passengers alone in the coach.

The back door opened, and McBroom's hulky form entered. "You still ain't found him?"

"No," Lynch said. "But he's gonna answer to me when he shows up."

"Maybe he took off for some reason."

"Yeah? And where would he go?"

"The line shack, I suppose."

"You're probably right. Well, anyway, when he comes back, he's got some tall explainin' to do. We need him here."

McBroom nodded, then said, "Can I talk to you a minute, Dyar?"

"Sure. Come on into the front car."

The two outlaws sat down at the rear of car number one, where Grabow and Banning paced the aisle.

"What is it?" Lynch asked.

"We got a U. S. marshal in my car, and he's got a prisoner handcuffed to him. Seems to me we could use another man, since Vic's gone who-knows-where. How about we set the prisoner free and let him join us? I'm sure he'd be glad to."

"Don't doubt that. What's his name?"

"Dunno, but if he's in trouble with the law, he'll fit right in."

"Okay, do it."

McBroom stood up. "You don't care if I do away with the tin star, do you?"

Lynch grinned as he rose to his feet. "Why ain't I surprised that you'd like to do that?"

"Well, the only good lawman's a dead lawman, I always say."

"Yeah, you do always say that, don't you?"

Merle McBroom entered car number one and stood over Treg Taggart and Ridge Holloway. Both men looked up as McBroom said, "The boss and I have decided we want your prisoner let go. Gimme the key to the cuffs."

Taggart shook his head. "Don't have it. I lost it somehow after I cuffed us together. We can't be separated till we get to Denver. What do you want him for, anyway?"

"None of your business," McBroom said, heading toward the coach's wood bin, which was located in a small compartment at the front door.

Taggart turned to Holloway and whispered, "I'm gonna tell him the truth about us, and I'll be free of you, lawman. I told you you'd never get me to Canon City!"

Holloway did not reply, but he was praying for God's protection.

McBroom returned, bearing a large ax. The passengers watched as he made Taggart and Holloway stretch the chain over the edge of the seat. One hard swing cut the chain in two.

Taggart grinned and said, "Now, I wanna tell you somethin', McBroom."

"Shut up!" he snarled. Then he looked at Holloway and asked, "How would you like to join the gang and cash in on some of the gold?"

"Listen to me, McBroom," Taggart said. "This whole thing is all mixed up."

"What're you talkin' about?"

"The truth is, I'm the prisoner, and he's the U. S. marshal. You see, we were in a stagecoach on our way to Grand Junction, and—"

McBroom slapped Taggart's mouth, staggering him. "Shut up, you yella-bellied liar! Don't give me some cock-and-bull story! You badge toters ain't nothin' but a bunch o' yella-bellied crooks!"

"You gotta believe me! I'm tellin' you the truth!"

McBroom slapped him again, then grabbed him by the front of his coat and dragged him toward the front door. The passengers looked on, eyes wide. Taggart was helpless against McBroom's ox-like strength. McBroom jerked the door open, pulled the terrified Taggart through, and slammed the door. He held Taggart at arm's length, cocked his revolver, and rammed the muzzle against Taggart's midsection.

Time stood still in the mind of Treg Taggart. He thought of Ridge Holloway's words— *"This masquerade will backfire on you, Taggart. The wicked shall fall by his own wickedness"*—and realized the utter truth of them.

Everyone on the train heard the gunshot.

Ridge Holloway was standing with the other three outlaws in car number three when McBroom returned and closed the door behind him.

An elderly woman glared at McBroom and mouthed, "Murderer!"

"Well, wanna join up?" McBroom asked Holloway.

"You bet!"

"So what's your name?" McBroom asked.

"Holloway. Ridge Holloway."

"Okay, Ridge Holloway, you're assigned to the next car. C'mon."

Breanna, Autumn, and Lulu got a clear view of Ridge Holloway when he preceded Merle McBroom through the door. All three were shocked to see him. The shock was equally as powerful to Ridge. He met their startled gazes with his own and shook his head furtively, using his eyes to tell them not to show that they knew him.

The other three outlaws in the car came toward them, and McBroom said, "Fellas, I'd like you to meet Ridge Holloway. He was shackled to a deputy U. S. marshal, on his way to Denver, but I fixed that. Deputy's lyin' dead out in the snow. Dyar told me to offer Ridge here the opportunity of joinin' the gang, and he took me up on it. He'll take Vic's place for the time bein'."

McBroom went to car number one and brought Lynch back to meet Ridge Holloway. He also brought Ridge a Colt .44 revolver, which Ridge tucked under his belt.

It was almost dawn, and the storm was easing up. Hodge, Sibley, and Kalbaugh left Holloway to guard the passengers in car number two alone. They wanted to confer with their boss since the storm appeared to be passing.

Ridge was glad for the opportunity to talk to his friends. He stood over them and told them what had happened. Lulu felt a touch of sadness, knowing that Treg had been shot.

Breanna explained why Autumn was being taken to Denver, and Ridge said, "The Lord is going to work everything out, Autumn. We'll get through this and be on our way to Denver soon."

"I know the Lord will take care of us, Ridge," Autumn said. "It's just so good to see you again."

"Likewise. I've thought about you a lot."

Breanna was relieved to know there was a lawman amid the outlaws. Her prayers were beginning to be answered.

Morning came with a clear sky and a sub-zero temperature. The wind had piled snowdrifts in some places against the train and hollowed out bare spots in others.

When the outlaws emerged into the biting air, they found that the team and wagon were missing. Lynch was sure, then, that Cochran had slipped out into the storm and taken them to the line shack.

Lynch pulled Grabow and Banning aside and said, "I want you two to go to the shack. Bring the team and wagon back here and tell Cochran I appreciate him thinkin' of the horses, but I wish he'd talk to me before he goes off on his own. The snow's deep where it's drifted, but other than that, it ain't too bad. We'll load up the gold and let the train move on."

"Okay, boss," said Banning. "We'll be back in a few minutes."

It took the two outlaws nearly an hour to trudge their way to the line shack. To their surprise, they found no sign of the team and wagon, nor any trace of Vic Cochran. All they could do was make their way back to the train. Lynch was going to be furious. There was no way to haul the gold without the wagon.

TWENTY-ONE

The Mexican watched through the frost-lined windows of coach number two as Ord Grabow and Errol Banning plodded southward through the snow. Dyar Lynch had called Clarence Judd and Ray Sibley to stay with him in coach number one. This left Les Hodge, Marlon Kalbaugh, and Ridge Holloway in number two, and Lionel Ruppert, Ervin Dill, and Merle McBroom in number three.

Engineer Todd Bandy, fireman Dorsey Lowe, and the conductor were brought into coach number one so they could be on hand to move the train out once the outlaws were gone. Most of the passengers were asleep.

Breanna Baylor dreamed as she slept. She and John were together on a snow-covered mountain side, frolicking in the snow. She made a snowball and threw it at him. He ran toward her, laughing, and batted the snowball aside. Suddenly they were in each other's arms, their lips about to blend in a sweet kiss. Breanna awoke with a start.

She found herself in the railroad car with Autumn asleep on her shoulder. She looked at the Mexican across the aisle and found him looking at her. He smiled and turned toward the frosty window.

She studied him for a long moment, appraising his wide shoulders and the long black hair that dangled on them.

Ridge Holloway paced the aisle while Hodge and Kalbaugh stood near the front in conversation. He paused beside Breanna, drawing her attention away from the Mexican. Ridge looked at the sleeping Autumn and whispered to Breanna, "Isn't she the prettiest little thing you ever saw?"

"Yes, she is," Breanna nodded, smiling.

Ridge moved on, wary of giving himself away to the outlaws.

While Ridge was turning around at the rear of the coach, the Mexican removed his sombrero and laid it on the seat next to the aisle. He listened for the deputy's footsteps and pushed the hat onto the floor, causing Ridge to step on it.

"Hey! Look what you deed, gringo! You knock my sombrero on zee floor and step on eet!"

"I didn't knock it on the floor! It fell, and I couldn't avoid it!"

"You lie!" the Mexican shouted, and he grabbed Ridge around the neck and took him to the floor. Hodge and Kalbaugh scurried toward them.

"Ridge, it's John Stranger!" the Mexican whispered. "We need to find a way to talk!"

Ridge Holloway couldn't believe his ears. "Okay," he whispered. "I'll think of somethin'."

"Hey Pancho!" Kalbaugh bellowed, laying hold of Stranger's collar. "Break it up!"

By this time, everyone in the car was awake and looking on.

Stranger let go of Ridge's neck and stood up. "Thees hombre knock my sombrero on zee floor and step on eet! I do nawtheen to heem!"

Breanna had seen the Mexican flip the sombrero onto the floor. Why was he starting trouble?

"No sense makin' trouble, Ridge," Kalbaugh said. "We're gonna be gone pretty soon."

"Sorry, I just don't cotton to long-haired Mexicans. He grinds me the wrong way."

"Forget it," Hodge said. "He isn't worth wastin' your energy on."

The front door of the coach came open, and Dyar Lynch stuck his head in. "Holloway, we're about to run out of firewood in my coach. Engineer says there's more in the caboose. How about gettin' some for me?"

"Sure," Holloway grinned. "How about if I make this Mexican carry an armload?"

"Fine with me. Just get it done," Lynch replied, and was gone.

Ridge pulled his gun, leveled it on Stranger, and said, "Put your hat on. We're gonna get some wood for my boss."

The line shack stood on a high crest overlooking a sweeping valley to the south. When Grabow and Banning found no sign of the wagon or of Vic Cochran and were about to head back, Banning pointed to the far side of the valley and said, "Look down there."

Grabow spotted a wagon at the edge of heavy timber, dark against the snow. "What the—? What's it doin' clear down there? Must be a couple miles from here."

"I don't know, but we'd better get to it."

When they finally reached the wagon two hours later, they found that the horses had been attacked and killed by wild beasts. The tracks in the blood-splattered snow showed that it was wolves.

"No sign of Vic, though," Banning said, looking around. "You don't suppose them beasts dragged him away and ate him somewhere else."

The sight of the blood and the paw prints in the snow had taken Grabow's mind back to the day he fed Jack Slattery to the wolves. He was thinking what an awful way it would be to die when he realized Errol was saying something to him.

"I said you don't suppose the wolves dragged Vic off somewhere else and ate him, do you?"

"Must've. He had to be the one drivin' the wagon."

"But if Vic was drivin' the team, what was he doin' clear down here?"

"Maybe the blizzard had him blinded," Grabow suggested. "What're you thinkin'?"

"That maybe somethin' else happened to Vic, and them horses just took off 'cause they were scared of the storm."

"Could be."

"Well, whatever," Banning said, "we better go tell Dyar what's happened. He's gonna throw a real tantrum when he finds out we ain't got no horses to pull the wagon."

The going was slow as the two men trudged up the slope toward the line shack. The wind was picking up again, driving its knife edges through their heavy coats. The sun shone in a clear sky but seemed to give off no heat. Banning swore as they labored through the calf-high snow, pressing northward.

Movement on the timbered ridge above them to the right caught Grabow's eye. His blood chilled when he saw several pale-eyed wolves watching them from the edge of the trees. "Don't make any sudden movements, but take a look up to your right," he said.

Banning recoiled when he saw the gray beasts eyeing them. "Wolves!" he gasped. "We gotta get outta here!" He lunged forward, and Grabow grabbed his arm.

"No, you fool, go slow! If you run, they'll attack for sure!"

Banning whipped out his revolver.

"Don't!" Grabow said. "We'll be all right if we just walk slow. Friend of mine—well, the one who was supposed to show up at the line shack—he knows a lot about wolves. Said they'll only attack humans if they feel threatened or smell human blood...or if they're starving. If those are the same wolves that ate the horses, they sure can't be starvin'. So let's just keep on real slow, and they won't bother us."

The outlaws trudged northward, but they did not leave the wolves behind. The pack stayed close by, slinking amongst the timber. It had been downhill to the wagon, and now they were halfway back to the shack and the climb was steep.

"Wait a minute," Banning gasped, stopping to catch his breath.

"Gladly," Grabow said, hauling up a couple of steps behind him. He let his line of sight trail to the wolves at the edge of the timber. Their number had grown. At first there had only been six or eight. Now there were more than a dozen.

Banning watched them with wary eyes. "Ord, I don't like the looks of this. They're stalkin' us."

"Maybe they ain't the ones that ate the horses."

"What'll we do?"

Three more wolves showed up from the dense woods, and the pack moved out into the open. They watched the men and fanned out forming a half-circle directly ahead of them, blocking their path. Their pale eyes seemed to penetrate those of the two outlaws.

Grabow's face went as white as the snow. He kept picturing the scene at the Elk Mountain cabin when the wolves converged on Jack Slattery. It put ice in his blood.

Banning's trembling hand lowered to the handle of his revolver. He was breathing hard, staring in terror at the gray line of wolves spread out before him.

Grabow was some six feet behind Banning and a couple of steps to his left. He slowly slipped his revolver from its holster and lined it on Banning's back. Banning turned to say something and saw Grabow. His eyes bulged in fear and anger as he whipped his gun out of its holster.

Grabow's gun roared and the slug hit Banning in the left thigh. He jerked with the impact, but managed to bring his own gun to bear and fired.

The bullet chewed into Grabow's right side, knocking him down. Swearing, Banning staggered and fired at Grabow again, missing him by inches. Grabow rolled over in the snow, raised his gun, and shot Banning in the stomach. Banning buckled and fell to his knees, gripping his midsection with his free hand. He looked at Grabow through eyes of hatred and tried to bring his gun up, then toppled onto the snow.

Grabow gripped his side and tried to stand up. He heard a deep-throated growl behind him and turned to see the whole pack of wolves only forty feet from him. Ahead of the pack, less than a dozen feet away, stood a huge male, looking at him with menacing eyes that seemed alive with fire. The beast growled again, slavering and licking its chops.

It moved closer, stopping barely six feet from him. The rest of the pack moved in slowly. Grabow tried to raise his gun, but his arm would not move. The wolf's ears were laid back and its hackles were raised. Its fangs protruded from a lip-curling snarl.

The wolf sprang at him, growling and snapping.

One long scream echoed over the frozen mountains and died suddenly as the frenzied wolf pack converged on Ord Grabow.

Dyar Lynch was fit to be tied. It was almost noon, and the wagon still wasn't there. He paced back and forth in the baggage coach in front of the boxes filled with gold and swore repeatedly. He had sent Ervin Dill and Lionel Ruppert to find Grabow and Banning over two hours ago, and they still had not returned.

Merle McBroom was the only gang member in the baggage coach with Lynch. Nervous because his boss was so upset, McBroom said, "Dyar, you want I should go and see what's happenin' at the line shack? Somethin's happened to them guys. I just know it."

Lynch stopped pacing, looked at the big man, and said, "I can't afford to send anybody else. Besides, what could've happened to 'em? This is raw mountain country up here. Ain't no lawmen traipsin' around these peaks, and ain't no rival gangs up here, neither. Them boys must be havin' a hard time findin' the team and wagon. For the life of me, I can't figure out why Vic would take off with 'em anyhow. They'll be showin' up pretty soon. They just *have* to."

In the coaches, the other gang members devoured what food was left on the train, refusing to share it even with the few children on board. The passengers were allowed to move about and stretch their legs as the outlaws observed them with watchful eyes.

In car number two, Ridge Holloway was teamed with Clarence Judd. Ridge positioned himself at the rear of the car to be close to Autumn and her family...and to John Stranger when it was time to begin carrying out Stranger's plan. Judd was at the front of the coach.

"How long's this going to go on?" one of the male passengers near the front asked Judd. "You can't keep all these people cooped up on this train forever."

"We don't like this situation any better than you do, mister. The boss has four men out right now tryin' to find the horses and the wagon. Once they get back, we'll unload the gold and you people can be on your way to Denver."

The heatless sun was slanting low in the sky when Dill and Ruppert showed up, telling Lynch they had found what was left of Ord Grabow and Errol Banning about a mile south of the line shack. Moving on, they had found the wagon and what was left of the horses. They had pushed and pulled the wagon toward the shack as best they could, and it was now near the remains of

Grabow and Banning. They were exhausted, but if Dyar would send more men, they could get it closer before dark.

Lynch thought about it. He could have the men carry the gold from the baggage coach to the shack a little at a time, but that would take much too long. It would be better to bring the wagon to the train. He decided to wait till morning. He would cram all the passengers into one car so two men could guard them, freeing the other gang members to bring the wagon. They would unload the gold, then push and pull the wagon to the line shack.

The wood supply on the train was running low, but the crew was optimistic that there would be enough to see them to Denver if they were able to move on the next morning.

When darkness had fallen, Ridge Holloway stood at the rear of car number two, leaning against the door, arms folded over his chest. From time to time, he and Autumn Lynne exchanged furtive glances. Autumn thought of Doug Price and how quickly he lost interest in her when he learned she might never walk again. And here was Ridge Holloway, who cared for her even though she was paralyzed and might remain that way.

Autumn bit her lip. No! She must not give in to never walking again. The Lord would use Dr. Lyle Goodwin to restore the use of her legs. She *would* walk again. And if Ridge felt toward her what she saw in his eyes, they would have a wonderful and happy life together.

When darkness had settled over the mountains, John Stranger was ready to put his plan into action. Breanna looked at him as he slumped in the seat, sombrero tipped over his face. She had never seen a Mexican with such long legs.

As a signal to Ridge that he was ready, Stranger lifted the sombrero for a moment, adjusted himself on the seat, and settled back down. He could hear Ridge walking the aisle, and just as he drew abreast of him, Stranger stuck his foot out and tripped him.

Ridge stumbled, caught himself on a seat, and whirled and spat, "You tripped me, Mex!"

Stranger sat up quickly, pushing the sombrero to the back of his head, and said, "You are wrong, gringo! I deed no' treep you. I only stretch my legs."

Holloway seized Stranger by the front of his coat and jerked him to his feet, causing the sombrero to tumble to the floor. He pulled the Colt .44 from under his belt, cocked it, and snarled, "That's it, Mex! You've had it! Outside!"

The Lynnes, Lulu, and Breanna looked wide-eyed, mouths gaping as Ridge spun the Mexican around and shoved him toward the back door. From the front of the coach, Clarence Judd saw the passengers looking back at the scene and yelled, "Everybody stay in your seats!"

Holloway pushed Stranger through the door, slammed it shut behind him, and both men raised their voices at each other, making sure they were loud enough to be heard inside the coach.

Autumn's eyes were fixed on the door, and she jumped with a start when a gunshot was heard, followed quickly by another. Nelda gripped Roy and ejected a tiny squeal.

The door came open, and Ridge entered, tucking the .44 under his belt.

Judd looked at him from the other end of the coach. "Guess he won't be a problem to you anymore, eh, Ridge?"

"Man messes with me once, he's in deep trouble. He messes with me a second time, he's dead!"

Suddenly the front door opened and Dyar Lynch came in with Merle McBroom on his heels. "I heard shots! You fellas know what happened?"

"Yeah. Ridge done shot that long-haired Mex."

"Kill 'im?" Lynch asked looking at Ridge.

"Yeah."

"Where's the body?"

"Outside."

Lynch walked through the coach and out the door. McBroom and Holloway followed.

Lynch looked on both sides of the platform but saw nothing. "So where is he?"

Ridge pointed to the right side of the coach at the deep ravine. "I tossed him over the edge."

By the light that flowed from the coach windows, Lynch and McBroom could see marks in the snow all the way to the lip of the crevice. They had no reason to doubt Holloway's word.

Lynch laid a hand on Holloway's shoulder and said, "I like you, kid. Maybe after you get your hands on some of the gold, you'll wanna join us permanently. I like a fella who don't mind killin' a guy who gets in his way."

While Ridge was outside with Lynch and McBroom, Nelda looked at Autumn and whispered, "I can't believe what's happened to Ridge. I thought he was a Christian, but…no Christian would do what he did to that poor man."

Tears spilled down Autumn's cheeks. "I don't understand what's happening here either," she whispered, "but I know that Ridge is a kind, good, and decent man. He's a deputy U. S. marshal, and a good one…and he's a good Christian, too. I tell you, there's more to this than we're seeing. And I might as well tell you something else. I'm in love with Ridge, and he's in love with me."

Both parents looked shocked.

"Autumn, you can't possibly know you're in love with him. You haven't known him long enough!" Roy said.

"What?" Autumn whispered incredulously. "You've told me time and again, Daddy, that you and Mother fell in love at first sight, and both of you knew it!"

Roy Lynne's face crimsoned. "This is different. From all appearances, Ridge Holloway has joined these outlaws. There's no future for you with him."

✳ ✳ ✳ ✳ ✳

After discussing the killing of the Mexican with Ridge Holloway, Dyar Lynch did some switching around, positioning some of his men in different cars for the night.

At about nine o'clock, McBroom went to car number two, leaving Judd to watch car number three alone. He asked Holloway and Kalbaugh if Ruppert and Dill had passed through their car recently. They had gone to see Lynch in car number one, but should have returned by now. Holloway and Kalbaugh hadn't seen them.

"I thought Les Hodge was here with you two," McBroom said, looking around in the coach.

Kalbaugh shook his head. "Naw. He was with us till about half an hour ago, then he said he needed to talk to Dyar. He left and hasn't been back, so he must still be with Dyar."

McBroom stomped toward the front door, mumbling something about Lynch having a convention in his car. He entered car number one and found Lynch at the rear door, and Ray Sibley at the front. Some of the passengers were asleep, while others talked in low tones and still others sat in silence.

"Dyar, where's the others?" McBroom asked.

"Who ya talkin' about?"

"Who do ya think? Ruppert, Dill, and Hodge."

"I thought Ruppert and Dill were in your car."

"Well, they ain't. They left, sayin' they needed to see you."

"When was this?"

"'Bout forty minutes ago."

"Well, I ain't seen 'em. And Hodge is supposed to be with Holloway and Kalbaugh in number two."

"They said about half an hour ago, he left to come see you."

Lynch shook his head. "I ain't seen him, neither."

McBroom scratched his head. "Well, where can they be?"

"Well, unless they've pulled a disappearin' act like Vic did, they're probably wanderin' around outside...or maybe they're in the baggage coach lookin' at the gold."

"I'll take a lantern and make a little search, okay?" McBroom said.

"Yeah. Tell them to take their places. I want Ruppert with you and Clarence for the night, and I want Dill with me and Ray."

"I'll tell 'em. There an extra lantern in this car?"

The lantern was provided, and Merle lit it and moved out onto the rear platform. He held the lantern at shoulder level and moved down the metal steps into the snow. There was a swishing sound behind him. Startled, he turned to see who or what it was, and the barrel of a revolver cracked him on the temple. He crumpled to the snow in a heap.

Fifteen minutes later, Lynch called Sibley to the rear of the car and told him that McBroom should have been back by now. He asked Sibley to step out onto the platform and see if he could locate him. The lantern would be easy to spot.

Sibley looked on both sides of the train, then returned to Lynch and said there was no sign of McBroom or the lantern.

A small sensation of panic started flickering in Dyar Lynch's chest. Some of the passengers watched and listened as he said with a shudder, "Ray, somethin' strange is goin' on. One of us has gotta stay in here and keep an eye on these people. You go bring Kalbaugh from the next car. We'll leave him here on guard while you and I do some searchin' together."

CHAPTER

TWENTY-TWO

❖———◆———❖

While Marlon Kalbaugh stood guard in number one, Dyar Lynch and Ray Sibley searched the engine, the coal car, the baggage coach, and the caboose. Finding none of the missing men, Lynch was puzzled and frightened. Not only had Vic Cochran disappeared mysteriously, but Les Hodge, Lionel Ruppert, Ervin Dill, and Merle McBroom had vanished into thin air. Besides himself, Lynch had only four men left, including his newest addition, Ridge Holloway.

Lynch's fear drove him to order all passengers crammed into car number one. Clarence Judd ushered everyone from car number three through car number two at gunpoint. Once those passengers had passed into the first car, Marlon Kalbaugh stood at the front door of car number two and said, "All right, let's move, folks. Everybody into the next coach!"

Ridge Holloway was at the rear. As the passengers at the front began filing out, he called to Kalbaugh, "Marlon, we have the little lady who can't walk back here. Make them save a seat for her in the next car. Once everyone else is out of this coach, I'll carry her to her seat."

Roy Lynne set angry eyes on Ridge. "Oh, no you won't! I don't want your filthy murdering hands on my daughter! I'll carry her!"

Kalbaugh shouted at Roy, "You just get yourself into the next car, mister!"

Roy knew better than to argue. "I'll make sure you have a place to sit in the next car," he said to Autumn.

Roy burned Ridge with hot eyes as he ushered Adam, Lulu, and Nelda up the aisle. Nelda regarded him with disgust, and Adam and Lulu ignored him.

Breanna was about to follow them when Ridge leaned close and whispered, "If you can get the message to the others, tell them everything is under control. The Mexican isn't dead. It was a plan he and I worked out to thwart the robbery...and it's working!"

Autumn heard Ridge's words and a smile broke over her face.

"I knew it was something like that!" Breanna whispered. "And so did Autumn. Didn't we, honey?"

"Yes!" she said as tears misted her eyes. To Ridge she whispered, "I love you!"

"I love you, too. It's going to be all right. Believe me!"

"C'mon, folks!" bellowed Kalbaugh at the front door. "Let's get a move on!"

When the Lynne group reached the door, Kalbaugh said, "Ridge, go with 'em and make sure there's a comfortable seat for the little cripple. Since her daddy doesn't want you to carry her, I will."

"I'll take care of getting her seat, but don't worry about the other. I'll be back to carry her."

Ridge was pleased to see that the men were giving seats to the women and finding places to sit on the floor. Breanna, Nelda, and Lulu were given seats, and there was a spot next to Breanna for Autumn.

When Ridge pushed the door open to car number two, what he saw filled him with wrath. Kalbaugh had Autumn cradled in his arms and was trying to put his lips to hers. Autumn squirmed and twisted her face away, begging him to put her down.

"Kalbaugh!" Holloway shouted. "Put her down!"

"I don't like the tone of your voice, pal."

"I said put her down!"

"All I was doin' was tryin' to get me a kiss."

"I don't want you kissin' her and neither does she."

"Now, just what business is that of yours?"

"She's my girl, that's what business it is!"

"You're lyin'!"

Ridge stood directly in front of them in the aisle and said, "I'm not lyin'!"

"Aw, c'mon. You got on this train, shackled to that lawman. Be some coincidence your girl bein' on the same train."

"It's true," Autumn said. "I am his girl. Now put me down."

Kalbaugh swore. "How could an outlaw have a nice girl like you?"

"An outlaw couldn't, but a lawman could!" Ridge said, whipping the gun from under his belt. "I'm a federal marshal, Marlon, and you're under arrest."

Kalbaugh swore again and threw Autumn at Holloway. She screamed as their bodies collided. The impact knocked Ridge's gun out of his hand as he and Autumn went down to the floor. The gun slid under the seats, out of sight.

The outlaw had gone off balance when he tossed Autumn at Holloway, and he stumbled back against the wall between the seats. While he struggled to right himself, he clawed for his gun.

Ridge slipped out from under Autumn and charged Kalbaugh, swinging a haymaker. The punch connected with Kalbaugh's jaw, driving him back against the wall. Ridge then brought his foot up and kicked the gun out of the outlaw's hand. It sailed toward the front of the car and landed with a clatter somewhere near the door.

Kalbaugh leaped at Holloway, swinging his own haymaker. Ridge dodged it, and slammed him on the nose. Kalbaugh's eyes watered, but he came back with a solid punch to the chin, driving Ridge across the aisle.

While the two men fought, Autumn crawled down the aisle toward the rear of the coach to avoid being stepped on. Her lifeless legs slid over the floor behind her like two lengths of rope. She looked for Ridge's gun, but it was nowhere in sight. She could see Marlon's gun lying near the door, partially under a front seat, but there was no way to get to it with the two men fighting in the aisle.

Holloway and Kalbaugh were in a tight clinch when the front door burst open. Clarence Judd had come to see what was going on. Kalbaugh caught a glimpse of him and shouted, "Help me! This dirty skunk's a lawman!"

Judd swore and went for his gun. At the same instant, Ridge flung Kalbaugh against him, throwing both outlaws off balance. Ridge glanced behind him. Autumn was a few feet away, looking on with terror in her eyes.

Ridge landed a punch to Kalbaugh's jaw, knocking him against Judd again, then looked around for his gun. He could not see it, but he could see Kalbaugh's gun near Judd's feet.

Kalbaugh, mouth bleeding, came at Ridge again. He met a solid punch that staggered him to one side. Ridge saw Judd reaching again for his gun and lunged at him, grabbing his wrist. They wrestled in a circle, slamming the door, then bounced against the front seats. Kalbaugh, breathing like a wild beast, jumped in.

Suddenly Autumn remembered the revolver the Mexican had given Breanna. She twisted around, laid her head against the floor, and looked under the seat where they had been. The medical bag was still there, but it was fifty feet away. Autumn could crawl there, but it would take too long. Soon the two outlaws would overpower Ridge and kill him.

Almost without thinking, Autumn drew her legs up under her, grasped a seat, and pulled herself to a standing position.

Clinging to the seat and balancing on her newfound legs, she gasped, a sudden intake of breath, high in her chest. She lifted one foot and took a step, using a seat to steady herself.

The sounds of the death struggle launched her forward. She let go of the seat, took a step, and walked, then ran to the seat where she and Breanna had been sitting. Tiny needles were prickling her legs as she bent down, snapped open the bag, and took out the revolver. She held the gun in both hands and swung it around, stiff-armed.

Kalbaugh had Ridge in a hold from behind and was dragging him away from Judd, whose back was to the door. Murder was in Judd's eyes as he yanked his weapon from its holster.

Ridge was giving Kalbaugh a difficult time. He had stiffened his legs and driven Kalbaugh backward against the window between the front wall and the first seat. Autumn had a clear shot at Judd.

Her gun roared, and the slug tore into Judd's wrist, splintering bone and knocking the gun from his hand. He howled in agony, grabbed his wrist, and flopped onto the front seat.

Ridge looked at Autumn in amazement. She was standing, supported only by her legs!

Autumn swung the smoking muzzle, lined it on Kalbaugh's face, and took three steady steps forward. "Let go of him!" she hissed.

Fear showed on the faces of the passengers in car number one when they heard the gunshot. Breanna had just given Ridge Holloway's message to the Lynnes and Lulu Taggart when the shot was heard. Every eye was fixed toward the rear of the coach.

Dyar Lynch held his own gun at the front of the coach and said to Ray Sibley, who was at the rear, "Go see about it...and be careful."

Sibley's gun was in his hand. He nodded grimly and opened the door and stepped out onto the platform. Closing the door behind him, he crossed to the platform of car number two.

Before he could reach the door, a steel-like hand seized his ankle and yanked him to the snow-packed ground. A swift blow to the head with a gun barrel sent him into unconsciousness.

Inside coach number two, Marlon Kalbaugh reluctantly released Ridge Holloway and stepped aside. "Sit down beside your pal!" Autumn snapped while keeping her gun aimed at Kalbaugh.

Kalbaugh took one look at Judd's wrist and concluded that the girl must be a crack shot. Slowly but steadily he sat down beside Judd, who was bent over in pain as he held his bleeding wrist.

While Autumn held the outlaws at gunpoint, Holloway rummaged around in the coach until he found enough cloth to gag them. He used their own belts to bind them, then wrapped up Judd's shattered wrist to stop the bleeding. Both Autumn and Ridge were surprised that no other outlaws came in response to the shot.

When Kalbaugh and Judd were secure, Autumn lowered the gun. Ridge took her into his arms, held her tight for a moment, then kissed her softly. "I love you, Autumn Lynne."

"And I love you, Ridge Holloway."

Roy, Nelda, Adam, and Lulu were praying that Autumn and Ridge were all right. They also asked the Lord to forgive them for not having more faith in Autumn's assessment of Ridge Holloway...and in Ridge himself.

Dyar Lynch still stood at the front with the gun in his hand, his face showing the strain he was feeling. Sibley had been gone for five minutes. *Where was he? Who had fired the shot? Was anybody shot? If so, who?*

He could wait no longer. Since he couldn't leave the car, he shouted Sibley's name at the top of his lungs. When there was no response, he shouted it again.

Still no answer.

Panic seized him, and his voice rose in pitch until he was screaming Sibley's name. Lynch's wild cries covered the sound of the door opening behind him. The passengers were shocked to see the Mexican step inside, a cocked revolver in his hand. Hatless, his long black hair dangled over his forehead and down to his shoulders.

Dyar Lynch saw the reaction on the faces of the passengers and realized they were looking at something behind him. He cut off his screams and started to turn. But the cold muzzle that pressed tight against the back of his neck checked him. His eyes darted rapidly back and forth as a soft, deep voice said, "Hand me zee gon, señor, or you eat a bullet from zee wrong side!"

But the Mexican was supposed to be dead! Lynch's heart banged his rib cage as he lifted the revolver shoulder high and released it to the Mexican's hand.

The Mexican grabbed him by the collar and yanked him through the door. The passengers gave a rousing cheer and applauded the dark, mysterious man. Breanna's heart was in her throat. There was something about that man...

"Maybe the Mex will handle the rest of the gang, too!" one of the men said. "But we dare not venture out to see. We'll have to wait till he comes back and tells us it's all over."

"Listen to me!" said Roy Lynne, raising his voice. "The man named Ridge Holloway is not an outlaw!"

"What?" gasped a woman. There was a buzzing among the passengers.

"He's a deputy U. S. marshal. He and the Mexican have been working together all this time to free us from these beasts!"

Another cheer filled the coach.

✳ ✳ ✳ ✳ ✳

In car number two, Ridge sat Autumn down and said, "Lynch isn't screaming for Sibley any more. You wait here. I've got a feelin'—"

"Señor Reedge!" came the Mexican's voice from just outside the front door. "I jos' look through zee window! You have zee bad hombres tied up, I see. Deedn' wanna frighten you! I come een now?"

Autumn and Ridge smiled at each other. "Sure!" Ridge called. "C'mon in!"

From where they sat on the left front seat of the coach, bound and gagged, Marlon Kalbaugh and Clarence Judd looked on owl-eyed as the Mexican came through the door.

"Hey, you do real good, Reedge! You handle both of zees hombres!"

"Well, it really wasn't me who handled them. It was Autumn."

"Autumn?"

"When she saw the danger I was in, she ran back and pulled the gun out of Breanna's medical bag. Take a look at Clarence's right wrist and you'll see—"

"Wait! Did I hear you right? Autumn *ran* and got the gun?"

Autumn's brow furrowed. The Mexican had suddenly lost his accent.

"You heard me right," Ridge said. "When she saw that these two were bent on killing me, she got up off the floor, ran back there, and pulled out the gun. Her father taught her how to use a handgun years ago. She shot the gun out of Clarence's hand and put a stop to Marlon's effort to strangle me."

Autumn studied the Mexican as he looked at her and said, "So you found what it took to restore your desire to walk again. Praise the Lord. He answered our prayers for you."

"Mr. Stranger!" Autumn gasped, smiling.

Stranger lost the stoop and rose to his full height. "In person, Autumn. Let me see you stand up."

Autumn rose to her feet and took a step into Ridge's arms.

"Marvelous!" Stranger said. "Dr. Goodwin just lost a patient!" He paused, then said, "I've watched you two eyeing each other. I was pretty sure what I saw was love growing."

"Were we that obvious?" Ridge asked.

"To me, at least," Stranger said. "Apparently none of these hoodlums saw it."

Kalbaugh and Judd glowered at Ridge and grunted through their gags.

"Oh!" said Stranger. "I got so excited about Autumn walking again that I almost forgot what I came in here for. I came to tell you that the gang is completely out of commission."

"Really!" gasped Autumn.

"Even Lynch and Sibley?" Ridge asked.

"Lynch is lying outside in the snow with a knot on his head. He's tied up, and no doubt still out cold. Sibley's hog-tied at the line shack along with the others...just like I told you I'd do it."

"Do the passengers know they're free of these beasts?" Autumn asked.

"Well, they know I took Lynch by surprise and jerked him out of the coach. And they know Sibley hasn't come back. But, of course, they don't know about Kalbaugh and Judd here."

"Let's go tell them!" Autumn exclaimed. "I want Mother and Daddy to know that it's you in that wig and bushy mustache, Mr. Stranger!"

The tall man shook his head. "They can't know right now, Autumn. I have my reasons for asking you not to tell them until— well, until Ridge says you can."

"I don't understand," she said, a puzzled look on her face.

"Me either," Ridge said.

"I'll explain it to you when we're alone, Ridge. Right now, there is much to do. I'll take Kalbaugh and Judd to the caboose, along with Lynch. You go pick four men from among the passengers. Tell them to bring lanterns and meet me at the caboose. I want them to help me bring those men in the line shack down here. We'll put them in the caboose, too."

"Will do," Holloway said.

"While you're doing that, send a half-dozen or so of the men out front to remove the barricade…and tell the engineer and fireman to get the boiler hot. They need to be ready to move out within the hour."

"Sounds good to me," Ridge said. "Come on, Autumn. Let's go show your family what's happened to you!"

"Ah…may I make a suggestion?" Stranger asked, brushing the long hair of the wig from his forehead. "It's going to be quite a moment for Autumn's family when they learn she can walk again…for Breanna and Lulu, too. That moment should be a private one. I'll take these hoodlums out of here, then you go enlist the men to do as I said. While we're all doing what needs to be done to get this train moving, you can bring Autumn's family and friends in here for the surprise."

"Great idea," Ridge said.

"I'll wait here, Ridge," Autumn said. "I'll be standing when you bring them in."

"John, before you go, can I ask you somethin'?" Ridge said.

"Sure."

"Would…would God call a deputy U. S. marshal to preach?"

Stranger grinned. "I think He already has."

"Oh, Ridge!" Autumn exclaimed, throwing her arms around him.

While Autumn clung to the man she loved, Ridge told her what the Lord had been doing in his heart. He would go from being one kind of minister of God to being a better one. His pastor in Denver had books he would lend him, and Ridge was sure the church would sponsor him to start a church in Delta…if the people of Delta would have Ridge Holloway as their pastor.

Autumn hugged him tight and said they would look at Ridge as the answer to their prayers.

Stranger removed Clarence Judd and Marlon Kalbaugh from the coach. The young couple was alone and shared a sweet, velvet kiss. Then Ridge held Autumn close and said, "I realize we haven't known each other a terribly long time, but I do know my heart. And...well, Autumn, would you...would you consider being a preacher's wife?"

Autumn smiled and ran the tip of a finger along the edge of his chin. "I would if the preacher was you."

"Then I'll make it official. Miss Autumn Lynne, will you marry me?"

"Yes, Deputy U. S. Marshal Ridge Holloway—soon to become the *Reverend* Ridge Holloway—I'll marry you!"

TWENTY-THREE

Autumn Lynne stood in the aisle of car number three, her heart thundering in her breast. She thanked God for what He had done and waited for the moment her family would come through the door.

Less than a minute after Ridge had gone to the other coach, she heard the people cheer and applaud. Moments later, she could hear men's voices and caught sight of lanterns winking outside the windows. None of the men entered car number two. Apparently Ridge had asked them to take lanterns from elsewhere.

Her heart pounded harder when she heard the familiar voices of Ridge and her family. She stood up straight, threw her shoulders back, and waited breathlessly. The door came open, and Nelda entered first, with Roy and Adam behind her. Breanna and Lulu were on their heels. Ridge was last.

When Nelda saw her daughter standing, unassisted, she threw her hands to her mouth, squealed, and lunged for her with open arms. Roy broke into tears and hugged them both.

Breanna and Lulu looked on with shimmering eyes as the Lynne family stood holding each other, weeping and praising the Lord.

When the initial jolt was past, Ridge told them how Autumn had saved his life. He then said he was going to offer himself as pastor to the Christians in Delta who wanted to start a church.

There was more rejoicing. Roy and Nelda assured him he would be welcomed with open arms by all the people. They confessed how wrong they were to think he had murdered the Mexican and joined the gang, and they asked his forgiveness. Ridge forgave them and told them he understood why they had gotten the wrong idea.

Ridge then cleared his throat and said, "Mr. and Mrs. Lynne, I…ah…I want you to know that a few minutes ago when Autumn and I were alone here in this coach, I asked her to marry me. I realize we've only known each other a short while, but we both know we are in love and that the Lord has brought us together. I'd like to formally ask for your daughter's hand in marriage. After a proper courtship, of course."

Autumn's parents happily consented, and there was more rejoicing and congratulations.

It was just before midnight when all the passengers were back in their seats and the train began to chug up the side of the mountain.

Ridge excused himself when the Lynnes and Breanna and Lulu returned to their seats, saying he had to meet with the Mexican outside. Now that the train was rolling, Autumn was worried that Ridge was not yet in the coach. Breanna was thinking about the Mexican, whose sombrero still lay on the seat across the aisle.

The train had been in motion about five minutes when the rear door of the coach opened and Ridge entered. He stood in the aisle and said, "Well, our big adventure is over."

"Thank God!" said Lulu.

"Amen to that!" Nelda said.

"We can thank the Lord for seeing us through this ordeal," Ridge said.

"Yes, and thank the Lord for that Mexican," added Roy. "If it weren't for him, we'd still be at the mercy of those outlaws."

"Speaking of whom, where is he, Ridge?" Breanna asked.

"He's in the caboose, keeping an eye on the prisoners."

"Is he going to ride back there all the way to Denver?"

"No, ma'am. He's going to ride in the caboose all the way to Red Cliff."

"Red Cliff was the last town we passed through before we started up Vail Pass. It's westward...behind and below us."

"Yes, ma'am," Ridge nodded. "The Mexican and the conductor unhooked the caboose from the train with the engineer's permission. He'll roll the caboose down to Red Cliff and wire Sheriff Worland in Grand Junction to come and get the outlaws. They can stand trial in Mesa County as well as anywhere else."

"Ridge, you've known that Mexican before, haven't you?" Breanna said.

The coach rocked and Ridge used the seat to steady himself. He glanced at Autumn, then met Breanna's gaze. "Yes, ma'am."

"He's not really a Mexican, is he?"

"No, ma'am." Ridge reached in his shirt pocket and produced a neatly folded white handkerchief. He handed it to Breanna and said, "He asked me to tell you that he loves you, and to give you this."

Breanna's hand trembled slightly as she accepted the folded handkerchief. She unfolded it carefully, lovingly, already knowing what was inside.

The highly polished silver medallion was exactly the size of a silver dollar. Breanna released a shuddering sigh, her eyes suddenly bright with tears.

The medallion was centered by a raised five-point star. Around its edge were inscribed the words: *THE STRANGER THAT SHALL COME FROM A FAR LAND—Deuteronomy 29:22.*

OTHER COMPELLING STORIES BY
AL LACY

Books in the Battles of Destiny series:

☛ *A Promise Unbroken*

Two couples battle jealousy and racial hatred amidst a war that would cripple America. From a prosperous Virginia plantation to a grim jail cell outside Lynchburg, follow the dramatic story of a love that could not be destroyed.

☛ *A Heart Divided*

Ryan McGraw—leader of the Confederate Sharpshooters—is nursed back to health by beautiful army nurse Dixie Quade. Their romance would survive the perils of war, but can it withstand the reappearance of a past love?

☛ *Beloved Enemy*

Young Jenny Jordan covers for her father's Confederate spy missions. But as she grows closer to Union soldier Buck Brownell, Jenny finds herself torn between devotion to the South and her feelings for the man she is forbidden to love.

☛ *Shadowed Memories*

Critically wounded on the field of battle and haunted by amnesia one man struggles to regain his strength and the memories that have slipped away from him.

☛ *Joy From Ashes*

Major Layne Dalton made it through the horrors of the battle of Fredericksburg, but can he rise above his hatred toward the Heglund brothers who brutalized his wife and killed his unborn son?

Books in the Journeys of the Stranger series:

☞ *Legacy*

Can John Stranger, a mysterious hero who brings truth, honor, and justice to the Old West, bring Clay Austin back to the right side of the law...and restore the code of honor shared by the woman he loves?

☞ *Silent Abduction*

The mysterious man in black fights to defend a small town targeted by cattle rustlers and to rescue a young woman and child held captive by a local Indian tribe.

LOOK FOR
AL LACY'S NEW

ANGEL OF
MERCY

S E R I E S

featuring
Breanna Baylor.

AVAILABLE JULY 1995

Available at your local Christian bookstore

872